# BURIED ALIVE

J.A. Kerley worked in advertising and teaching before becoming a full-time novelist. He lives in Newport, Kentucky, but also spends a good deal of time in Southern Alabama, the setting for his Carson Ryder series, starting with *The Hundredth Man*. He is married with two children.

Also by J.A. Kerley

*The Hundredth Man*
*The Death Collectors*
*The Broken Souls*
*Little Girls Lost*
*Blood Brother*
*In the Blood*

# J.A. KERLEY

# *Buried Alive*

**HARPER**

*Harper*
An imprint of HarperCollins*Publishers*
77–85 Fulham Palace Road, London W6 8JB

www.harpercollins.co.uk

1

First published in Great Britain by
Harper, an imprint of HarperCollins*Publishers* 2010

A catalogue record for this book
is available from the British Library

ISBN 978-0-00-792613-8

Set in Sabon by Palimpsest Book Production Limited,
Falkirk, Stirlingshire

Printed in Great Britain by
Clays Limited, St Ives plc

**MIX**
Paper from
responsible sources

FSC
www.fsc.org

**FSC® C007454**

*To the Northside Trio:*
*Duane, Dave, and that other guy.*

# 1

R-rrrrr.

*R-rrrrr.*

I felt the phone before I heard it, a rusty saw rasping over my forehead, trying to rip an opening into my subconscious.

*R-rrrrr.*

My eyes opened to slats of maple flooring. Chair legs. A crumpled sock. I was on the floor, head in the living room, feet in the bedroom.

*"R-rrrrr."*

Behind me I saw blanket and sheet following like a tangled umbilicus. I had tried to crawl from my dreams again. I rolled to the phone on the bedside table before the saw took another cut.

"Carson Ryder," I mumbled, cross-legged on the floor and leaning against the bed. The clock showed 7.25 a.m.

on a Saturday morning. Outside, gulls keened above my beachside home as the Gulf of Mexico's waves slapped the shore a hundred paces distant.

"Detective Ryder, it's Nancy Wainwright at the Alabama Institute for Aberrational Behavior. I need your help."

I stifled a yawn as my mental Rolodex presented an image of a slender, fiftyish woman with long brown hair and penetrating, intelligent eyes behind round glasses.

"What can I do for you, Doctor?"

"Bobby Lee Crayline's here at the Institute."

I rubbed sleep from my eyes. "Again? Why?"

"He's going to be hypnotized."

It took a five-count for the words to materialize into a grammatical pattern and snap me bolt-upright with the phone tight to my ear. "Bobby Lee Crayline?" I knew my heart was fully awake. I could feel it pounding. "Who's doing this?"

"Crayline's legal team wants to regress Bobby Lee."

"Regressing Crayline could blow him off his hinges," I said. "Vangie told me Crayline was the tip of the one iceberg that she never wanted to see beneath the surface."

Vangie was Dr Evangeline Prowse, psychiatrist, the former head of the Institute, which housed and studied the country's most dangerous psychopaths and sociopaths. She'd been murdered in Manhattan two years ago, the circumstances strange and sad. Nancy Wainwright had been installed as the Institute's full-time director some months back. I barely knew her.

2

"You interviewed Bobby Lee in prison, right, Detective?" Wainwright continued. "Since you have a history with him, I thought maybe you could stop the procedure."

Another mental Rolodex spun, one hidden in a far corner of my skull, and I saw Bobby Lee Crayline, his green reptilian eyes studying me the moment I entered Holman Prison's visitation room. I saw his flattened nose and his scarred hands on the far side of the Plexiglas divider, hands skittering over the counter like restless tarantulas. I smelled the stink pouring like gasoline fumes from his jittering, tattoo-smeared body. I'd gone home after the unsettling interview and washed my clothes. Twice.

"Crayline's legal team won't listen to me, Doctor," I explained. "It's not much of a history and I'm just a homicide dick from Mobile."

"You're in that special unit. That has to count for something."

She was referring to PSIT, the Psychopathological and Sociopathological Investigative Team. The team was me and my partner, Harry Nautilus. Few outside the Mobile PD even knew of the existence of the unit called *Piss-it* by everyone but Harry and me.

"I doubt that will sway anyone," I said. "Even given Bobby Lee's obvious psychological damage."

Bobby Lee Crayline had been arrested seven months ago, at the age of twenty-eight, after his strange abduction of a colleague. His path had always led him in a disturbing direction, a history of breathless violence, starting in high school when he'd beaten two teachers a half-inch shy of death, one teacher today confined to a wheelchair. Though he'd avoided incarceration when it was proven both male teachers – a coach and an assistant – had taunted the sixteen-year-old when he didn't join the football team, Crayline was expelled from school.

Crayline spent the next few years winning amateur "Toughest Man" competitions, often dragged from atop opponents after the round ended. His reputation for crowd-pleasing megaviolence bought entrée into the XFL, Extreme Fighting League, a made-for-TV motley of pro wrestling, full-contact karate, and bar-room brawling. Two combatants fought in a circular, thirty-foot-diameter cage until one was vanquished, often in a shower of blood and teeth. I'd once watched three minutes of XFL before retreating from the television, wondering if the species known as *Homo Sapiens* – thinking man – had been hideously misnamed.

Bobby Lee Crayline's XFL career consisted of twenty-two bouts. He generally wounded his opponents in an early round, then toyed with them for several more, spitting insults and inflicting damage until the victim collapsed. Two opponents quit the league, humiliated. In the most notorious incident, one of Crayline's opponents died of a brain hemorrhage after the match. Because of the viciousness of Crayline's attack – he had to be pulled from the fighter after the bell – the incident was ruled manslaughter and Bobby Lee received a six-month prison sentence. I interviewed him the first week he was in prison, part of

4

my ongoing research. He was scary and uncooperative and I spent less than ten minutes in his company, which was fine.

A month into his sentence, a savvy lawyer got Bobby Lee transferred to the Alabama Institute for Aberrational Behavior. He remained there for two months before other legal wranglings set him free and he returned to the XFL.

Crayline had won all his XFL fights but his final one, vanquished in the third round by an imposing and experienced fighter called Jessie "Mad Dog" Stone. Bobby Lee Crayline disappeared overnight, no one knowing where he went or why. One waggish sportswriter opined that "Hell hath summoned Bobby Lee to the home office."

Bobby Lee Crayline's next public appearance was eight months later, in court, arrested at a remote rented farm in north Alabama's Talladega Mountains and charged with kidnapping. Chained inside a deep pit in a barn behind Crayline's house, covered with flies and sores and his own excrement, was Jessie Stone, the one man to ever best Crayline in a fight.

Within a month of Bobby Lee's arrest, three bodies turned up in the countryside where he spent his teen years, the victims shot to pieces, though nothing thus far tied him to the killings. The coroner put the time of death as approximately two years earlier and the investigation was ongoing. It had been conclusively proved that Crayline was in the area at the time.

But Stone's kidnapping did the trick: Bobby Lee

received a sentence of thirty years in prison and stepped into the big cage three months ago. And there he'd remained until today.

"When's this procedure supposed to go down?" I asked Dr Wainwright, shaking Bobby Lee Crayline from my thoughts. "The hypnosis."

"Today at eleven."

"Grab the reins and stop the session, Doctor," I said. "Tell the truth: Bobby Lee Crayline is a box that should never be opened."

"Can you help me convince the lawyers hypnosis is dangerous to their client?"

"You're giving me too much credit, Doctor. I can't just—"

"Ask anything. Just please come up here." It was a plea.

The Institute was west of Montgomery, almost three hours away. I sighed and looked at the anxious eyes of my dog, Mr Mix-up, standing at the doorway with his bowl in his mouth, tail fanning behind. He wanted food and his morning walk.

"I'll come on one condition, Doc. I can bring my dog."

"Whatever it takes."

I hung up and went to my closet; almost empty. I'd been waiting for today to play laundry catch-up. I plucked yesterday's shirt from the basket to check the aroma index. The shirt got to my nose before my nose got to the shirt. I grabbed from the casual side of the closet: patched jeans and one of Harry's cast-off shirts, penguins in sunglasses sipping martinis. He'd found it overly conservative. I found it overly large by two sizes, but comfortable. My socks having missed the wash, I went without, jamming my feet into battered running shoes.

I checked the mirror and saw my hair had gotten long again – how does that happen? The man looking back at me resembled a thirty-six-year-old refugee from a Jimmy Buffet concert.

I fed Mr Mix-up, loaded him into my old pickup, painted gray with a roller. I took a deep breath, fired up the engine and raced north toward the Institute, hoping to stop the worst idea I'd heard in a long time.

# 2

Pulling into the lot at the Institute, I noted two vehicles in visitor parking slots, one a big square Benz, burgundy, looking heavy enough to sink into the asphalt like stone through water, the other a gleaming silver Corvette of recent vintage. The juxtaposition reminded me of a brick beside a stiletto, blunt trauma versus puncture.

Nearby waited a brown van with a cage inside, a prisoner-transport vehicle from Holman Prison. It was early January and the temp was forty-eight degrees, the engine running to keep the heater blasting, native South Alabamians thin-blooded by nine months of what most locales called summer. When it dropped below forty degrees, we crawled into steamy bathtubs and hibernated until the magnolias blossomed.

Two bored-looking guards sat inside the van smoking

cigarettes. I trotted over, flashing ID and motioning to roll the window down.

"What you boys here for?" I asked.

The driver, a tight-eyed old gunbull with buck teeth centering fat jowls, pushed back his hat. "We brought Bobby Lee Crayline up from Holman. I 'spect he'll be back out here soon enough."

"You know he's here to be hypnotized?"

The gunbull's lips curled in a sneer. "Fuckin' legal bullshit to put him in a cushy mental hospital. Crayline should be hypnotized into thinking he's a campfire."

"Why's that?"

"Then we can shovel dirt over him until he goes out."

I sprinted back to my truck and opened the door, Mr Mix-up launching out like a torpedo, bounding at my heels, spinning in circles. Mix-up had drawn widely from the canine gene pool, his body thick and heavy in the chest, the hair tightly grained but with fluffy tufts behind his long legs and on his tail. His feet were oven mitts, his head a St Bernard with basset-length ears. His eyes were huge and inquisitive. His powerful, deep-chested body was spotted brown and white and black, the back legs brindled a rusty red. The first time I saw Mix-up I thought him a Dr Seuss character come to life.

"Hey, Detective, what the hell kinda dog is that?" the guard yelled out the window.

"'Bout every kind, I think," I said.

"An' probably some horse and ostrich, too," the guard noted, shaking his head in wonder.

I passed through security and headed to the sign-in clipboard to register. The registration sheet held three signatures, two from a firm named Dunham, Krull and Slezak. The firm was from Memphis, high-powered and low-oriented, defending anyone offering big money or big publicity. Neither category seemed to fit Bobby Lee Crayline, but I'd been wrong before.

"Who's in this meeting?" I asked Theotis Burns as he walked up. Theotis handled administrative operations of the Institute. He was forty-three, smallish in stature, and wore dark suits that flowed like liquid. Theotis reminded me of the rapper-entrepreneur Puff Daddy or P. Diddy, except P-whatever never worked in a venue with red EMERGENCY buttons spaced along the corridors.

"Dr Wainwright and three men," Theotis said. "One looks like a guy playing a movie star, got poufy white hair and whiter teeth. He's wrapped in two-thousand-dollar threads, pure silk. One's a chubby guy in a blue off-the-rack threads, round glasses, Hush-fucking-Puppies over gray socks. Radiates shrinknicity, gotta be the hypnotist."

"The third one?"

"A hard-looking guy, big, had to surrender a Glock 17 at the outside gate. Wasn't happy about it, either."

"What's your take, Theo?" I asked, knowing he kept a close ear to the ground.

"You know Bobby Lee Crayline was with us for a couple

10

months two years back, Carson? Just after he killed the guy in the ring?"

I nodded. "Vangie was studying him."

"Crayline's got one of those personalities that sucks everything to him. He started getting into people's heads and causing all sorts of trouble. He was never meant to be a permanent resident. Dr Prowse sent him back to prison. Then the appellate judge set him free."

"I figured he'd be back in the system," I said. "Took a couple years and a kidnapping – and maybe a few bodies pulled from the dirt in Alabama – but here he is."

"Doc Prowse thought a lot about hypnotizing Bobby Lee when he was here, Carson, but decided against it. She ever tell you why?"

I nodded. "Vangie was afraid he'd decompensate. That direct contact with his past might create conditions in which he'd become even more dangerous."

"He's barely wrapped as it is."

"He siphons off the worst impulses by beating the hell out of others, Theo. It's an escape valve."

Theotis shook his head and retreated down the hall. I led Mix-up to a small meeting room, tossed a biscuit on the floor. When he was rolling on the biscuit, his curious pre-chow ritual, I closed the door and turned down the hall toward the conference room.

I knocked and stuck my head inside. The room was spare, the lighting indirect, the cool air tinted with false lemon. Two men were at the table, one resembling country singer Porter Wagoner, hound-dog features beneath a white

11

pompadour. He had a booth-built tan and looked in his late fifties. Theo was right about the threads: Where Wagoner would have worn ten pounds of sequins, this guy was tucked inside three thousand bucks' worth of sedate gray silk.

Beside Pomp'n'tan was a tall and broad-shouldered guy in his mid-thirties. His eyes were deep-set and dark and when added to his thick eyebrows suggested a Neanderthal on steroids. His black suit was cut large, allowing easy access to the Glock he'd had to surrender.

A penguin-bodied man sat to the side with a briefcase in his lap. Bald with side fringes, pencil mustache, soft blue eyes behind thick trifocals. He was sixty or so, dressed in a formless suit. The hypnotist shrink.

"Where's Dr Wainwright?" I asked.

"The restroom," the Neanderthal said, eyeing me like a bum who'd stumbled into a wedding. "Wait outside and you won't miss her."

"I'll wait in here," I said, stepping into the room.

"This is a private meeting." He stood, hand blocking entry further than two steps. It was a bouncer's move and I'd never liked bouncers.

"I'm on the VIP list," I said.

"I said this is a private meeting."

When I started toward a seat the Neanderthal stopped me with a stiff finger at my sternum. Another bouncer move. I jammed my leg in front of his, grabbed his wrist and rotated like an ice skater starting a sit-spin. The Neanderthal went sprawling across the floor, sending two

12

chairs tumbling. He was up in a half-heartbeat, fists clenched, flashing I'm-gonna-kill-you eyes. I whipped out my badge wallet and ID.

"Not recommended," I said.

"What's going on here?" Doc Wainwright appeared at the threshold, looking between the upended chairs and my ID display.

"A get-acquainted session, Doc," I said.

"Sit, Bridges," said a voice behind me. Scarcely louder than the hum of the air conditioning, it was a command. Pomp'n'tan was studying me with interested eyes. He held a business card between index and second finger, as if slipping a tip to a bellhop.

"Read it to me," I said.

"Arthur Slezak, of Dunham, Krull and Slezak. Counsel of record for Robert Crayline. The gentlemen with me are Charles Bridges, who you just, uh, met. And this is Dr Walter Neddles, psychiatrist and certified hypnotist. May I see your identification, please?"

Slezak donned reading glasses and studied my particulars as I studied his hands: pink with perfectly manicured nails, on his left wrist a Rolex that cost as much as I made from January through June. I saw him frown, as if trying to grasp a memory.

"Mobile?" he said. "Aren't you a bit far from your jurisdiction, Detective?"

"I've asked this man to be here," Wainwright said, taking her chair at the head of the table.

"Why's that, Doctor?"

13

"Detective Ryder knows the danger Mr Crayline represents. He's against the hypnosis as well."

Neddles cleared his throat. "I assure you, Dr Wainwright, that I've hypnotized dangerous people. Terrence Crump, Ernesto Vasquez, Rhonda Sue Bolz—"

"I've met them all," I interrupted. "I tracked and arrested Crump, who attacked elderly women. Bolz was a hospital poisoner. Vasquez killed winos or railroad bums. Have you studied Bobby Lee Crayline, Doctor? His capacity for violence is on another level."

Slezak had a butter-smooth smile on his face. "If Mr Crayline is resistant to hypnosis, we're gone. All I'm requesting is the opportunity."

"What do you want to know?"

"That's private, except to say that Mr Crayline might know things he may not know he knows."

"That's suitably vague," I said, "You going to ask Bobby Lee about the three bodies found in his old hometown?"

"Purely circumstantial," Slezak pooh-poohed. "Never tied to Mr Crayline."

"So far," I said.

"I've decided this is too dangerous," Wainwright announced, finding her courage. "I'm sorry for your trouble, Mr Slezak, but I refuse to allow the hypnosis."

Slezak plucked out a sheaf of paper from the briefcase at his feet. He slid reading glasses over the lengthy nose and tapped the pages. "Did you know, Dr Wainwright, that the land beneath the Institute is leased from the state for a dollar a year? And there's a clause stating if the Institute poses a threat to the well-being of the local citizenry, the deal can be revoked?"

"We've never posed a threat to anyone," Wainwright said.

Slezak feigned confusion. "Did not a patient escape from this very institution just two years ago? A man who murdered his father and five women? Wasn't he a prime suspect in the death of Evangeline Prowse, the former director of this institution?"

"Jeremy Ridgecliff," Wainwright said, leaning forward, her voice tight. "The man was never loose in this area. And no one really knows what happened after his escape. Surely you heard the rumors regarding Ridgecliff's supposed role in the hotel explosion during the—"

Slezak cut her off mid-sentence. He snapped his fingers and turned to me.

"I know why the name Ryder sounds familiar. You were the cop sent to New York to stop Ridgecliff. Don't tell me you think the man is anything but a vicious killer." Slezak raised a white eyebrow, as if Ridgecliff's guilt was written in the sands of Time and anyone thinking otherwise was moronic.

"I do question Ridgecliff's guilt. Revisiting the women's murders could have different findings this time around."

"But isn't Ridgecliff still in hiding?" Slezak countered. "No effort to proclaim innocence? Never contacted anyone?"

My face grew hot and I looked away. I'd spoken to

15

Jeremy Ridgecliff a week ago, the seventeenth conversation I'd had with him since his escape. I actually spoke to him on a fairly regular basis, though I never knew where he was calling from.

It's said everyone has one big secret. Here's mine: Jeremy Ridgecliff is my biological brother, our kinship concealed by my long-ago name change and other obfuscations. Those who knew could be counted on one hand with digits to spare. I'd spent years hiding my ties to Jeremy and our childhood, only to be slammed into him in New York and made part of his escape mechanism. I had no idea where he was, only that he was brilliant enough to develop exacting mechanisms to avoid capture.

"Detective Ryder?" Slezak prodded. "You're not answering my question. Is Ridgecliff on the run from the law?"

"Yes," I said. It was all I could say.

Slezak gave me a lizard smile and turned to Wainwright. "A mad killer set loose, Doctor? Imagine if that fact was presented to the citizens who allow prime taxpayer land to be leased for a paltry sum. A funding backlash might ensue."

"We do important work here," Wainwright said. "You can't jeopardize that in order to—"

Faces turned my way as I stood and crooked a come-hither digit at Nancy Wainwright.

"Doc? How about a brief meeting in the hall?"

She followed me outside and I closed the door. "It's a

goddamn bluff," she said. "The slimy bastard won't do it."

"He might, just to show he can," I cautioned, having met too many Slezaks.

"Having to defend the Institute would wear me out," Wainwright sighed, leaning against the wall, arms crossed. "Upset the staff. Jeopardize serious research. The scum bucket has me by my weakest point."

"Slezak's crafted his whole life around exploiting weaknesses, Doc." I put my hand on her shoulder. "It's obvious they're gonna do the hypnosis somewhere. Here, at least you're in charge, right?"

She reached out to one of the EMERGENCY buttons recessed into the white walls, ran her finger lightly over its blood-red surface.

"For whatever that's worth," she said.

# 3

We adjourned to the observation room adjacent to where Crayline would be hypnotized, a one-way mirror allowing viewing. The room was small and dark. Speakers piped in conversations from the meeting room, the on/off switch beside the mirror. The set-up made me think of a recording studio without the electronics.

Slezak, Wainwright and I took chairs. We peered through the glass into the adjoining room and saw Dr Neddles and Bridges. The room was painted in soft and neutral tones, calming, perhaps to distract from several steel rings recessed into the concrete floor. Two chairs sat within, as well as a small round table. A sofa was to the rear.

"I want a guard in there," Wainwright said.

"Mr Bridges is an ex-Marine," Slezak said. "Very capable should extra restraint be needed. He'll stay."

Bridges puffed out his chest and jutted his jaw, looking

tough. Wainwright looked to me for a verdict. I knew Bridges was a contract employee for a firm like Dunham Krull, inhabiting a hard-edged world of bail bondsmen and bodyguards, repo men and bounty hunters. He'd be mean and hard and proud of the fact, since it was his sole selling point.

"We can live with that," I said.

Wainwright plucked a phone from the table beside her chair. "I'll have Bobby Lee brought in."

Crayline shuffled through the door a minute later, grinning as if he'd called the meeting. He was six-two or -three, two hundred ten pounds, wide shouldered but wasp-waisted. His head was shaved, the bright flesh webbed with scars. Some of the healed wounds looked decades old and I wondered how they'd been inflicted. He was wearing an institutional sweatshirt and pants, muscle-crowded arms and chest filling his shirt; his thighs pulsing against the fabric like beating hearts. Crayline radiated so much force that a blind person would have sat up straighter when he entered a room.

Crayline surveyed his surroundings with electric green eyes, as if determining whether accommodations and participants met his standards. He'd obviously been told of the lawyer's visit – his right – and the wrangling on the subject of hypnosis. He had just as obviously agreed to the procedure, probably to break the monotony of his day.

"Have a seat, Crayline," Bridges said.

Crayline turned to Bridges as if suddenly noticing him. "You're a big fella, aincha?"

"Big enough," Bridges said, putting challenge in his eyes and tapping the chair. "Sit."

Crayline turned his head away and whispered softly.

"What was that?" Bridges asked, leaning closer. "What did you say?"

Crayline whipped his head back around and snapped his teeth like a pit bull biting a chunk off a roast. Bridges startled backwards into the table, sending it skidding across the carpet. Crayline grinned. Bridges, red-faced with embarrassment, shoved the table back in place.

"Sit," Bridges repeated, voice taut with anger.

Crayline sauntered to the table and stood beside the chair, flexing his knees. Bridges slid the chair beneath Crayline's buttocks and he sat. Bridges had, without thinking, moved the chair to accommodate Crayline.

Control.

The guard affixed Crayline's leg chain to a D-ring beneath the table and retreated to the rear. Dr Neddles placed his open briefcase on the table and took the chair opposing Crayline. The prisoner had a sinus affliction, trails of syrupy yellow mucus draining from his nostrils to his upper lip. Neddles popped a few tissues from his briefcase.

"Would you like for me to wipe your face, Mr Crayline?"

Bobby Crayline drew his lower lip up and over the effluvium, scooping it into his mouth. He swished it between his cheeks as if sampling wine.

"Tastes like fresh oysters," he grinned, winking and swallowing. "I'm my own seafood restaurant."

Beside me, Slezak grimaced and whispered *Jesus*.

Crayline looked at the mirror as though seeing it for the first time. It seemed he was staring directly at me. Then he did something – I don't know what it was – like he'd directed energy into his eyes.

For a split second Crayline's eyes were those of a rabid wolf.

I blinked, looked again. His eyes were normal. My heart was beating faster. Bridges backed to the corner as Neddles produced a small musical triangle and its striker. "The sound starts a musical voyage, Mr Crayline. Each ring of the bell helps you float away."

"What if I ain't a floatin' sort, Doc?"

"You promised to let us try, Bobby," Neddles crooned. "Close your eyes and clear your mind until there's nothing in it but one clear and pure note . . ."

Crayline closed his eyes. The psychologist struck the triangle twice.

*ting, ting*

"Relax, Bobby Lee. Breathe like a series of waves. Warm and gentle waves . . ." *ting* ". . . Foaming and flowing around your legs . . ."

*ting . . . ting*

Triangle tinging rhythmically, Neddles continued his hypno-patter, trying for that peculiar mental seduction called the suggestive state. After several minutes, Crayline's head lolled to the side, his face softened, his eyes closed.

"My lord," Doc Wainwright said. "I think it's working."

Neddles set the triangle aside and reached in his pocket,

snapping open a folded page of questions. Crayline looked as close to benign as someone like that could get. We heard his breathing through the sound system, relaxed and regular. I was beginning to look forward to the show when Slezak stood and strode to the switch beside the mirror. He snapped the speakers off and the room went silent.

Wainwright scowled. "I have to monitor the procedure, Mr Slezak."

"It's privileged information," Slezak said. "I demand privacy with my client."

"How about I leave the room, Slezak?" I offered. "It'll be you and the doctor. That work?"

"No. Both of you please leave us until we're finished."

Wainwright looked into the adjoining room, saw all was calm. She frowned at Slezak. "We'll be right outside the door."

"Whatever makes you happy," he said.

Wainwright and I stepped outside. "You think he's really under?" I said. "I can't figure Crayline being hypnotized."

"Sometimes people who seem the worst potential subjects go under in a fingersnap. You can't tell who's a good candidate until you swing the watch."

"I assume Slezak never told you who he's really representing?" I asked.

"He suggested it was Bobby Lee."

"Bobby Lee wouldn't know Slezak from Muzak," I said. "Someone else is paying for all this."

I sat and read a three-day-old newspaper fetched from the employee lounge. Doc Wainwright busied herself reading case histories. I heard a sound from the room with Crayline, lifted my head and, hearing nothing, resumed reading.

After twenty-five minutes, I set the paper aside. Another sound, like a squeal, issued from the room. Then something louder, a moan. I looked at Wainwright.

"Privacy be damned," she said, turning toward the observation room. "Something's going on."

She entered with me at her heels. Slezak stood, his eyes sizzling with anger. "I want you both out, now!"

We strode past him like he was furniture and went the mirror. Bobby Lee Crayline was rolling his head like it was on gimbals. His mouth opened in a howl but nothing transmitted through the glass.

"Doctor Neddles touched something painful," Wainwright said.

"You're risking a lawsuit," the lawyer barked. "I'll have your . . ."

Slezak's voice tapered off as Crayline howled loud enough to hear. His body began to spasm. His fists were clenching and releasing. "Crayline's too deep," Wainwright said. "God knows what he's re-living."

Another cold and quivering howl pierced the glass. I slipped my hand to the switch on the wall, snapped the speakers on.

"I KILLED THEM WRONG!" Bobby Lee howled. "THEY'RE STUCK THERE FOREVER!"

Neddles looked confused; the words made no sense. Bobby Lee began leaping as if to touch the ceiling with his head. Great pumping leaps in time with his howls, like the floor was on fire. He'd compact himself, leap, repeat. Bridges was beside Crayline, trying to get an arm around the man's neck.

One of Crayline's arms flew wide, chain whipping through the air. My heart froze. Crayline had summoned a demonic reserve of strength and torn the ring from the floor.

"He's loose," I yelled.

I watched in horror as the madman head-butted Neddles, who collapsed like deflated skin. Bridges aimed a kick at Crayline's groin. He took it on his thigh, ducked, and shoulder-rammed Bridges into the wall, dropping him. Bobby Lee turned and stared into the mirror, his eyes radiating the rabid-wolf look I'd seen before.

He lowered like a bull preparing to charge.

"Oh Jesus," Wainwright whispered. I pulled her aside as Crayline exploded through the glass like a missile launched from hell. I dove for his shoulders, tried to snake an arm around his phone-pole neck. Doc Wainwright was screaming for the guards. Crayline bucked like a rodeo bull, sending me spinning across the room. When I spun back to the tumult, Crayline had Slezak's head under his arm, trying to snap the man's neck. I grabbed Crayline's arms, his biceps like living cannonballs.

Emergency horns blared. Guards exploded through the

24

door. Stun guns sizzled. A final howl from the subject, his voice a high tremolo, like a child sucked down a drain.

The hypnosis of Bobby Lee Crayline was over.

# 4

Wainwright and I stood in the bright Alabama sun and waited for a heavily restrained Crayline to return to the prison van. He was belted to a gurney, not allowed to stand. I'd fixed Mix-up's leash to his collar and kept him to my side.

Bridges stood a dozen feet away, humiliated by the man he'd been charged with controlling. Dr Neddles probably had a mild concussion, but was coherent and expected to do fine. The medics were putting a restraint collar on Slezak's neck. His face was ashen, like he'd looked into a grave and realized it was his.

"Coming through," the younger of the guards yelled, rolling Bobby Lee Crayline to the van. Crayline was grinning again, as if the gurney was a sedan chair and he was being borne aloft through adoring throngs. Mix-up lunged toward Crayline, like the man smelled of raw meat. I pulled my dog tighter against my leg and saw Bridges's knuckles turn white as Crayline rolled nearer. Bridges strode to the restrained Crayline and stared down at him. *Uh-oh*, I thought, tensing.

Bridges cleared his throat deep and spat thickly in Crayline's face. Said, "Try my oysters, faggot."

"Get back from him, now," the guard growled, shouldering Bridges aside as the gurney clattered to the van.

"How much inbreeding did it take to make you, Crayline?" Bridges yelled at the retreating prisoner. "How many generations of retards fucking their retarded sisters?"

Wainwright strode to Bridges, grabbed his arm. "Bridges! That's enough!"

But Bridges wasn't finished. "How was your childhood, Crayline?" he railed. "Bet you got used like a girl by all the men in your family. Bet you put on lipstick and begged for more."

The grin on Crayline's face was replaced by a blank screen. His head twisted back as he was hustled across the asphalt, his voice no longer giggly but rasping, the sound of a henchman's axe on the grindstone.

"You best move to another planet, girly," he hissed. "Bobby Lee's gonna fry your guts for his supper."

"Fuck you, you genetic moron," Bridges snarled. He strode to his Corvette and roared away. Neddles and Slezak limped to the Benz and followed. A minute later, the van with Crayline pulled away.

Wainwright and I watched the vehicle pass the checkpoints, then swerve on to the road a half-mile distant to become a brown speck against green fields. Wainwright fumbled in her purse and produced a rumpled pack of cigarettes, lit one.

"Didn't figure you for a smoker, Doc," I said.

"I have two cigarettes a week, Detective. I'm having them both now."

"I fully understand," I said.

"I owe you for coming up here," Wainwright said, exhaling a blue plume of smoke. "I know there's nothing I can do for you, but if ever there is . . ."

I waved her promise away and we stood quietly for a couple minutes to watch a jet pull a slender contrail from the west to the east. Wainwright lit her second cigarette from the first, squinted over my shoulder. Frowned at something. My eyes followed to a black rope of smoke rising into the sky perhaps five miles away. I knew there was nothing in that direction but cotton fields and pasture.

"What do you think it is?" Doc Wainwright said.

"Nothing good." I told her to call the local cops, then sprinted to my truck with my dog at my side.

From a quarter-mile away, the scene sent ice cubes clattering through my belly. The Holman van lay on its side in a ditch, orange flames licking from the windows and turning to smoke the color of raw petroleum. I saw a green tractor in the middle of the road and wondered if the vehicles had collided.

I pulled to the side of the road, jumped out, hearing the distant whine of approaching sirens. Mix-up followed, keeping a wary eye on the fire. The tractor was a John Deere with a trailer behind, piled high with hay bales. A farmer in blue overalls and work shirt knelt above the young guard, severely burned, his clothing smoldering. His face was pocked with shotgun pellets.

The farmer turned to me, his face a mask of terror. "I was in the field, saw smoke, drove over on my tractor. I pulled this man from the van. There's another man in there, a driver. I couldn't get to him, the flames . . ."

I looked into the fully engulfed van. A lost cause. I saw Mix-up in the corner of my eye, grubbing in the hay atop the trailer. The farmer started to touch the man, give comfort, but his hands couldn't cross the distance to the dying guard. He looked at me, helpless, almost in tears.

"I don't know what to do."

"Help's coming," I said, hearing the sirens, loud now.

# 5

Months passed with no new details added to Crayline's escape, save that the farmer mentioned hearing a motorcycle racing away in the distance as he arrived. It was theorized that a motorcyclist passed the lumbering Holman van and fired a shotgun into the windows. The speed limit on the stretch of road was thirty-five miles per hour. No matter what the van did when the driver lost control, the chances were Bobby Lee – strapped in from several angles – wouldn't get hurt too badly. I always pictured him laughing as his rescuer pulled him from the broken vehicle, like a guy getting off a roller-coaster.

It was a brilliant plan, probably hatched in Holman when Crayline discovered his upcoming trip to the Institute. Prisons had "alumni associations", and someone with the demonic charisma of a Bobby Lee Crayline would have outside connections, men who'd risk their lives to say they'd helped him escape.

In the meantime, people in Mobile were bludgeoned, stabbed, poisoned, shot and, in one memorable case, vacuumed to death. Harry and I investigated, putting in a lot of eighteen-hour days. Then, good news. Financial stimulus funds reached the understaffed Mobile Police Department and sparked the hiring of new officers. This allowed the promotion to detective of several deserving uniformed men and women. The workload decreased.

I was thinking about taking some time off, when my supervisor, Lieutenant Tom Mason walked to my desk. Tom had been trying to get me to take a lengthy vacation for years. I'd get close, but the caseload would balloon and I'd truncate my plans to a long weekend getaway. At least that's what I told myself. My partner muttered that I was an investigation addict afraid of missing a fix, but he muttered a fair amount.

But in truth, even I felt increasingly frazzled. Cases were becoming less a rush than a drudge. The slackening of pressure had me thinking it was finally time to take a break and get my edge sharpened.

"You and Harry have had a tough year," Tom said. "He got his head banged like a gong. You put in eighty-hour weeks on that case with Sandhill. Not to mention this current crop of madness."

"The point being, Tom?"

"The Department owes you forty-three days of accumulated vacation, Carson. Now, I can't order you to take time off, but I think it would be good if you gave it some thought and . . ."

"I'll do it," I said, clapping my hands.

"Do what?"

"Like you just said. Go on a vacation. What a great idea!"

Tom paused. "You will? Just like that?"

"It's brilliant, Tom," I said, standing to do a little shuffle-foot dance. "I'll start making plans."

Tom nodded and turned back to his corner office, stricken mute. I could tell he'd prepared an entire lecture on *Why Carson Ryder Should Take a Vacation.*

Tom paused at his doorway, fingers tapping the frame. He turned.

"You'd planned to take some time off, right, Carson? Is that it?"

I did cherubic innocence. Tom waved the question away and went inside his office, his long face heavy with puzzlement.

Which explains, in a roundabout way, how I ended up in Eastern Kentucky, hanging off the side of a mountain while being yelled at by a gnome.

# 6

"Hey Carson!" called a voice from way below my feet. "You get lost again? Yoo-hoo, Earth to Carson Ryder."

"I hear you, Gary," I called over my back. Above me I saw two hundred feet of Corbin sandstone, the leavings of untold millennia of alluvial flooding. I was climbing through the compressed floor of an ancient sea that flowed during the Mississippian era, 400 million years ago. My fingers clutched small handholds. My toes were wedged into clefts. At my back lay nothing more than air.

"Others are waiting their turn, bud. Come on down."

I pushed away from the rock face, dropping a foot until the rope through the bolt jolted me to a stop and I was lowered thirty feet to the ground. Gary, the twenty-five-year-old rock-climbing instructor, a diminutive guy who was part gnome, part mountain goat, grinned as my feet hit the ground. Pete Tinker, the other instructor from Compass Point Outfitters, grabbed the control rope and launched another aspiring climber up the cliff face. Gary patted my back.

"You seem to get lost up there, Carson. How was it?"

"I'm sweating like a sprinkler," I said, pulling my soaked tee from my chest to put air over my skin. "My muscles are quivering. My fingers ache. But I'm ready to go back up right now."

"I'm not surprised. A lot of folks don't have the physicality for rock climbing, the strength and elasticity. You do. But even more, you have an intuitive feel. You don't waste motion."

"I'm surprised to hear that. I feel clumsy as a first-step toddler."

Gary grimaced toward the young woman just sent up. She'd lost her grip and was spinning in the air as Tinker belayed rope and shouted instructions.

"These folks are toddlers, Carson. Four days of lessons and you're up and running. But you've done this before, I take it?"

I grinned. "I dated a climber a few years ago. She gave me the basics."

"She done good. But you're ready to move past the basics. You're coming back, right?"

"Try and keep me away."

I packed up my rented climbing gear and began coiling ropes. The eight other climbing students did the same under Gary and Pete's watchful eyes. We heard the labored grind of an engine and turned to an SUV arriving on the old logging trail connecting the main road to our cliff face. The insignia on the door read *US Forest Service*. We were on their turf, inside the Red River Gorge Geological Area of the Daniel Boone National Forest.

The high-sprung vehicle crunched to a stop and two occupants exited, a big, square-built county cop about my age, mid-thirties. His face was a broad, flat plain centered by a button nose, as if a normal nose had been sectioned and only the tip pasted to his face. The man's eyes were a gray wash and his mouth so lipless and tight I couldn't imagine it smiling. His belly rolled three inches over a wide belt hung with police implements. The cowboy boots were alligator and the hogleg pistol he carried would only be standard issue in a Wild West wet dream. His uniform was too many hours from an iron.

Beside him, in visual opposition, was a trim and tall older guy in a hard-creased green uniform that looked ten minutes from the dry cleaners. It took a second to register that he was a forest ranger. He had a relaxed and dreamy smile on a tanned and ruggedly pleasant face, leaning back to stretch his spine. But I noted his half-closed eyes vacuuming in his surroundings. It was interesting.

The cop went to talk to Pete and Gary. I carried on coiling rope and watching from the corner of my eye. The ranger had nodded to the instructors before leaning against the trunk of a hemlock, whistling to himself and studying the sandy ground.

I looked up and caught a hard and cold appraisal from the sheriff, like he found something offensive in my bearing. I feigned indifference and walked my coil of rope to the van. Turning, I saw the ranger cross my path to pick up a tiny foil wrapper, as if collecting errant litter. He tucked the foil in his pocket, looked down again, headed back toward the SUV.

I knew what he was doing, and it had little to do with litter collection.

"Sheriff Beale," the ranger said.

The cop turned from Gary, pushed back his hat. "E-yup?"

"We're done."

The big cop shot me another hard glance, then nodded and followed the ranger. They climbed in the Forest Service vehicle, pulled away slowly, the ranger at the wheel. As he passed in front of me, I smiled.

"Not the shoe prints you were looking for, right?"

His eyes held mine for a two-count. Then the eyes and the SUV were moving away and I tossed my second coil of rope in the van with the gear of the other students. They'd driven six miles from the outfitters in Pine Ridge. The cliff we'd been using for practice was only three miles from my lodgings, so I'd driven over on my own.

Gary shot a thumbs-up out the window, said, "See you later," and the van rattled away.

I stared up the wall of rock – for a brief moment wondering how far up I could get on my own – then came to my senses and climbed into my pickup, pausing to enjoy the view and the strange journey that had led me here, a *pas de deux* with fate, or perhaps blind luck.

After talking with Lieutenant Mason, I had been sitting at home and shuffling through a lapful of travel brochures snatched from rest stops over the years. They were heavy on entertainment-oriented venues: Branson, Orlando, Gatlinburg, and other places that made me break out in a cold sweat. I was wondering if I should just put Mr Mix-up in the truck and start driving à la Steinbeck when the phone rang.

"*Mr Ryder? This is Dottie Fugate at RRG cabin rentals up here in the Kentucky mountains. Feel like a little vacation getaway?*"

"I, uh . . . What?"

"*You stayed with us a while back, right?*"

My family had lived in the area for four months when I was a child of seven, following my father in his job as engineer and bridge-builder. Then, almost a decade ago, at age twenty-seven, I'd returned before joining the MPD, a self-imposed weekend retreat to sort out a jumble of warring factions in my head. It hit me that I must have stayed at an RRG cabin.

"The last I was in your neighborhood was nine years ago, Miz Fugate. You keep records that long?"

She laughed. "*Yep. An' ever' year we drop all the previous guests' register cards in a hat and my daughter pulls out a winner of free use of a cabin. She plucked out your name. I sure hope you can come back and stay with us.*"

Clair Peltier, a pathologist for the state of Alabama and my significant sometimes other, believes in the concept of synchronicity, thinking a webwork of logic underlies the fabric of the visible world, a fluid and spiritual mathematics with a sense of humor. She would have explained that my seeking a vacation spot and one arriving via phone was synchronicity: it was not luck, but an item on the universe's to-do list.

To me it was just weird. But it had dropped in my lap, and it was free.

"You got any cabins available, say, next week?" I asked.

I heard pages flipping, Dottie Fugate checking a calendar.

*"Choice is tight, cuz it's summer tourist season, but we got one open starting Saturday. It's in a holler in the backcountry and damn remote, to tell the truth."*

"I'll take it."

I started the engine and my truck ascended from the valley through pine and hemlock and maple, passing sheer rock faces where vegetation wouldn't grow. I saw huge house-sized chunks of rock that had toppled from the ridges eons ago. The dark boulders sat in the forest like sentinels, and I recalled that during my brief childhood stay in the mountains I had imagined the boulders whispering to one another during the night, not through the air, but the ground.

I headed back to the cabin, stomach growling, breakfast burned away by hauling my ass up rock faces. The road was asphalt, potholed, crumbling at the edges, but a main county road nonetheless, the shoulders dappled with wildflowers. I curved past a cliff face and cut on to a tight lane, the truck's springs squealing as the tires dropped from asphalt on to rutted double track of dirt and gravel.

Directly ahead, the road seemed to disappear, the effect of a precipitous winding drop into the tight cleft between two mountains, a hollow, or what locals called a "holler". I eased down until the lane flattened out. Another few hundred feet and the road forked. To the left was the only neighboring dwelling, a sizeable log cabin visible through the trees.

The right-hand path took me a half-mile deeper in the hollow to my cabin, slat-sided and roofed with dark green metal. Behind, three towering hemlocks pushed into the blue sky, taller by a third than the surrounding white pines and oaks. The dark, raw-wood cabin looked native amidst the forest, as if it had sprouted on its own.

I climbed the porch and pulled my key, for the first time noting that the keychain had a label with the cabin's name. Vacation retreats were given names – *Rocky Ridge, Timbertop, Braeside* and so forth – mine apparently named by its remote placement.

*Road's End.*

I heard a hellacious din from inside and saw a blur of frenzied motion at the window. I sighed and opened the door.

A tornado blew out.

"Jesus, ouch, damn . . . calm down, Mix-up."

Having saved my dog from the euthanasia needle with about a half-hour to spare, many would have figured his wild-eyed, slobbering delight was joy at greeting his savior, but jubilant chaos was his default setting: spinning in circles, bumping my legs, rolling on his back, a dog that delighted in everything.

Mix-up thundered between my legs, and I went down. When my head was on his level he began licking it like a beef roast.

"Stop, dammit. No, Mix-up. Sit! SIT!"

A strange thing happened, something I didn't expect in a hundred years.

He sat.

His body twitched, but his haunches stayed glued to the ground. I stood, staring at the phenomenon. For a year I'd been working on commands, Mr Mix-up immune to my imprecations. I'd say *Sit,* he'd thunder in circles. I'd say *Stay,* he'd follow me like my pants were made of bacon. I'd throw a stick and yell *Fetch*, he'd roll on the ground and pedal his legs at the sky.

A couple months ago I'd spoken about Mix-up's recalcitrance to his day-care lady, Lucinda Best, who volunteered at the animal shelter from which I'd rescued him. She'd recommended a nearby obedience school and I'd taken him thrice-weekly for a month, a hundred and fifty bucks' worth of watching other dogs learn to heel, fetch, sit and stay while Mix-up went his merry way.

It appeared he'd managed to learn something, though. Did one of his many breeds have a learning lag time?

I held up my hand and quietly said, *Stay*. I backed away. He stayed. I back-stepped down the drive for fifty paces, hand up, repeating my command every few seconds. I stopped, gestured my way, said, *Come here*.

He exploded toward me. When he was two dozen feet away I thrust my hand out, said *Sit*.

He skidded to a stop in sit position. I backed away again, keeping him in place with the *Stay* command. I found a foot of busted branch on the ground, threw it down the drive yelling *Fetch*!

He tipped over and began pedaling his paws at the sky.

"Two out of three ain't bad," I told him, rubbing his belly. "Let's go grab some chow."

I opened the cabin door and went inside, the air cool and smelling of wood and my breakfast bacon. The walls were pine decorated with cheap buys from local flea markets: a red-centric quilt, a sign advertising Texaco Gasoline, calendar-style photos from the Gorge stuck in a variety of dime-store frames. The living room had a vaulted ceiling, with loft space above. Dormers let light pour in. The dining room and kitchen made one long unit.

I showered away the morning's sweat and grit. Afterwards, I went to the kitchen area and lashed together two sausage and jalapeno cheese sandwiches. I cracked open a cold Sam Adams and dined in a rocker on the sun-dappled porch, serenaded by insects, birdsong and the tumble of water over rock in the nearby creek. Swallow-tailed butterflies skittered through the warm air.

Somewhere on the ridge above the cabin a woodpecker drilled for bugs.

I leaned back in the rocker and set my bare heels on the railing as something puzzling happened in my neck and shoulders. At first I didn't recognize the feeling, then it came to me.

They had relaxed.

# 7

I spent the remainder of the day hiking in the Gorge, watching Mix-up bark after squirrels and turkeys and splash through the creeks. With the wide blue sky a constant companion, we pushed through green thickets of rhododendron, crossed slender ridges no wider than my truck, yawning drop-offs on both sides. We climbed up and down the steep grades until my knees went weak and we had to return.

I hit the mattress at eight thirty, worn and weary and happy as a clam.

In the morning a strange chirping roused me from my dreams, the sound resolving into the cellphone beside the bed. I thumbed the device open and put it to my ear.

"Hello?"

"—ot a police emer—cy," bayed a female voice, the lousy reception chopping out half of her words.

"I can't hear you," I said.

"We have—lice emerg—" the woman repeated in a twangy mountain accent, giving no sign she was receiving me.

The phone showed a half-bar of reception. I'd quickly learned cell signals were haphazard in the mountains, wavering. I sprinted out the door and up the hill beside the cabin, yelling, "Hang on!"

When I'd put fifty or sixty feet on my altitude, I looked at the phone and saw another strip of bar on the meter.

"This is——Cherry of——of Kentucky. We need you——mergency."

"I can't hear you!" I yelled.

"GPS—ordinates are . . ." I pulled out my pen, focused on nothing but hearing. The coordinates were spoken twice and I managed to get them, I hoped.

"Who is this?" I yelled. "Identify yourself."

The call warbled, howled, beeped and died. No caller number had registered. My head whirled with questions as I stumbled down the hillside. Who had my caller been? Who knew I was vacationing in Kentucky?

Wait . . . the caller thought I was in Alabama. That made a lot more sense. Just to be sure, I grabbed my brand-new, bought-for-the-trip GPS and entered the coordinates.

The position was maybe four miles from the cabin. My caller had been local. There was nothing to do but holster my weapon in the back of my pants, leave my dog a fistful of snacks to distract from my leaving, jump

44

in the truck with the GPS set for the coordinates, and hope for an answer to the mystery.

I followed the jittering GPS arrow until turning on to a gravel road. The gravel crunched under my tires for four miles, diminishing to dirt studded with pebbles. I rounded a copse of pines and saw what remained of a house. Small, single story, rickety porch, brick chimney at one end, the mortar etched thin by the elements. The paint had been scoured away, leaving bare wood turned barn-side gray. I saw a leaning utility pole behind the house, its insulators made of glass, the line part of the rural electrical grid installed in the 1930s, finally allowing many Appalachian families entrance to the twentieth century.

A black power line stretched from the pole to the structure. I saw bright copper connections at the insulator, like the line was an illegal tap, jury-rigged. It fired up alarms in my head as I exited my truck. I double-checked my GPS readout: This was where the woman had directed me.

"Hello?" I called.

Nothing answered but distant crows, though for a few seconds I heard a distant siren. I approached the house with eyes down, wary of snakes in the overgrown weeds. The porch was side-slanting, creaking with my footsteps. The mesh had rotted from the listing screen door.

I slipped my gun from my back-of-belt holster and pushed on the door. It grated open over warped floor-boards. The living room was a clutter of rotted furniture

45

and wood lath and plaster fallen from the walls and ceiling. With the windows boarded, there was little light. I smelled an overwhelming stench, like foul meat mingled with feces. My stomach churned and I tied my red bandana handkerchief over my nose and lower face. The flies were a cloud of dots racing in circles.

A rectangle at the back resolved into a door opening as my eyes adjusted to light strained through holes in the roof and corners of the window boards. There was a light switch on the wall, cracked and dirty. I flipped it, but nothing happened.

I stepped into a dark room centered by a bed, a human shape across it like an X. Thick wires bound the wrists and ankles to posts at the corners. The stench could have made a buzzard retch. I fumbled in my pocket for my butane lighter, scratched up a flame. My feet snagged in a wire on the floor and I kicked it aside as I moved to the head of the bed, my flame shivering in the wretched air, dying as my thumb slipped from the trigger.

I knelt beside the bed, flicked the lighter on again. A man's hideously shattered face stared at me from between wood-spire bedposts. The broken visage was hideously distorted, eyes bulging from the sockets, the mouth holding a frozen scream.

Ghosts were pouring from the nostrils and mouth.

I recoiled in horror, losing my footing, stumbling over the scummy floor. I regained my feet, unsteady in my motions, staring at white plumes exiting a dead man's face. I was turning for the door when it exploded open.

I spun as a body slammed into me and I was again on the floor, the muzzle of a gun pressing into my forehead.

"GET YOUR HANDS BEHIND YOUR BACK. NOW!"

I complied. A hand pressed my face into the filthy floor.

"He's got a gun," a second male voice said. I felt my weapon slipped from my waistband.

"It's OK," I said. "I'm a co—"

The hand behind my head slammed it to the floor, crushing my words against my face. "SHUT THE FUCK UP!"

Hands yanked me upright. Blood from my floor-slammed nose started running into my mouth and down my throat. I gagged. My captor spun me into a wall, holding my collar so tight I couldn't breathe or speak. His face filled my vision, eyes ablaze with anger, breath so close it filled my nose. It was the big sheriff from yesterday, the one named Beale.

"You murderous son of a bitch. You sick fucker." He yanked the bandana from my face, stared, turned to the second cop. "I saw this bastard yesterday with the Compass Point students. The fucker knew we was checking footprints, made some smart-ass remark." He slammed my head against the wall. I saw stars and heard plaster crumble to the floor. "You planning to get one of the kids alone, smart-ass? One of the women, maybe?"

"Easy, Sheriff Beale," the second man's voice said, a younger voice.

The angry man's eyes glared into mine. I could smell his anger as his hand tightened on my neck. I was being

47

strangled. The room spun away toward darkness. Running footsteps from somewhere . . .

"BEALE!" a woman's voice commanded. "Get your hands off him. Now!"

"This is my county, Cherry. You can't tell me what to do."

"I can pinch off the money tit, Sheriff. Wanna explain that to the voters?"

A pause. The hand let go. I dropped to my knees and choked breath into my lungs. Even the stinking air in the room tasted good.

"Cuff him, Officer Caudill," the woman ordered.

I didn't say a word as the bracelets slapped on, fearing any utterance would cause the hulking sheriff to attack. When I could look up, I saw the sheriff stewing in the corner. Beside him was a cop in his mid-twenties, rangy, with jug ears poking from short yellow hair. The older cop looked homicidal, the young one just looked nervous.

A strong flashlight from across the room filled my eyes, held by the woman who'd kept me from strangulation.

"Lord," the voice behind the blinding light said. "What is that stink?"

The beam shifted to the ruination of the victim's face. Gray ghosts continued to stream from his lips and nostrils.

"What the fuck's coming out of him?" the sheriff named Beale whispered.

I watched the shape behind the light step toward the body, tentative, like a superstitious person forced to walk beneath a ladder. She bravely edged her fingertips into the shapes poring from the victim's nostrils and mouth.

"It's smoke," she whispered, amazed. "No, wait. . . . It's wet. I think it's steam."

The woman passed the light to the young cop. "Go down the body inch by inch, Caudill."

She sidestepped beside the corpse as the light revealed a body toned and powerful, with melon-round shoulders and hawser-thick trapezoids. The chest was deep, the waist slender. The legs were spread wide.

She tripped as I had done.

"Point the light to the floor. What's down there?"

The light found a heavy and outdated electrical conduit snaking from a wall socket toward the body. The light tracked the conduit upward to the bed where it disappeared beneath the victim's thigh.

"Get over here and put some illumination between the glutes," the woman said.

"Excuse me?"

"Light the guy's asshole."

The cop angled the light into the crevice between the victim's buttocks. The cord entered a wooden handle protruding from the anus. I heard hissing, like water boiling, and saw red-brown rivulets running from the body's rectum to the mattress as steam misted upward. It was the second most bizarre sight I'd ever seen. The first was what was happening a couple feet upward.

"What's up his ass?" Beale said.

"An industrial soldering iron," Caudill said. "My granddaddy had one. They're about sixteen inches long and glow red-hot when they're plugged in."

The woman said, "Then unplug the damn thing. Get the suspect outside and stick him in my cruiser for the time being. I'll call Frankfort for a forensic unit."

Beale manhandled me outside and jammed me into the back of an unmarked cruiser as the woman tapped at her cellphone. I leaned forward and looked through the Plexiglas divider into the front of the cruiser, relaxing a bit at seeing familiar turf. There was the usual radio equipment, miniature computer terminal and input pad, about the same as Harry and I had back in Mobile.

A stack of books on the passenger seat caught my eye and I sat forward to read the titles on the spines. All were on law enforcement, with most of the books written by people familiar to me. The third volume down was a just-published compendium featuring case histories of sociopaths penned by the cops who tracked them down. Written for law-enforcement agencies, the book had sold quite well for a special-interest publication.

I looked up. The woman was at the corner of the porch and thumbing her cellphone. She studied the screen and rolled her eyes. I took it there was no signal to be found.

In the light the woman was in her early thirties, an inch or two above medium height, slender. She wore a blocky black pantsuit that looked straight from the rack at Wal-Mart, black cross-trainers, with a gold badge slung around her neck on what appeared to be a length of clothesline. Her hair was an unruly shag à la early Rod Stewart, red, probably the real thing given her creamy complexion and dusting of freckles.

She looked my way. Stared, like making a decision. She walked over, her eyes a mixture of curiosity and contempt, her voice pure country.

"We caught you standing over the body, fella. Anything you wanna talk about?"

She was hoping for an on-scene confession. Instead, I nodded toward the book in the passenger seat. "Interesting-looking book up there, Detective. *Serial Killers by Their Captors*. Is it yours?"

She glanced at the stack of books, then back to me, figuring I was working some kind of angle. Or playing with her. I noted her sea-green eyes looked in slightly different directions, a mild strabismus. Though the declination was subtle, it was unsettling, like one eye was looking at me, the other at something on my shoulder.

"The book's mine," she said. "Why? You figuring to add to it?"

"Did you read the case history of Marsden Hexcamp and his followers? The cult from coastal Alabama?"

She stared at me for a five-count. "I read that chapter."

"I wrote it," I said, leaning forward to jiggle my cuffs. "Can a brother get a little love here?"

# 8

We were in a bilious yellow meeting room in the Woslee County Police Department. It smelled of boiled coffee, tobacco smoke, and drugstore aftershave. Donna Cherry, head of Eastern Kentucky Combined Law Enforcement, Region 5, sighed and dropped the phone into the cradle after checking my background with the Mobile police. She leaned cross-armed against the wall and stared at me with the offset eyes. The call hadn't made them any friendlier.

"Let's start again, Ryder."

"Come on, I'm not really a suspect, am I?" I argued. "You just verified that I—"

"I verified you're a cop. What I didn't verify was how you happened to be on the scene of a murder before the locals arrived."

"You called me, dammit. My cellphone rang and you gave me coordinates. Asked for help."

"That's a bald-faced lie, Ryder. I never called you."

"You have a distinctive voice," I said, mentally adding *nails on a blackboard*.

She glared at me, angry I wasn't breaking down and confessing to God-knows-what, then stood with the eyes still hammering hard. I felt the silent pounding as she paced behind my back. She sat across the table, her question bag re-filled.

"You said the call confused you, Ryder. If so, why didn't you call back to ask for more information?"

I was getting irritated. I'd received a cryptic call for help, ran to offer assistance, was being grilled for the effort.

"You blocked your number. But you know all this, don't you, Detective Cherry? You're gaming me for some reason."

"I AM NOT GA—" She caught herself and took a couple seconds to compose, tapping clear-polished nails on the desk. I saw anger in one eye, bewilderment in the other, averaged it out into exasperation. "How could I call you without knowing your number, wise guy?" she asked.

"I've told several locals I'm a Mobile detective, gave them my cell number. The people at Compass Point Outfitters. A lady at the service station in Pine Ridge. Dottie Fugate at the cabin-rental company."

"So what?"

"I know how the country grapevine works. One of them called you, said 'Guess what, there's a homicide dick vacationing in the area.'"

53

She gave me incredulous. "You're saying when faced with a homicide my first thought was to call the big-city detective?"

I gave her my most sardonic smile. "You called me, lady. I didn't call you."

She put her elbows on the table and leaned forward. "If *I* called *you*, why didn't anyone expect you on the scene, Einstein? You figure that one out?"

Actually that one bothered me a bit. But I was working on theories. "The cell connection was lousy. You didn't realize your message got through. When you found me with the body, my face under a bandana, you figured me for the perp."

"And not the hotshot hard-on from Mobile."

"Your words, not mine," I said. "But let's get back to my question: Why are you gaming me?"

"I am not running a game here, Ryder," she said slowly, as though explaining something to a child. "I did not call you anonymously because you're a big-time detective who writes books and all. What I am trying to do is reconcile your story with your actions."

Cherry seemed truly convinced she hadn't called me. I wondered if the woman had two personalities, each with its own line of sight. I decided to bag my confrontational attitude and appeal to her rational side, if there was one. I pulled out my cellphone, thumbed to *Call History*.

"Let's try a timeline," I said, holding my phone screen so Cherry could see the info. "There's my call, at 6.57 a.m.

It says *Caller Unknown*. My only call today, the call from, uh, the woman with the distinctive accent. When did you get the message about the body, Detective Cherry?"

She scrabbled through the papers in front of her, plucked up a sheet. I saw her eyes juggling information. "We received information at six forty."

My rational side lost out to my hand slamming the table. "But you people didn't arrive until almost seven thirty!" I barked. "Ten minutes after I did, even though you were notified before my call. Did you stop for breakfast along the way?"

Her jaw clenched and she looked away. "Our notification wasn't by, uh, traditional means. It took some time to, uh, deal with."

"The message came by carrier pigeon?" I asked.

"Not your business."

"The hell it isn't. Someone called me with your voice and sent me to a crime scene and now I'm halfway to being accused of the murder."

"No one's accusing you of anything, Ryder," she said, adding: "Not yet."

"Then I can escape the Donna Cherry Memorial Madhouse, right?"

The eyes blazed, the jaw clenched. She stood stiffly and nodded toward the door.

"You're free to go."

I stood, started to walk away, paused in the doorframe. I turned round and lit my eyes with false bonhomie.

"The next time you know I'm in the neighborhood and want a consultation with the hotshot hard-on from Mobile, Detective Cherry, just call and use your real name. It won't be hard ..." I made the thumb-pinkie phone sign, wiggling it beside my cheek. "You've got the number, right?"

I winked and walked out the door.

The next morning I awoke to birdsong and the cackling of crows, the sound so full and rich it pushed aside the weirdness of the preceding day's events. The air through my open window smelled of pine and rising dew. The clock showed 6.23. Mix-up scampered out for the performance of his morning duties.

After showering and dressing and gulping down my coffee, I met Gary for a two-hour lesson on the cliffs. I returned feeling pumped and happy at half past ten, noting a man sitting in one of the rockers on the porch, patting my dog's head.

It was the ranger who had been with Sheriff Beale the day before I'd been summoned to the murder scene. He smiled and stood as I pulled up. I stepped to the porch and shook hands with Lee McCoy, senior ranger for the Red River Gorge area of the Daniel Boone Forest.

"I heard about what happened yesterday," McCoy said, producing a zip-locked bag with a two-inch stack of pink ovals inside. "I figured it'd be good to give you a more proper mountain welcome."

"Country ham?" I asked, studying the package.

He grinned. "Pepper-rubbed, cob-smoked, finished off with a year's hanging. Fry a minute in hot butter starting to brown, flip over for another minute. Your mouth'll think it's stepped into heaven."

I cradled the ham to my chest like a cache of diamonds and ran it to the fridge. The best country hams rarely see store shelves but are traded in the shadows by cognoscenti. I poured coffee and we sat on the porch, chatting about weather and light topics. Something seemed a bit amiss in the proceedings – I was, after all, a man with an unknown connection to a dead body, but McCoy seemed oblivious to my conflicts, more concerned that I was having a good vacation experience. But perhaps his loyalties rested with the tourism industry. I asked McCoy how long he'd been with the Forest Service.

"Twenty-seven years. All in the Daniel Boone Forest, a good half stationed here in the Gorge. I grew up in Clay City fifteen miles west. I used to ride my bike here before I could drive."

"You must know every step in the Gorge."

He winked. "The Gorge keeps a few places hidden. That's its nature. Today I'm heading into the backcountry to check a stand of white-haired goldenrod."

Maybe it was something in me that harkened to child-hood, Smoky the Bear and Ranger Rick or whatever. Maybe it was McCoy's spiffy, hard-creased uniform, or the cool wide-brim hat, but my cynicism melted and my heart skipped a beat at the prospect of hiking alongside a for-real forest ranger.

I sighed like a jilted teen. "Jeez, I'd give my eyeteeth to tag along."

He smiled. "We'll be out for a few hours. Best to pack a sandwich."

I grabbed my daypack and a canteen before McCoy had a chance to change his mind.

"You bringing your pup?" McCoy called through the door. "Dogs aren't allowed in Natural Bridge Park, but they're fine in the Gorge."

I whistled Mix-up to my side and we jumped into McCoy's official Jeep Cherokee, driving out of the long valley, coming to the split where the road wandered back to the only other cabin in the hollow. McCoy nodded toward the cabin as we passed.

"Had a chance to meet Doctor Charpentier, the fellow who lives there?"

"Never seen him."

"He spends hours in the forest, hiking and thinking. If you see him, stop and say hello. A brilliant man. I've never known anyone to absorb information so quickly."

"Charpentier is a medical doctor?"

"A psychologist from Montreal who took early retirement. He moved here for the climate, finding Canada too cold, the South too hot. Doctor Charpentier thinks Kentucky has the perfect temperature, and our forest reminded him of Canadian woodland."

McCoy pulled up out of the hollow and drove north. He entered the national forest and wound down to the bottoms, the Red River to our left as we angled southeast.

Whenever the canopy of trees opened, I saw looming cliffs studded with pine on the ridges.

"Beautiful view," I said.

"Depends on your perspective." McCoy nodded at a cliff face thirty stories above the valley. "We've got a problem with people falling off cliffs. Doped-up locals and drunked-up college kids, mainly. They camp on the ridges for the view, forget where they are, walk over the edge. Last week a man took a two-and-half gainer from the top of that cliff to the bottom. I was on the rescue team. Or maybe body-recovery team is a better term. I've personally recovered over two dozen."

McCoy slowed as a huge recreational vehicle moved toward us in the other lane, crowding the centerline. McCoy slipped past, pulled off the road and stopped the engine. We'd reached the trailhead. It was after we'd exited and gone to the rear to grab our packs that McCoy made his first mention of the grisly events of yesterday.

"I heard you had to spend some time with Detective Cherry," he said. "She was surprised at your appearance."

"It was a surprise to us all," I said.

McCoy cleared his throat. "Did Detective Cherry mention there'd been a death prior to the man in the shack? A very similar event?"

"No, Lee," I said, more interested than my face let on. "We never quite got around to police chit-chat."

"It was a week back. Sonny Burton drove a snack truck, chips and pretzels and such. He went missing for two days. His truck was found in a hollow, Sonny underneath it, hands frozen on to the front tire parked on his chest. Even though he was dead, his mouth was open, like he was screaming. There were a couple boot prints on the ground, what you noticed me looking for the other day. I guess you're tuned to stuff like that."

I nodded. "Two murders in a short span of time is probably unusual around here, but not freakishly odd anywhere, unfortunately. What makes you sure Burton is connected to the guy from yesterday?"

"The way the police received notice of both crimes."

The point Cherry hadn't discussed. "How?" I asked.

"Through coordinates on a geocache website. The location of Sonny Burton's body was listed on a geocaching site with geographic coordinates. A couple teen kids found him."

"Geocaching is hide and seek with a GPS, right?"

McCoy nodded. "It's a recent craze. People hide things, trinkets, a log book. The coordinates are posted on the web. You use a GPS to find the cache, usually adding a trinket to a bunch of trinkets, or signing the book. There are big national geocaching sites, and little regional ones. The site where Burton's coordinates were posted is called East Kentucky Geofun. It's run from a computer server and operated by a kid in Stanton."

"Cherry checked him out, right?"

"A sixteen-year-old techie – not involved. The site runs itself: Anyone with internet access can post on the site anonymously. Some local kids saw the new coordinates and went out expecting to find a standard cache, a box of trinkets or whatever."

"But instead found a guy with a truck parked on his sternum. The same happened with the guy in the shack?"

"There were differences," McCoy said. "Not much, but . . . It's odd. Geocache listings are in a standard format for the website: the name of the cache, the coordinates, and the name of the person or persons placing the cache."

McCoy had my attention. "How are these different?" I asked.

The ranger reached in his pack and produced a sheaf of folded pages. "Let me show you the format of the typical geocache . . ."

He unfolded a page and handed it to me. Geocache entries copied from a computer screen. The format was simple.

### Haystack Rock

N XX.XXXXX° W XXX.XXXXX° / Johnny Cache

McCoy said, "It's the name of the cache, the waypoint or coordinates, and who placed the thing – in this case a humorous handle. Standard stuff for a geocache." His finger tracked down the page. "But down here is the entry that led the kids to Sonny's body . . ."

$$=(8)=$$

N XX.XXXXX° W XXX.XXXXX°

"A strange symbol and the waypoint," McCoy explained. "That's all. The computer registers when the cache is placed, so that's automatic."

"Any idea what the eight denotes? Time of day, a campsite number, the infinity symbol on its side?"

He shrugged. "Donna Cherry and I spent hours trying to make sense of the number and symbols, together and individually. Nothing."

"You and Cherry work together?"

"I have law-enforcement powers in the national forest. Plus I know the area better than most anyone else."

I tapped the second set of coordinates. "This also showed up on the geocache site leading to Soldering-iron Man?"

"Not exactly. The coordinates were different, of course, but so was the number in parentheses."

=(5)=

N XX.XXXXX° W XXX.XXXXX°

I stared at the pad and did all I could in the face of the information, which was shrug.

We pulled on our daypacks and for four hours I followed McCoy on his rounds: checking stands of white-haired goldenrod, a species only found in the Gorge; checking erosion blocks designed to keep sections of trail from gulleying; noting a deadfall across the path so the maintenance crew could tend to it with a chainsaw, and looking in on the occasional backpacking camper or campers to make sure they were following rules about campfires and so forth.

Interspersed with these bouts of "business", McCoy pointed out a few things I would have seen on my own, and a hundred more I wouldn't have noticed. At a cliff face he explained strata, naming the epochs and conditions that had created the demarcations. He showed me where Native Americans had built camps and villages. He pointed out caves cut by underground streams, rolled away logs to display salamanders and other hidden critters.

We paused for lunch on a high ridge, the panoramic Red River Gorge spreading below like a postcard from Heaven. Mix-up chomped jerky sticks and took a nap. In minutes we pulled our packs back on. We were descending switchbacks on a curving trail when I saw a slender, white-bearded man approaching on the right-turning path ahead, visible across a slight ravine. His shoulders were wide, hips slender. He wore large sunglasses, a wide-brimmed safari hat, a blue shirt and khaki pants. He carried a walking stick and had a set of compact field glasses strung from his neck. He moved with ease, as if the trail were a city sidewalk.

"That's Dr Charpentier," McCoy said, sounding pleased. "You'll enjoy meeting him."

I saw Charpentier pause to study something in the trees, then resume his approach. The trail curved behind a stand of rhododendron and I lost sight of him.

We kept walking, but the trail remained empty, as if

Charpentier had vaporized. I turned back to McCoy and a hundred feet behind saw Charpentier moving away with carefree grace. For a split-second I wondered if some mystical forest physics had occurred, Charpentier passing through us like neutrinos through the earth.

"Uh, Lee. . . ." I said. "How did Charpentier do that?"

McCoy pointed up the hillside. "A spur trail goes to a campsite above. He walked past us up there."

"Charpentier's antisocial?"

"Focused. When he's thinking about something important, he doesn't stop to chat."

I shot a final look at Charpentier. He'd turned our way with field glasses to his eyes. I had the uneasy feeling they were trained on me.

In return for being my guide, I offered to fix supper for McCoy and he was happy to accept. We'd have a nice conversation, I figured, though it might veer into an area the ranger wasn't expecting, one including the irritable Miz Donna Cherry.

I found a roadside stand offering silver queen corn, tomatoes, sugar onions, banana peppers, new potatoes the size of golf balls, and a local offering called greasy-grits beans. The grocery store provided smoked hocks. I cooked the beans, potatoes, onions and hocks together in stages, steamed the corn. I sliced the tomatoes and mixed them with sautéed peppers and onion, drizzled vinegar and olive oil over the concoction.

McCoy arrived at seven bearing two bottles of wine,

red and white, just to be prepared. We ate like stevedores and I asked questions sparked during the hike. We retired to the porch to watch the falling sun light the sky behind the western peaks. I leaned back in my chair and set my heels on the porch railing. Mix-up gnawed at a ham bone, a dog in bliss.

"Lemme ask a question, Lee. Sheriff Beale about took my head off when he found me at the scene. It wasn't the height of professionalism. What's his story?"

McCoy took a sip of wine. Sighed. "Roy's daddy was sheriff, granddaddy before that. Roy's part of a lineage that connects to a different time, back when a sheriff made up the rules as he went along, favors for kin and friends, revenge on enemies. Roy's daddy died six years back, slammed by a heart attack while bedded down with a friend's wife."

"So Beale Junior got the sheriff job?"

"There was an interim sheriff for three years until the term ran out and it came election time. Like his daddy, Roy's kin to half of everyone in the county. I reckon every relative that voted for Roy figured no one else in their right mind would."

"Doesn't inspire confidence."

"Roy's father and grandfather were stubborn and humorless men. Hard as flint, the both of them. Roy's soft as a pillow, so he has to act the role he's seen. Sometimes when I hear Roy talking and swaggering, it's like hearing a high school student doing Henry V. The only problem is, I saw it done by Olivier."

I laughed at the analogy. McCoy leaned back and folded his arms over his chest, studying the darkening sky. "Thankfully, Donna Cherry is in charge," he said. "Sort of."

"I noted she sometimes seems to out-rank the locals, sometimes not."

"The state police and county agencies are stretched thin by budget problems. The state created Eastern Kentucky Combined Law Enforcement, where professionals help coordinate law-enforcement efforts in rural regions. We're in region five, Cherry's region. She was working in Berea, population of fifteen thousand folks or so. But she's originally from here in Woslee County, the first in her family to attend college, about the first to finish high school."

I put my hands behind my neck, stared into McCoy's eyes. Smiled.

"Does Donna Cherry often use you as her spy, Lee? Or is this something new?"

He froze in his rocking.

"Pardon?"

"You stopped by this morning out of nowhere. Took me on a hike. Asked me a lot of questions. Probably would have asked me to dinner if I hadn't invited you. This was all at Cherry's suggestion, right? I can almost hear her voice. 'Couldja get close to Ryder, Lee? Make sure he ain't turned from a psycho tracker to psycho killer.'"

It was a poor impersonation of Cherry. My brother

was a natural mimic and could have nailed the voice. McCoy cleared his throat and turned, embarrassment coloring his face, no attempt to lie his way free.

"Donna wanted me to take you out on the trails and get a read on you. She thinks I'm a decent judge of character."

"And your verdict?"

He nodded toward the table inside, still set with dishes. "I'm pretty sure insane killers can't cook that good."

"Did Cherry make any judgment on her own?" I asked. "About *moi*?"

McCoy colored with embarrassment again. "She said we had to check, but that you were probably too, uh, goofy to be a killer."

# 9

The next morning I arose to the *rat-a-tat* of a wood-pecker's beak against a nearby tree. The proverbial early bird, up and working at daybreak. I stretched and yawned and recalled a passing storm during the night, hard rain pounding the metal roof of the cabin, keeping me awake for a few minutes until lulled back into delicious sleep.

My first week was more than half gone, the free week. I had three more weeks of vacation coming. I'd initially planned to take the freebie in the Gorge, then head some other direction. But I was enjoying the mountains, the climbing lessons, the hikes with Mix-up. And, truth be told, the background hiss of a murder investigation was comforting as well, like an old companion in the neighbor-hood.

Donna Cherry was an interesting cipher too.

I showered and ate and drove to the RRG offices in

the micro-town of Slade, hoping to wangle an extension of my lodging. A bell on the door caught the attention of a teen guy in a corner chair. He scampered behind the desk.

"Miz Fugate around?" I asked.

He tipped back a ball cap. "She's gone visiting up in Ohio, a sister by Springfield. She ain't due back for a couple–three days. I'm in charge while she's gone. Can I help you?"

"I wonder if it's possible to add another couple weeks to my stay?"

He frowned. "It's busy season cuz most schools are out. We're pretty much rented tight. What cabin you at?"

"Road's End."

"Lemme look at the reservations." He pulled a book from beneath the counter and thumbed through pages. "You say you rented Road's End for the week?"

I nodded. "I won a week's rental. Miz Fugate's daughter picked my name from a hat."

"According to the book, you got the place for a month. Says clear as day in Dottie's handwriting, rent paid in cash."

"I never paid a penny, cash or otherwise."

He pulled off his cap and scratched his head. "Tell you what, put down a deposit for two weeks an' I'll check with Dottie if she calls. If she's already given it over to you for free, I'll tear up your deposit check. Call here in a couple days and I'll let you know. But from what I'm seeing, I figure it's yours. You sure no one else paid for you?"

"Like I said, I won the stay in a contest."

"Sure don't sound like Dottie. Mebbe she's easing up in her old age."

"I guess," I said, not knowing what I was guessing at. I wrote the check and headed for the door, perplexed but not dwelling on it. I was halfway out when the kid called to my back.

"S'cuse me, Mr Ryder? Did you say your name got pulled from a hat by Dottie's daughter?"

I nodded. "I was the lucky one."

"I never heard of Dottie having any kids."

I shrugged, wandered out the door. The sun was clean and bright and smelled of pine from the breeze blowing down from the ridges. Then, as if from nowhere, I smelled something coarse and off-key. I looked around for garbage bins, before it hit me the foul scent was a memory of yesterday, blowing not in the wind but through my brain.

I wondered if the poor tormented man had been ID'd. And what his story was. I figured a few minutes of talking to Miz Cherry wouldn't hurt my vacation mentality and called the Eastern Kentucky Combined Law Enforcement, Region 5.

I got an answering machine, a pre-digital model with tape speed problems.

*"This . . . is . . . the . . . Easternkentuckycombinedlawfrcmtiveplslve. . . . a . . . message . . . and . . . wewillgetrightbato . . . you."*

I sighed and hung up. McCoy had given me the number

for his mobile phone so I tried that. He answered on third ring.

"Hey, Lee, I need to see Cherry. Where's her office?"

"East side of Campton, just through the light on the highway. There's an antiquey type of place, a Dairy Queen, a dollar store. The EKCLE office is just past. Look close or you'll drive right by."

"Where you at?"

"Out by Courthouse Rock, checking on nesting areas for hawks."

"Wish I was there. No new stars on the GPS horizon, I take it?"

"You mean symbols and numbers? Nope. Just the good old normal kind."

I drove past the EKCLE offices my first try, then came back around. The office was in what appeared to be a defunct used-car dealership: a gray single-wide trailer on a half-acre of faded asphalt. I saw a plain blue Crown Victoria Police Interceptor model parked outside, the unmarked cruiser Cherry had been using at Soldering-iron man's murder scene.

I parked and walked the steps to the door, entered. The trailer's living area had been converted to an office, probably back in the car-dealership days, with paneled walls, grubby blue carpet, a window-unit air conditioner with water stains beneath it. A map of Kentucky centered on one wall. There was a round table surrounded by five mismatched chairs at one end of the room, an old metal

71

desk at the other. Two battered filing cabinets flanked the desk. The air reeked of tobacco seeping into the woodwork over decades.

Cherry was at the desk pushing a pencil. She wore a white lacy top. Her earrings were turquoise bangles and complemented the red hair. She looked up, frowned, went back to her work.

"What can I do for you, Ryder?"

"I was gonna buy a used car, but it looks like your inventory's low."

She set the pencil down. Spiked me with the left eye, brushed me with the right one. "Something on your mind?"

I spun a chair to the front of her desk and sat. "Thank you for sending Lee McCoy to inspect me yesterday. We had a great hike and a fine supper, which you doubtless know."

"I didn't send him to—"

"Your spy confezzed," I said in my Hollywood Nazi, which sounded closer to Scottish. "I br-r-r-roke him."

She rolled her eyes. "Lee's so straight they use him to calibrate plumb-bobs. Given your appearance on the scene, I wanted him to sniff you over, Ryder. No apologies."

"No apology requested. It's what I would have done."

"Really? I'm amazed I did something a big-city detective would do. My day is made. Thanks and bye."

I kept my seat. "Any ID come through on the body?"

"There's a problem. The fingers were burned. The prints were damaged."

I saw the case materials arrayed on her desk. Felt a rush of adrenalin. I said, "McCoy told me about the murder of the snack-truck guy. How about I take copies of the cases back to my cabin and check for anything you might have missed."

"Excuse me, did you say 'missed'?"

I nodded toward the remnant-store surroundings. "I'm just trying to be helpful, Detective. This is hardly the forefront of law enforcement."

Donna Cherry brushed back a bright lock of hair from her forehead and leaned forward with her elbows on her desk. "It's true that I work in a thirty-year-old trailer that smells like cigars. I got a busted answering machine and a vehicle with a hundred forty thousand miles on it. I spend half my time trying to cement jurisdictional alliances with politicians who can't spell either word. But guess what, Mister Big-city Hotshot? This program is eight months old and serious crime in my territory is down seventeen per cent. How y'all doing in Mobile?"

She snatched up the pencil. Looked down at her work.

"Have a nice vacation, Detective, but please have it somewhere besides my office."

73

# 10

I made it two steps from the trailer before turning back inside. Cherry didn't look up. I stood in front of her desk and did my best contrite look, a good one, because it was real.

"Now what am I doing wrong?" she said, still writing.

"Absolutely nothing. You're obviously a professional doing exceptional work with limited resources, Detective Cherry. Mobile's not generally considered a major metropolitan area and usually I'm the one considered a hick and a yokel. I've never been on the other side and I guess I was seeing how it felt. It was stupid and small and I apologize for my general everything."

She looked up and stared at me with the off-centric eyes. The left one still didn't like me, but I think the right one was coming around. She started to speak, but was interrupted by the phone, grabbing it up.

"This is – Oh, hi, officer, what's—"

Her face darkened. She asked several questions and hung up. "Come on," she said, standing and pulling her weapon from inside the desk. "Maybe you can be useful somehow."

"What is it?" I followed her to the door.

"Judd Caudill reports a new addition on the geocache website. He and Beale are heading there now. It's in the national forest so they alerted McCoy. Number eight is back."

I buckled my seat belt as Cherry swooshed away, the big engine sucking air and burning tires. Cherry drove like a female version of my partner, Harry Nautilus: with total confidence and less-than-total control. As with Harry, I pulled the belt tourniquet-tight, holding my breath and closing my eyes when the situation warranted.

After fifteen wild minutes, we rounded a bend with tires flinging gravel into the trees. I saw McCoy's SUV parked beside a Toyota compact with a Transylvania University sticker on the bumper.

"Uh-oh," Cherry said. "Civilians. Probably saw the coordinates online."

She pulled a large shoulder bag from the trunk of the cruiser. I offered to carry it but she waved me off. We jogged down the sole path for several hundred feet to a shallow meadow at the base of a cliff. We found McCoy, talking to a young male and female in T-shirts and hiking shorts, she wearing a floppy Tilley hat, he a Cincinnati Reds ball cap. I saw a GPS unit clipped to his belt.

The girl was the kind of distraught that shivers, stops, starts shivering again.

"We were looking for a new cache," the girl said, holding her shoulders like she was hugging herself. "It was on the Gorge-area site. We were looking upstream where the coordinates directed us. But we didn't see anything. Then we came down here and we-wuh-wuh-wuh . . . We saw . . . that thing in the water."

Her words drowned in a spasm of shivers. McCoy tossed me his GPS. It was a good one, displaying the site in the manner shown on the net:

$$=(8)=$$

$$N\ XX.XXXXX°\ W\ XXX.XXXXX°$$

Eight again, not five. The local coordinates.

I handed the device back. McCoy flicked his eyes toward a line of oaks. Cherry and I headed that way, finding a meandering creek on the far side of the trees, pools separated by shallow, rocky runs, the water maybe a foot in depth. Floating face-down in a pool was a woman's body. It was slender and well maintained. Strands of false blonde hair drifted in a Medusa circle around the head.

I stepped into the water for a closer look. The victim wore a black leather corset, black boots, a black collar. Hooked to the collar were several yards of blue climbing rope. I held the dripping rope up for display. Cherry grimaced.

We heard voices. Beale and Caudill had arrived. The two cops ran over and looked down.

"Shit," Beale said, looking disgusted. "Let's pull it out."

"Let's deal with the kids first," Cherry said. "Get them gone."

The girl was still speaking, wiping her eyes with a tissue. "No, we j-just saw the coordinates. We were at M-Miguel's Pizza and Ken was on his laptop. W-we saw a new cache had been added, so we turned on the GPS and went l-looking."

She dissolved into shivers and tears. I saw Cherry catch Beale's eye, nod toward the couple. Beale looked back, confused.

"What you want?"

"Get their statements, Sheriff Beale. Did they see anyone else on the way here? Cars, hikers, that type of thing."

He patted his pockets. "Got something I can write in?"

Caudill said, "There's a pad in the car, Chief. I'll go fetch it."

"Bring me a goddamn pen, too."

Cherry and I trudged back to the body. She opened the bag and pulled out evidence bags, latex gloves, scene tags, a camera and other necessaries, photographing the scene from every possible angle. We splashed into the creek and wrestled the woman from the water and laid her supine on the ledgerock.

She was a woman who had been attractive while alive. Even at her age – which I guessed as late forties – her body was well-sculpted, slender and heavy-breasted. Her black corset laced through the front, plump white breasts spilling from hard cups. The boots were knee-length, laced. A black leather collar circled her neck, and centering the collar was a stainless steel O-ring. The blue rope was attached to the ring with a carabiner.

"Captive somewhere?" Cherry suggested.

"Looks that way."

"The boots are maybe three sizes too big," she said, wiggling the boots as water dripped out. "Plus that corset get-up isn't laced tight, and doesn't look like it would. One item's too small, the other's too large."

"You don't think the boots and boogie gown are hers?"

"No," Sheriff Beale interrupted from behind us. "Not a chance."

Cherry and I turned. Beale had finished his note duties and dismissed the kids. "You know the victim, Sheriff?" Cherry asked.

"Tandee Powers. Lives in Hazel Green, not too far from here. Churchy lady. Used to be a teacher who did stuff for orphan kids and that. Took a real pervert to dress her like a whore."

He looked sick and walked away, acting like he was checking the bushes for clues. We inspected the body, noting some bruising and several deep scratches, but no major wounds. The local ambulance company arrived, ready to transport the body to a nearby funeral home. It needed chilled storage until the Kentucky crime lab could add it to their backlog.

When the body was gone, we scoured the area for evidence. Cherry and I walked with our heads low, studying. Beale and Caudill stomped in circles. McCoy wandered with his GPS unit in hand. I watched him head upstream until he disappeared around a bend. Finding nothing in the vicinity of the body, the four of us trotted after McCoy.

We found him staring into a pool of muddy water, sixty feet long or so, twenty wide. At the downstream end was a rough concrete dam, three feet high, crumbling where it met the shore. In the middle was a horizontal metal wheel, two feet in diameter. The wheel operated the gate, a solid door that controlled water flow.

"Weird," I said, seeing a small man-made pond in the middle of a thickly forested nowhere, stark rock cliffs rising at our shoulders.

"Not if you know the history," McCoy said. "Fifty years ago one of the logging companies kept a crew shack by the base of the cliff. This was their swimming hole. I've taken a dip here a time or two." He pointed to the center of the pool. "That's where the GPS coordinates actually lead, oddly enough."

"You mean the waypoint is in the pond?" I said.

"Might not mean much. GPS units aren't accurate to more than a couple dozen feet, the older ones are worse."

"But the other coordinates were almost dead-on, right? The ones leading to the first bodies?"

He nodded. "Under fifteen feet, all of them. For GPS, that's an arrow dead-center in a target."

I looked at the wheel on the dam gate. Wheel and screw rusted. Probably unused in decades. "Let's see if we can open the gate," I said to Beale. "Let some water out."

"Hunh?" Beale said.

"Give it a shot," Cherry said, suddenly interested.

Beale looked unhappy, but splashed into the eight or so inches of water below the dam and stood beside me, taking one side of the wheel as I grabbed the other. Beale needed a better deodorant. We slammed ourselves into the task, but the wheel was frozen solid with rust.

McCoy appeared, dragging eight feet of rusty railroad track, the small gauge used in logging operations.

"There was a spur track here," he said, grunting the metal over the ground. "Old rails are still scattered around."

I saw his intent and helped wedge the rail in the wheel. Archimedes said, "Give me a place to stand and I will move the earth." He was talking leverage, and so was McCoy. The ranger stripped off his shirt to keep the rust from smearing his uniform. Though in his early fifties he looked as hard and limber as a top-flight tennis pro.

"Again," he said, planting his feet against the wet stones. "On three. One, two . . ."

This time we threw ourselves into the task with several feet of leverage on our side. The wheel made a grating squeal, then began turning, puffs of rust falling away in the breeze. Water trickled from beneath the rising gate, then poured through. We stepped away.

In fifteen minutes most of the bed was visible. I rock-hopped toward the center and looked down at an assemblage hanging from the inner side of the dam.

"What is it?" Cherry said from the shore.

"The base of the dam is riddled with decay. Pieces of the metal lathe, a mesh of rebar, are exposed. Someone wired a pulley to the rebar three feet down."

Cherry walked to the dam, jumped atop its one-foot width, edged out to where I was standing. She crouched and studied the bright metal pulley, obviously brand new, its frame wired to a rusted loop of rebar. She thought for a five-count, stared at me.

Whispered, "Oh my God."

The others stood on the shore and stared between us, not yet seeing the horror.

Two hours passed. Beale and Caudill returned to the department. Cherry seemed reluctant to leave the scene. The three of us stood between the cruiser and McCoy's SUV.

"The rope and the pulley, Detective," McCoy said, looking at me. "You're surmising that . . ." His words were replaced by grim pictures in his head. "You can't be serious. It's . . . insane."

"It fits the evidence," I said. "The killer looped a rope through the pulley, tied on a carabiner and hooked it to the woman's collar. She was in the water, four feet deep

81

at the end of the pool. When the rope was yanked, the victim was pulled under water. Repeatedly, I figure. Why else rig a system where you can pull someone under, then loosen the rope to let them get to the surface again?"

"That's . . . torture."

"So is having a soldering iron jammed up your fundament. And who knows what happened before the truck was driven on to the first victim."

Cherry nodded down the road. "Why was she taken from the pool and put downstream? Was it to confuse us?"

I saw McCoy's mind working. "The edges of the dam are eaten away, erosion. There were pocket storms last night, heavy and fast. This creek drains about eight square miles of mountainside watershed."

"The creek flash-flooded," I said.

"The body started out in the pool, then rising water pushed it past the dam. The victim was left at the co-ordinates, but washed downstream a couple hundred feet. The coordinates were exact when the killer departed, some time before the storm hit."

"Marking kills with creepy GPS coordinates," Cherry said, shaking her head. "Dressing a body in sex clothes. Boiling someone's insides with a soldering iron. This is beyond me, Ryder. You write books about this stuff. What's your take?"

"It's about control. The perp controls the victims through torture and making them conform to an image, as with the woman's garb. He controls us, too, through the geocache game. We don't discover bodies, he sends us to them."

"Killing as a game?" McCoy said, looking ill. "Torture as play? Control through dead humans? What sort of world do you live in?"

"Same one you do, Lee," I said. "I just see it through the basement window."

Cherry sighed. "Let's go take a look at the victim's digs. See if she was as churchy as Beale thinks."

We made one stop along the way, a tiny and weather-beaten log house a mile down the road, the only other dwelling in the area. The place looked like a relic from the 1800s, save for the silver propane tank nestled against its side and well over a dozen handmade bird-houses dangling from the row of maples in the side yard. Some were raw wood, oak and cedar. Others were painted in reds and blues and greens. It was like an avian subdivision.

"You know who lives here?" I asked as Cherry rolled into the drive.

"An elderly woman, gotta be mid-eighties. I stopped by the only time I was ever out here. Last year when I took the position, I drove every road in the county. She was on her porch. A very old-school mountain woman."

Cherry knocked several times, shrugged. No one home. We headed on our way to Tandee Powers's house.

The victim lived six miles distant, in what Cherry described as an "ancient trailer built a couple decades before Noah's Ark". It was back in a tight ravine, down one more gravel road with weeds growing between the tire lines.

83

We swept around a bend. Cherry said, "Oh shit."

I looked up and saw the smoldering remains of a trailer. Muttering to herself, Cherry pulled in. We exited and kicked through pieces of wood and charred aluminum.

"It burned down in the night," McCoy said, crouching at the edge of the burn field and studying the remains of a box spring and mattress. "No one could see flames back here in the hollow, and the smoke wouldn't show on a clouded night. It was probably destroyed before the rain hit."

Cherry walked over and stood above McCoy, looking into the wreckage. Her shoulders were slumped.

"That's one thing about old trailers," she sighed. "They burn two ways: hot and to the ground."

# 11

Cherry returned me to my car and waved off my offer of conversation to pass the time while she did paperwork. I went back to the cabin to empty Mr Mix-up, passing Charpentier's house. A lone figure was visible behind the cabin, hoeing in the garden. I waved, but the psychologist was too absorbed in his task to notice.

I'd been back at Road's End all of ten minutes when McCoy appeared. I held my fingertips an inch distant from my ear holes. "If you tell me there's another cache on the site, Lee, I'm not gonna listen."

"No, thank God. But I got to thinking about the, uh, unusual aspects of the crimes. Do you think Dr Charpentier could help? He's a psychologist."

I thought a moment and shrugged. "He may be a clinician who specializes in smoking cessation or phobias, or autistic children. There are all sorts of specialties, Lee, few helpful when dealing with monsters."

"Are we missing a chance by not asking, Carson?"

The ranger had a point. I hopped in McCoy's SUV and drove the thirty seconds to Charpentier's cabin. The doc was still in his garden, bent over with his back to us, weeding a potato mound. His waist was slender, suspenders running from loose khakis to shoulders broader than I remembered from our near-meeting in the forest.

"He looks in good shape," I noted.

"When he arrived in late winter, Dr Charpentier removed an acre of trees. Cut them, split them into firewood. He rented equipment to pull the stumps. The soil is clay, and he had truckloads of topsoil brought in, all for his garden. He seems a natural at backyard agriculture, a man given to nurturing. When he's not in his garden or working on his land, he's in the forest, studying."

"The cabin looks older than a few months."

"It was built a decade ago by the Brazelles, a pair of retired optometrists from Dayton, Ohio. Beautiful folks, but Mr Brazelle, Theo, developed Alzheimer's and it became too dangerous for him in the woods. Sad. The property was on the market for less than a month when Doc Charpentier bought it. The land extends behind the cabin for a couple thousand feet, almost as wide. The cabin sits on thirty acres overall."

"Charpentier lives there full time?"

"He travels occasionally. I think he's writing a book.

Though he mostly keeps to himself, he can be surprisingly social. I've seen him at the park lodge talking Plato with vacationing philosophy profs from Western Kentucky University. The next afternoon he's drinking beer and trading off-color stories with the crew cleaning out his septic tank."

"Doctor Charpentier?" McCoy called as we stepped closer. "Hello . . . Doctor?"

The hoe kept its rhythmic pattern, Charpentier oblivious to our presence. "He's wearing a headset," I said, seeing the telltale white cord trailing from his ears. "An iPod or something."

Charpentier kept his back to us as we approached, the hoe chopping merrily away. A dozen feet distant, behind chicken-wire fencing, I saw stands of tomatoes and rows of cabbages. Sugar baby melons vined along the ground, looking like green cannonballs peeking from the leaves. There were hutches to the side, chickens perhaps, or rabbits. Further back, along the tree line, I saw white boxes nestled in the trees: bee hives. Charpentier seemed a man who enjoyed being self-sustaining.

When we were within a dozen feet of the Canadian psychologist, McCoy called out.

"Doctor? Doctor Charpentier?"

Charpentier half turned and saw us. He was wearing a red bandana under the floppy white hat, a sweatband. His face lit with the prospect of visitors and turned away as he set his hoe against a nearby wheelbarrow and pulled the buds from his ears.

McCoy said, "Doctor, I want you to meet one of your temporary neighbors. He's renting Road's End."

Charpentier turned fully to me. He stripped away the sweatband, then removed his sunglasses. My knees softened and a hiss rose in my ears.

Charpentier was Jeremy Ridgecliff. My brother. Two years gone from the Alabama Institute for Aberrational Behavior, an escapee.

Jeremy grabbed my hand in his right hand, his left hand under my forearm, steadying me. His palm was as hard and dry as oak. His eyes twinkled with delight.

"So pleased to meet you, Mr Ryder," he said, his voice inflected with a French accent. "Have you journeyed far?"

My first attempt at speech was a dry hack.

"I'm sorry, sir," Charpentier smiled. "I didn't quite catch that."

"Our guest is from Mobile, Alabama," McCoy offered. "He's a police detective. Part of his work involves psychology. A subject we'd like to talk to you about. We have a problem in the Gorge area, and may be able to use your expertise."

"My, my . . . I'm so infrequently useful these days. Anything I can do to help will be an honor, Detective, uh . . . I'm sorry," he said, flicking the ear buds at his neck. "I play my music too loud and my ears take a few moments to recover. You said your name was Carton? Is that like Sydney Carton in the Dickens novel, *A Tale of Two Brothers*?"

"Carson," McCoy corrected. "It's Carson Ryder. And wasn't that *A Tale of Two Cities*, Doctor?"

Jeremy clapped his hands. "Of course. My subconscious mingled the title with two characters in the story, Charles Darnay and Sydney Carton. They were close as brothers." Jeremy looked at me with amusement. "I forget, Mr Ryder . . . which man sacrificed himself for the other?"

"I don't recall," I said, trying to keep my voice steady.

My brother struck the exaggerated profile of a ham actor. "'Tis a far far better thing I do now than . . ." He turned back to me. "Or something suitably noble. Now then, Mister *Carson* Ryder, what sort of detecting do you do that involves psychology?"

"Homicide. Plus I also work a special unit that tracks psychopaths and sociopaths."

"Oddly enough, I've had a bit of experience there," my brother said, innocent as a starling.

Ten minutes later, Jeremy and I stood side by side on the porch of a fictitious Canadian psychologist and watched as McCoy drove away, Jeremy waving and calling *adieu*! Claiming other duties, McCoy had dismissed himself after the length of a glass of iced tea.

When I heard McCoy's vehicle finish grinding up the steep lane to the top of the ridge, I turned to Jeremy.

"Explanation time, brother," I said.

# 12

I followed Jeremy inside. The living room was a huge space, stone fireplace holding one end, bookshelves the other. Windows reached from the shelves to the vaulted ceiling peak. The wood walls shone softly, polished to a buttery gloss. The furniture was more delicate than the cabin; a couch, sofa and chair set on a braided rug inscribing an oval on the oak floor. A low table set centered the grouping. A chrome lamp arched fifteen feet from its base in the corner to the shade floating over the table. To the rear I saw a well-appointed kitchen with hanging pots, a beaten copper counter.

Though the exterior proclaimed rustic, the interior said Manhattan loft, reminding me that, in Manhattan, my brother had scammed a delusional paranoiac man into stealing from his brother-in-law. The take amounted to tens of thousands of dollars that he'd used in his escape and subsequent hideaways, but even the whole sum would have been nowhere near what this place cost.

"This must have cost a fortune, Jeremy," I said. "Where'd you steal the money?"

Jeremy turned to me, his eyes guarded and cryptic. "I've learned a modest trade."

"You? A trade?"

He gestured me upstairs to a room devoid of décor, like a cell, or a place where attention was riveted on a single task, no distraction allowed. The shades were drawn, everything lit solely by a bank of computer screens, four in all. The monitors sat on a long desk with a single ergonomic chair, a keyboard angled in front of the chair. The same screensaver played on all monitors, a white line inscribing random shapes against the dark.

My brother, who spent the bulk of his time in dark spaces in his mind, preferred this sort of room. The warm and bright furnishings downstairs were just a stage set for visitors. Jeremy crossed to the desk, tapped a button, turning the screensaver into charts and graphs, stock symbols and prices ticking in the corners.

"You play the stock market?" I asked.

Jeremy grinned, his eyes cold in the glare of the monitor images. "The market has but two states, Carson: scared child or blustering drunkard. I feel which one's in charge and place my bets accordingly. Yesterday the blustering drunkard opened the shop. I bought a medical firm at four bucks a share. Just before noon I sold at six and a half. At one the scared child took control, and my former med stock plunged to under three within a half-hour. I shorted on another stock that promptly dropped a third of its value. Yesterday I made over four thousand dollars pressing keys on my computer. I've become quite the little capitalist, brother."

"Under the name of Charpentier, no doubt."

"The process of creating the identity involved a child who died in Moose Hat in 1963, plus a few brilliantly manufactured certificates from the underground market."

"So you started your stock operation before you arrived? That's how you made the money to buy this place?"

Jeremy smiled as if he hadn't heard my question. He clapped a hand on my shoulder, squeezed it to the point of pain.

"Come, Brother, let's have a drink to celebrate our joyous reunion."

We retreated downstairs where Jeremy fetched iced teas and we sat in the living room. Though resembling a handsome and distinguished professor in his late forties, the eyes, voice and mannerisms were fully Jeremy's. I felt if I could grab the top of his scalp and pull, the professor would become a limp costume in my hand, my forty-two-year-old brother revealed, naked and scheming.

"The way I'm figuring things, Jeremy," I said, "you tricked me here."

He crossed his long legs, a man at ease. "The last we talked, you were planning a vacation, but dithering over destination. I went to the cabin-rental place and bought you a contest to win. The owner, Dottie, thought it all very cute. She said, 'He won't really believe I kept his name for nine years, will he?' I said, 'Hon, this guy believes in love.'"

"You mimicked Donna Cherry's voice. Sent me to the crime scene."

"I heard them nattering on my police-band radio, talking about a dead body, where it was located and so forth. They seemed confused and I thought you should meet the local constabulary."

"Why?"

He looked at me like I was the one not making sense. "Aren't dead bodies your field of endeavor?"

"I got there first, Jeremy. I could have been killed."

"Don't be so dramatic. Did you like my interpretation of Miz Cherry's voice? I hybridized Scarlett O'Hara with a cat in heat. Is the lady prettier than her voice?"

"Yes," I sighed. Talking to my brother was like talking into a whirlwind of conversational snippets.

"She'd have to be. Are you fucking her yet?"

"*What?*"

"If she's pretty, you've commenced a charm offensive to get into her pants, Carson. You need the attention."

My brother was fascinated by love and sex. Whenever we spoke on the phone, he pressed me about women. If I mentioned a recent date, I was in love. He had endless arcane theories on love and sex, always revolving around a damaged psyche. Mine, of course, never his.

93

"Drop it, Jeremy. I have no interest in the woman."

"You've already targeted her," he said. "Part of your childhood damage manifests in a shy roguish charm you use to warm yourself with temporary lovers, Carson. You gain them through various sensory buttons and words, then get to hide within them."

"I don't need to hear your old—"

Jeremy put a soft innocence in his eyes and stared shyly at the floor. "*I don't know for certain, ma'am,*" he said earnestly. "*But maybe I can stop by your house later, just to check on things. Would that be all right with you?*"

My breath halted in my throat. It was my voice coming from my brother. It wasn't like hearing a recording, but freakish, like eavesdropping on me from inside myself. My brother re-assumed his face and smiled wickedly.

"Then, Carson, once inside Miz Cherry you'll feel a momentary sense of safety and control. Maybe even—"

"We're talking about you," I rasped, my mouth dry. "Why did you want me here?"

"We're brothers," he said innocently. "We should spend time together. Thus my gift of a vacation."

"You know what I think, Jeremy?"

"Usually. But go ahead."

"I think maybe you heard details of the first murder, the snack king, on your little radio. Heard enough to figure out it was a horror-show scene. You got spooked about law-enforcement types running about, doing things like studying newcomers. Figured you'd feel better if I was around to keep an eye on things for you."

"You're so suspicious, Carson," he crooned, flicking lint from his collar. "It can be an irritant at times."

# 13

I returned to my cabin and slept. Just past daybreak, I took Mix-up for a walk, arching over the ridgeline bordering the cabin and winding a circular route to the side of Jeremy's home. It seemed still and content, no more than a quiet refuge in the woods. I heard another vehicle entering the hollow. When I saw it was Cherry, I sprinted after her, catching up as she angled down the slender lane to the cabin.

"You started sleeping in the woods with the dog, Ryder?" she asked as we stumbled to the road from the undergrowth. "You gone feral?"

"We were hiking. Anything happen yesterday after I left?"

"Beale asked the FBI in. There's a team finishing a case in West Virginia. They're coming here in a day or two. An important guy like you must have worked with the Feds, right?"

"I've been run under their bus a time or two. I've also worked with feebs with the smarts to collaborate instead of control. You never know what you're going to get."

"The Special Agent in Charge will be a fellow named Bob Dray. I've heard good things about him, a pro who listens to local input. I spoke to Agent Dray today; Bob, he said to call him. He's from North Carolina, knows mountain folk. I think we'll get along fine."

"You got lucky. Anything else going on?"

"Today I'm interviewing more friends of Tandee Powers. I'm heading to see a woman named Berlea Coggins. I know her a bit. Thing is, she lives with her invalid daddy, and I need someone to distract him."

"He eavesdrops?"

"He stares at my ass and clicks his false teeth."

That alone sounded worth the trip. "Let me put on a clean shirt," I said.

The Coggins's small house smelled of medical balms and lavender candles. Television, couch, end tables, recliner, coffee table, all lined the wall with geometric precision. There were no bookshelves, but doilies aplenty, plus wooden wall plaques laden with homilies: *Worry Ends Where Faith in God Begins, Faith Makes Things Possible, Not Easy, If You're Smoking in Here, You Better Be on Fire,* and so forth. A painting of Christ hung above the couch, the frame plastic, with a small nameplate at the bottom saying *Jesus of Nazareth.*

Miz Berlea Coggins was a skinny and plain-faced

woman in her late thirties, a prominent mole adjoining her nose and a mouth that appeared to have come direct from sucking a lemon.

Miz Coggins's father, Mooney Coggins, peered from around a corner, a wizened man in an electric wheelchair, oxygen tank in back, plastic tube running to his nostrils. I saw him grabbing glances at Cherry's hindquarters as if branding it in his memory – for which I could find no fault – but his teeth remained civil.

When Cherry asked about Tandee Powers, the old man gave me a twisted leer. He began opening and closing his hand, holding it high to make sure I noticed. Thinking dementia, I turned back to Cherry and Miz Coggins, the latter's mouth tight as she answered Cherry's question.

"I dunno I should say such a thing about poor Tandee. Ain't nothing can be done about things now, let her rest in peace."

"Miss Coggins, you know me. It's not my place to hurt someone's reputation, but to find out who killed Miz Powers."

Berlea Coggins went to an old spinet piano, a bible resting on top. She touched the book as if drawing solace, then turned, her eyes down.

"It was a dozen years back or so. Tandee led the church home-school committee, and I was secretary. There was a meeting with a sister congregation down in Franklin, Tennessee. The church sent Tandee and me, bought us a room at the Red Roof Inn."

Her hands began to fidget, like she was knitting with

invisible yarn. "Tandee and me had supper with the other church folks, but the big home-school meeting came the next day, so we went to our room for bed. When we was getting undressed Tandee started talking about . . . about men and what they liked to do."

"Sex?"

"Just jokey gossip. We put on our nightgowns and Tandee kept talking about how a man she used to know would sneak on up behind her and try and, uh, slide his hands over her . . . her . . ." Miz Coggins turned crimson.

"Her bosom?" Cherry said.

"Yes. And then she . . . Tandee . . . showed what happened."

"She touched you?" Cherry asked.

"It didn't seem so awful, both us being ladies and all. I was laughing cuz it was funny how men try and get their way with ladies."

"What happened next?" Cherry asked.

"Tandee dropped to her knees and yanked up my night gown. She tried to kiss me on my . . . my womanness. I pushed her away and told her if she didn't leave me be, I was going to run down the hall screaming."

"What happened?"

"We never spoke of it again. We hardly ever spoke to one another, neither."

I stepped away to give Cherry some woman-to-woman time with Miz Coggins. I walked past the old man, nodding politely. The clasping hand had returned to his side. He thumbed a button and the wheelchair whirred back against the wall.

"Hey, boy," his voice hissed to my back. "C'mere."

I turned. Cherry was still engaged with Miz Coggins. I went to the wizened old gent. One blue-white claw of a hand waved me closer and I leaned down until we were face to face.

"That Cherry woman's sure got a high round ass on her, ain't she? You tapping that keg, boy? Goddamn, I would. I'd slurp it up like a three-scoop sundae."

"Excuse me, sir. I have to go make some notes."

I had three steps between us when the old guy cackled out a whisper. "I knew that lady y'all are talking about, Miz Powers. I knew her inside and out, you get my drift."

I turned, walked back. "Sounds like you knew her pretty well, sir."

His eyes lit with humor. "Tandee Powers had one a these on her." He did the strange hand motion again, opening and closing it rapidly. "That's how Tandee's pussy was," he grinned. "It just kept goin' and goin', like that battery bunny on them commercials. Man or woman, didn't make no difference. Just keep that pussy working. Weren't many people know that about Tandee Powers, but I did."

"May I ask how?"

He stuck out his tongue, unfurling an appendage rivaling Gene Simmons's taste organ. Had I been in water I would have run for the shore screaming *alligator!* The old guy let it dangle a few seconds, then slurped it back between his lips. He wiped his mouth on his shoulder and grinned up at me.

"This was when Tandee was in her thirties. I was twenny years older, but my pecker and tongue could party all night. Wanna see it again?"

"That's OK. How often did you and Miz Powers see one another?"

He shivered his hand, meaning *not much*. "I was married back then, had to sneak around. My wife'd go off to visit her kin in Missouri and Tandee an' me'd run up to the gamblin' boats on the Ohio River, get a room. When me and Tandee got together, buddy, it was something to see and hear."

"When was the last time you and Miz Powers were, uh, together?"

"Been over fifteen years." He paused. "Tandee started gettin' too nasty for me."

One wrinkled claw was rubbing beside his zipper. I nodded my thanks and moved quickly away. Cherry had her hand on Miz Coggins's shoulder as she passed over one of her cards. Ms Coggins nodded and retreated to the kitchen. Cherry and I let ourselves out. The fresh air was a welcome relief.

"You get anything else?" I asked her.

"Just what you heard: Tandee Powers was probably a lesbian."

We got in the cruiser. Cherry fired up the motor. "Actually," I said, "she was probably a nymphomaniac.

Surreptitiously screwing a small group of the like-minded of either gender. Between appearances at church socials, of course."

Her head spun to me. "Where'd that come from?"

I looked toward the house. The old man had whirred to the door in his scooter. He was parked at the threshold, winking at me, his hand tickling in his lap as he slurped that monster tongue in and out.

"I see you made a new friend," Cherry said as she backed down the drive. "He seems happy you visited."

# 14

"What's the next step, Detective?" I asked when we'd put a couple miles between us and the tongue.

"I want to make sure I get everything tight for Bob, I mean Agent Dray. So I'm heading back to Sonny Burton's crime scene to make sure there's nothing I missed."

"Deep in the woods, right?" I didn't like the idea of Cherry alone in the forest with a psychopath on the loose. There had been cases of law officers being stalked and cut down when the moment presented.

"I'll be fine. Lee McCoy said he'd go along."

"I'm not doing anything," I said.

We arrived at Sonny Burton's murder scene a half-hour later, back a long fire lane. The nearest house was a mile away, down a long hollow. Hemlocks soared above, filtering the light into a gentle yellow that turned the nearby creek to gold. The upslope on the far side of the creek was covered with ferns so delicate they seemed more a green mist than rooted plants. The air smelled of pine. I found the beauty of the setting at horrible opposition to what had happened here.

Burton's case file described a good ol' boy, as we called them in the South. He worked hard and played harder. He liked to fight and had been a boxer in high school, earning a partial boxing scholarship to a small college. He hunted and fished and owned the best bass boat in Woslee County, the finest shotgun. His Dodge Ram 350 dualie pickup boasted more chrome than any other truck for miles. He loved Vegas. When time was limited, he'd hit the gambling boats on the Ohio River. Burton gave to local charities. Bought ads in high school yearbooks. He drove his snack truck in the county's Fourth of July parade, the white step-van third in line behind the honor guard, the fire truck and police cars, and ahead of the band, VFW marchers, and the winners of the "Cutest Baby" contest.

Burton had been married four times, each link in the marriage chain under two years in length, with one union lasting all of six weeks. From a psychological standpoint, serial marriage could mean several things, none of them attractive.

Cherry and I inspected the area as she detailed what she'd found upon arrival: Sonny Burton's body beneath the truck tire, chest almost flattened, innards squeezed out through his mouth and lower opening. Lee McCoy – the first to notice the murder scene's location on the geocache website – had been pacing beside the truck when Cherry arrived, frustrated by his helplessness.

I knelt beside a flat chunk of stone, three feet by five or so. Faint but fresh-looking scratches were inscribed in the stone, geometric, like something square had rested on the rock, scarring it.

"What are these, Cherry? The scratches on the rock?"

"I figured they came from the killer moving the truck around. Driving over the rock."

I scratched at the stone with my fingernail. "It's dolomite, a dense sandstone. Rubber tires wouldn't scratch dolomite."

"My, my, Ryder. You're a geologist as well as a detective?"

On our hike McCoy had pointed out dolomite layers in the Gorge strata and demonstrated how hard it was for sandstone. I probably should have mentioned that fact. Instead, I patted the stone as if drawing secrets from it with my fingertips.

"Something hard rested here, metal, I suspect. The object would have been a couple feet from Burton's head. That would place it beneath the forward section of the truck's frame. Would you know if the frame is—"

"Don't ask. I didn't study truck design."

I paced a circle around the stone, eyes not leaving its surface. "I've got a hunch about these scars. But we need to go to the Woslee impound and look inside Burton's truck."

"I got another idea." Cherry pulled out her phone and dialed. Tossed the phone to me. "Tell Caudill what you need."

The young officer arrived soon after, cradling a black cylinder and a two-foot metal pole beneath his arm. "A twenty-ton bottle jack," Caudill said. "Bolted behind the driver's seat in Burton's step van. The handle was back there, too."

The hydraulic cylinder was welded to a square steel base. I set the base on the stone. The scratches lined up with the base. Cherry studied the match-up and I saw the pictures enter her imagination.

"Oh lord, Ryder . . . the truck wasn't driven on to Burton. It was lowered."

I nodded and pushed the handle into the jack, marking the jack post with a pencil. I cranked it up, checked the distance traveled. Six or seven cranks moved the post an inch. I stood back and looked between the scene photos and the ground.

"Crank the truck up eighteen or so inches. Put Burton beneath the tire with his hands behind him, helpless. Lower the truck in one-crank increments. With each crank the tire dropped a fraction of an inch. Burton might even have been conscious to hear his ribs break as his chest caved in."

"Tortured," Cherry whispered. "Like Tandee Powers. And John Doe with the soldering iron." She crouched beside the stone. "Why use his truck? There have to be easier ways."

"The truck was symbolic to the killer. He was probably talking to Burton as he lowered the truck, getting off on the control. Making Burton beg and scream."

Cherry grimaced. "What the hell would the killer say, Ryder? 'Here comes the snack truck'?"

We turned to a roar of engines and crunch of gravel. Beale raced up in his SUV. Behind him was a second SUV from the sheriff's department driven by a fat guy with stained teeth and the weasel-eyed look of a natural sycophant; every department had at least one. I saw outlines of two tall people in the second, figured it was more of Beale's small force.

Beale skidded so close to my feet that I stepped back. He jumped out and strode to Caudill.

"What the fuck you doing here?" Beale spat.

"R-Ryder needed a jack from Sonny's truck," Caudill stammered. "He wanted me to bring it out."

"Why are you taking orders from some fuckhead with no jurisdiction." Beale swatted Caudill's hat from his head. "Who you work for, boy?"

"Y-You, Sheriff."

Cherry stepped forward. Though I'd seen the flash in her eyes when Beale slapped the hat from his hapless deputy, she was dealing with politics and needed to walk a thin line.

"It was important to get the jack out here, Sheriff. Detective Ryder made the phone call to Officer Caudill, but he made it for me."

"Cuz you're in charge of things, right?"

"A combined effort, Roy. We do a better job when we're united."

"You like being in charge, don't you?" Beale sneered. "Makes you feel important."

His voice was so condescending I was amazed Cherry kept her cool. "It's a task force, Roy. I'm not specifically in charge."

Three passengers emerged from the second vehicle. Two were men in dark suits and dark ties, the third a woman in the feminine version of the uniform, black pinstriped pantsuit and navy blouse. She was five eleven, maybe six feet tall, with the kind of blonde hair that doesn't grow naturally, bright enough to shame a lemon. The hairdo truncated above her shoulders, curling forward into points like horns. She liked makeup, but needed more skill at blending face into neck, giving the impression of a mask with cobalt blue eyes and purple-pink lips. It was not an unattractive mask, the cheekbones high and features even. She looked fit. I put her in her middle forties, but fighting it tooth and nail.

The new arrival inspected the sudden-hushed scene while slowly unwrapping a stick of chewing gum. She popped the gum in her mouth and smiled without a touch of mirth.

"You're right about not being in charge, Detective Cherry," she said, displaying a gold shield with an eagle above. "I am."

The Federal Bureau of Investigation had arrived. It appeared Bob Dray had missed the boat or had a sex change.

# 15

The Special Agent in Charge was named Gloria Krenkler. It turned out Dray's case lingered into extra innings and Ms Krenkler had been placed in his slot.

"I'm happy to meet you, Agent Krenkler," Cherry said, hand out. "You're a welcome addition to the team."

The cobalt eyes studied Cherry like Hernán Cortés viewing the welcoming natives. "Team?" she said.

Time for the official meet'n'greet amenities. I pasted my most charming smile on my face and waved across the dozen feet. "I'm pleased to meet you, Agent Krenkler. I'm Carson Ryder and I'm sort of, uh, consulting on the case."

The eyes studied me through a slow and silent five-count, like she was sorting items into boxes and trying to figure out what container I'd require.

"Ah yes, the vacationing cop who received the call from nowhere. Who called you?"

I shrugged. Krenkler said, "I heard it was Detective Cherry."

Beale grinned and I realized he'd fed Krenkler his version of events.

"That was my initial belief," I said. "I was wrong."

Krenkler arched a perfectly drawn eyebrow. "Really? I heard Detective Cherry discovered you were nearby and called for help." Krenkler turned to Cherry. "You'd call a vacationing cop before you'd call the FBI?"

"I assure you that I didn't call Detective Ryder," Cherry said evenly.

"But he was surely called by *someone* in local law enforcement, right?"

"That's the safe guess, Agent Krenkler," Cherry said. It was a subtle poke, and if Krenkler recognized it, an impression didn't register. Cherry continued. "However Detective Ryder was alerted, he's been tremendously generous with his time and input. We all owe him a debt of gratitude."

"I just arrived," Krenkler said, affecting puzzled. "Why do I owe him anything?"

There was an uncomfortable silence, no one wishing to venture an answer. I cleared my throat. "It's true," I said, trying to steer back toward civility. "I've simply been helping gather what little evidence has presented. In fact, new evidence came to light about the methodology of Mr Burton's murder, and Detective Cherry and I were documenting it for the Bureau's review."

Krenkler approached me with arms crossed. She stopped

a foot away, an uncomfortable incursion of personal space. "And just where is this new evidence, Detective Ryder?"

I gave it two slow beats.

"You're standing on it, ma'am."

Krenkler looked down. Her icepick-pointy black flats were dead-center on the dolomite. She stepped back and we studied one another, neither happy with the input.

She said, "I'm sure you'll be glad to get back to your vacation, Detective Ryder."

"I can help here, Agent Krenkler. I've had experience with—" I was addressing her retreating back. She gestured Cherry to her with a crooked finger, as if summoning an errant child. They spoke, Cherry's face growing red. I walked to the other agents with my hand out. The older man shook my hand and mumbled, "Rourke." The other kept his hands in his pockets and nodded to the air beside my head.

I leaned against a hemlock until Krenkler dismissed Cherry. We drove away, her knuckles white on the steering wheel.

"What's going on?" I asked.

"It's officially Krenkler's investigation," Cherry said, voice tightly controlled. "She was officially asked to take over by Beale, who is officially in charge of the county and officially allowed to request any assistance he needs."

"And you are officially what?" I asked.

"Fucked."

It was the only word she said on the drive back.

# 16

Two days passed. I resumed my climbing lessons and after-noon hikes, occasionally seeing a law-enforcement vehicle speed by, Beale's county mounties or one of the FBI's dark cruisers. The Bureau berthed at two cabins by the park. It looked like they'd brought in a couple additional agents, or maybe clerical types to keep the paperwork straight.

I knew they'd start by interviewing anyone who'd ever had a beef with Burton or Powers or who'd done time in prison or psychiatric observation. They'd check locals with violent backgrounds. Evidence – what little there was – would be shipped to the Bureau's labs, waiting for that one hit: the partial fingerprint, the molecule of DNA in Burton's truck or on Powers's clothing.

I hoped the Feds could identify Soldering-iron Man, the anomaly, the victim with no known ties to the area.

Gloria Krenkler and I hadn't harmonized at our initial

meeting and I'd judged her harshly based on my natural aversion to arrogance. I had been wrong about people before – often to my detriment – so I called John Morgenstern, a long-time FBI buddy. Harry and I had met John when he instructed us in behavioral psychology years ago. He was a straight shooter who gave me background info, knowing I'd never pass it on.

"Carson!" came the happy exclamation at the far end of the line, the Bureau's training academy in Quantico, Virginia. "How they hanging?"

"Off a cliff this morning, John. I'm on vacation in Kentucky, getting in some rock climbing."

"Keep a tight grip, buddy. What can I do for you?"

"Got a mean case nearby and I've got a fingertip in the proceedings. A state detective got bumped hard by one of your field agents, Gloria Krenkler. I was just wondering about Krenkler's capabilities."

"She's been based in the New York office for over a decade. Working mail fraud, mainly, heavy detail work, sitting at a desk and poring over reams of paper. We're short-handed, homeland security issues. I imagine it was felt she needed to get back out in the field a bit and—"

"You're giving me everything but an answer, John."

Morgenstern loosed a long sigh. "Let me put it like this, Carson: Krenkler's smart, but not creative. She makes up by being dogged, getting the job done a half-inch at a time. If Gloria Krenkler was an auto mechanic she'd tear down the engine to get at the tailpipe."

"I sense a need to control. Anger issues, perhaps."

A pause. "You're the one with the psychology degree."

"Just between you and me, John, do you respect Gloria Krenkler's abilities?"

"She can get the job done."

"Do you like her as a person?"

"Enjoy your mountains," he said, hanging up.

I decided to grab lunch at the lodge. When I arrived, McCoy was there, perhaps who I'd been hoping to see. He gestured me to his table. I sat and ordered.

"So, Lee," I said, handing the waitress my menu, "you're probably spending a lot of time with the FBI, right?"

He frowned over his coffee. "Agent Krenkler views me with curiosity, like I'm a two-headed calf. She can't understand why an adult would spend his life in the woods, even asked me if I had a 'Boy Scout complex'. She grilled me for a half-hour on the murders, but that was it."

That Krenkler didn't see McCoy's worth was inexcusable. "How about the website?" I asked. "Monitored day and night by the Feds?"

He nodded. "They tried to reverse-track the listings, but it was a dead end."

Meaning the killer knew enough to cover his electronic trail. "What's Cherry up to?" I asked, trying to keep my voice professionally disinterested.

"I spoke to Donna yesterday. She seemed embarrassed about being removed from the case so I kept the conversation short."

I'd been dismissed from investigations before. Even if

you'd been doing a kick-ass job, you felt like a dolt. What made it worse was knowing lack of progress in the case would be blamed on the initial investigators. *"We're having to go back and re-check all the sources,"* I heard Krenkler complaining to her supervisors. *"Detective Cherry left a lot of loose ends."*

I returned to the cabin and found Mix-up snoozing on the porch. I didn't have to shut him in the cabin when I left, finding he never ventured far. When I'd whistle, he was always at my side within a minute, often soaking wet from the creek. He did the same back on Dauphin Island, and I wondered if my genetic boullabaise of a dog carried a homebody species inside, or was loath to wander too far from his beloved food bowl.

I considered calling Donna Cherry – only to offer a sympathetic ear, of course – but heard my brother's words as clear as he'd spoken them in person:

*"If she's pretty, you've commenced a charm offensive to get into her pants, Carson. You need the attention."*

I decided what I needed was a drive through the mountains. Mix-up seemed content snoozing in the sun, so I left him to his dogdreams and followed my muse, circling through the Gorge until the road somehow dumped me several miles distant, in Campton. Being so close to Cherry's office, I was compelled by civility to stop and wish her well.

She was at her desk, hair pulled back in a streamlining of red, a pair of silver earrings bobbing against her milky cheeks. She wore a white blouse and dark pantsuit that would have turned any buxom starlet *du jour* into a sexless manikin, and I wondered if Cherry was – consciously or not – aping the drabness of the Feeb's palette.

She looked up and I thought I saw a spark of smile, quickly extinguished in favor of nonchalance. I spun a chair in front of her desk, where I saw a grouping of photos from Powers's death scene.

"You're back on the case?" I asked.

Cherry shrugged. "I figure Krenkler's first day push-away was a shot over my bow, making sure I knew my place."

"Which is?"

"Making multiple copies of all case materials," she said, keeping her face and voice emotionless. "Making runs for coffee and burgers. Smoothing the lady's way into interviews with locals."

"Ever think she's keeping you close to keep you open to blame?"

"That thought has occurred, Kemo Sabe. I'm watching my flank."

*I've watched it a time or two*, my mind said. My mouth said, "Krenkler making any headway?"

Cherry leaned back in her chair and sighed. "She wants to do all the interviews herself, like I'm too incompetent to ask a question. Trouble is, she's got this imperial atti-tude. And she's got all these guys in dark suits with her every step she takes, no idea how scary it is to a lot of the populace."

116

"People clam up the second Krenkler appears," I said.

Cherry nodded, silver earrings bouncing. "They pretend to be as dumb as she thinks they are. It seems to validate her suspicions, so she treats them even more like ignorant children and the circle keeps spiraling down. She has no concept of mountain folk."

I nodded understanding. Any group from a relatively isolated and low-money background learns the ritual as a form of protection. When you don't know how the rulers will use information, the best play is playing dumb. To the well-heeled, knowledge is power. To the poor it's usually just a target on their backs.

"What's Beale doing?" I asked.

"He's turned the Woslee police force completely over to Krenkler. She uses them for errands. She uses everyone for errands."

Cherry's cellphone rang. She pulled it from her jacket. "What? Where? How bad?" she said, listening between the words. She snapped the phone shut and shook her head.

"Caudill's got a problem. Some preacher has gone O.K. Corral and is holed up in a church shooting anything that moves."

"Anyone hurt?" I asked.

"A county worker brush-cutting a side road got hit in the thigh. He found cover under the tractor, but Caudill can't get to him. Uh, Ryder . . ."

"I haven't been to church in a while."

# 17

Within a minute we were on the Mountain Parkway, Cherry standing on the pedal, the speedometer in the hundred-ten-plus range. We veered on to an asphalt road that was barely a car and a half wide, changed direction on a switchback, climbed a couple hundred feet, swerved off on to a dirt road.

I saw a trio of wooden crosses in the distance, the center cross twenty feet high. Behind them, on a rise of three mowed acres, was a single-wide trailer with a large cross painted in white across its front. A hand-lettered sign said *Solid Word Church*. A hundred feet behind, at the edge of a woods, was a second trailer, living quarters, a small garden to its side.

A slug thudded into the side of the cruiser.

"Damn!" Cherry yelled. "Get down."

She aimed the car into a steep drainage ditch beside

the road, a few feet of cover. I saw a single-lane bridge two hundred feet ahead, a county-cop SUV and dark FBI cruiser on the far side. The occupants were safe behind a four-foot rock wall. Caudill and the Feds.

We jumped out as a round thudded into the dirt. Cherry pulled up a walkie-talkie, waved it at Caudill. He pulled his own unit from his belt.

"What's the story, Caudill?"

"We been stuck here since I called you. I've got two ambulances waiting a quarter-mile away."

"Where's Beale?"

"Hunting squirrel."

"Who's in there, Buddy?" Cherry said. "Who's the shooter? Over."

"It's Brother Tanner."

"Ezekiel Tanner?" Cherry said. "Uncle Zeke?"

Cherry set aside the communicator and stared at the church.

"You're related to the guy in there?" I asked.

"His father was my uncle's wife's cousin's brother third removed or something like that. I can't keep it all straight."

"He's a for-real reverend?"

"Self-ordained. Zeke has always seemed more sick with the spirit than inspired by it. He used to give the blessing at family reunions. You ever been eight years old and told you're gonna end up as cooked as the supper chicken, only in the devil's oven?"

"I had my own problems. You got field glasses in the cruiser?"

Cherry thumbed the trunk mechanism on her keys. I duck-walked to the trunk, lifted the lid. A shot from the church blew out half the light bar as I found a set of high-powered binocs. I scrabbled back to Cherry's side and peered over the top of the gulley, staying low.

The church-trailer was atop a rising hill, a small rocky creek at the base, a hundred feet from us. A narrow asphalt county road angled the side of the church. Between church and creek and slender lane, the scene was postcard pastoral. Until you saw the big green John Deere tractor tipped into the gulley, its bush hog attachment like a giant lawnmower on its side. The injured operator sprawled beneath the tractor, his right leg red with blood. He wasn't moving.

Another shot rang out. A headlamp exploded on the tractor, glass raining down on the wounded man.

"AVANT THEE, SATAN," screamed a voice from the church. "Yea though I WALK through the VALLEY I FEAR NO EVIL!"

It was Cherry's turn to duck-walk to the trunk, returning with a bullhorn. She aimed the cone over the wall. "Zeke? This is Donna Cherry. You remember me, right? I always loved your preaching."

"BITCH DEVIL!" the man screamed, punctuating his words with a volley. "SPAWN OF SATAN! WHORE OF BABYLON!"

"Not working," she said, ducking back down as the guy started talking in tongues. "ARM-A-LACKEE TATALODO. SHEM PAYLA RAS! HARWHALLA DEEM-ADAYDA!"

120

"He's losing whatever's left," Cherry said. "Mad as a hatter."

"The guy under the tractor looks passed out," I said. "Probably in shock." I gauged the width of the creek, deep-cut banks, the creek a good yard beneath the level of the land.

"I think I can get to the wounded man with the car," I said. "There's a rise I can use as a ramp."

"Jump the creek? No way. You'll plant the nose in the creek bed. Even if you make it, you'll have to drive in front of the church. He'll pop you like Dick Cheney shooting a caged bird."

I studied Cherry's car, the big Ford Crown Vic cop cruiser with a roaring four-point-six liter V-8 and the beefed-up frame and suspension. Harry and I had done enough unlikely feats in our succession of Crown Vics that the Motor Pool considered us *persona non grata*. I scuttled to the cruiser, pulled myself inside, studied a downslope over meadow grass to the creek-jump east of the church, then the two-hundred-foot run to the toppled tractor.

Ducking low, I jammed the gear stick into reverse, pulling out of the cover as the windshield exploded. He had the range. I pushed the accelerator to the floor and heard the big V-8 scream. I roared into the field below the church, the creek rushing at me.

I hit the rise, the car bottoming out, grille lifting in rebound. Airborne. Then: Thunderous boom, shocks breaking, sideways-skidding, passenger door popping open on busted hinges.

I'd crossed the creek.

Now to pass the trailer. I saw the rifle barrel hanging out a front window, ready to pick me off through the open door . . .

Change of plans. I skimmed the car across the front of the trailer, cheap pasteboard construction versus serious Detroit iron. The Crown Vic peeled open the trailer like a jack plane slicing pine. A tire exploded. The hood popped open. My face filled with steam from the radiator. Tire flapping, I aimed the wobbling vehicle toward the wounded man.

And then I was out and rolling beneath the tractor. Touching the man's throat. Feeling a pulse, thank God.

I saw Cherry and Caudill racing to the listing trailer with guns drawn. A warning shot, Cherry baying *Stay down!* The ambulances were moving in. It seemed odd that I didn't see the Feds.

I stood and was doing fine for about three seconds, until adrenalin buckled my knees and I sat flat on my ass like a swami.

# 18

Cherry and Caudill had stormed the trailer when they'd seen Tanner on the floor, moaning, grabbing at his belly. In what seemed like seconds – and with no resistance – the pair had the reverend subdued.

The bush-hog operator was rushed toward a hospital in Jackson. The paramedics from the second bus were trying to get Tanner stabilized. We'd figured the guy was having a psychotic episode, but it seemed he had serious physical problems as well. He struggled to pull in breath, then rolled to his side and began shaking.

Krenkler walked up, looked at the reverend. "Jesus," she said, wrinkling her nose. "What's wrong with him?"

"What's wrong with you?" I said, anger rippling through my guts.

"What's that supposed to mean?"

I said, "The only people I saw crossing the field to the church were Cherry and Caudill."

"And?"

"Three armed and experienced FBI agents and you sat on your thumbs."

Krenkler looked on the verge of a yawn. "It's a local matter. Not our problem."

"*What?*"

"We're here to stop a psychotic torturer, not a local head case. There were no new inclusions on the geocache site and Officer Caudill told us the victim was emotionally erratic. Ergo, it fell under local jurisdiction."

"That's bullshit," I said. "Fellow law-enforcement agents and an injured man were at risk and you squatted behind a wall and watched it like a croquet match." I looked at the two other agents. They were turned away, like this scene wasn't happening.

Krenkler's mouth twisted into an ugly shape. "Get out of here, Ryder. That's an order."

"It's not your jurisdiction, Agent Krenkler. You just said so."

The mouth twisted tighter but any response was interrupted by the preacher convulsing so powerfully he knocked one of the attendants from the ambulance. The sick man projectile-vomited a sticky curd the color of dead blood. It kept coming, a deluge, like a drainage pipe had broken in his guts.

"My God," Cherry whispered.

"His vitals are failing," one medic yelled to the other,

eyes tight to the monitors attached to Tanner. "Oh shit, he's shutting down, cardiac arrest."

The medics applied the shock paddles. Nothing.

Applied them again.

After four tries, they shook their heads. The bus pulled away. Somewhere in there the FBI had departed to do things in its jurisdiction.

McCoy appeared, called by Cherry. Caudill and I followed Cherry into the torn and listing church-trailer, McCoy standing aside and watching us work. There were no pews, only folding chairs in disarray. At one end of the floor was a plywood pulpit, painted white, a hand-painted cross on the front.

"Look for drugs," Cherry said. "The rev was acting like a guy on PCP or meth."

Caudill was scrabbling through a metal cabinet. "Bullets and bibles. Wonder why he stopped shooting?"

"He got too sick," Cherry said. "Dry-heaving like his body was trying to push something from his gut."

"Demons," I suggested. "Unfortunately, they were in his head."

"Let's check his house," Cherry said. "Nothing's here."

We walked the fifty steps to the trailer where Tanner had lived. A two-box life. We went our separate ways and I checked a closet.

"I've got six boxes of ammo at fifty rounds per," I noted. "Another box of nines for the Browning. Was Tanner expecting a revolution?"

"Paranoia." Cherry lifted a 3 × 5 index card, a hole

punched in one corner, a loop of string tied through the hole.

"Got something?" I asked.

"A note that says *Bless you Brother for your constant inspiration*. From one of the flock, I expect." She tossed the note aside and studied a pan on the stove.

"Tanner's last meal. Chunks of chicken, potato, carrot, mushrooms, gravy. Hope he said grace."

We stepped into the dining area where I reported finding nothing of merit, Caudill the same. We heard a clanging of silverware and turned to see McCoy in front of the stove. He'd fished something from the stew with a fork, holding the specimen at eye level, studying it in the light through the window.

"I don't like this mushroom," he said.

We bagged the stew and went outside. Cherry's cruiser was a jumble of useless metal and Caudill took us to his department, loaned Cherry a county car. She drove me to her office.

"Tanner was really half-crazed?" I asked.

"Like I said, Uncle Zeke was touched by the spirit, though some might say walloped so hard he lost all worldly perspective. You and I see gray, mostly. Zeke only saw white and black, Good and Evil. And Evil was always winning." She paused to watch a hawk spiral in the sky, turned back to me. "When I see things like Soldering-iron Man, I think maybe Zeke was on to something."

"Tanner was always that way?"

"Zeke started out gentle, a young pastor in tune with his flock. But maybe twenty years ago everything became repent this, repent that. He got strident on the salvation message, screaming at everyone to get saved before the devil got them. I always had this feeling . . ." She frowned, trying to find the words.

"What?" I asked.

"He wasn't preaching to a flock so much as to himself."

Cherry dropped me off. I stepped up to my porch, pulled my keys. A fortune-cookie-sized strip of paper had been taped across the lock with small and precise words penned over it. Though the words were in French, the language didn't matter: My brother wanted something, and that always meant *Now*. If I blew it off, he'd end up at my cabin at three a.m., shrieking in the window.

My shoulders slumped. I turned and trudged to Charpentier's cabin. I knocked on the thick door of Jeremy's home, heard *entrez-vous*. My brother was sprawled on the couch wearing a purple robe, his long feet tucked into a pair of battered hiking shoes with laces removed. He had a cup of coffee at his side and a computer on his lap. He looked up, closed the computer.

"What do you want?" I asked.

"Company."

"I'm a little tired right now."

My brother's nose started quivering like a hound's nose. "You stink of sweat and gunpowder, Carson. I smell a woman, too. Have we gone burrowing for love in the cherry grove?"

I saw his emergency-band scanner on the table. "You know what happened, right? You were listening."

He held up his hand, thumb and forefinger a half-inch apart. "A bit. I heard cops and medical people. A man died, correct?"

"Yes. Badly."

"Tell me all about it, brother."

"I was visiting Cherry and she got a call about a man with a rifle shooting at—"

"Not all three acts, Carson, just the final one. What was the death like?"

"The man was sick. Convulsing. His heart stopped in the ambulance. Drugs maybe. Or it just chose that moment to go."

Jeremy's brow furrowed with curiosity. "Was the death interesting?" he asked, eyes alert.

"Interesting?"

"You know . . . a sense of drama. Of theater. Or, as deaths go, was it just . . .?" he fluttered his tongue dismissively.

"I don't need this right now," I said, not wanting to revisit a man's demise for the odd pleasures of my brother. I walked out the door and kept moving.

# 19

The next morning found me sitting in the lodge restaurant at Natural Bridge Park, McCoy and Cherry across from me, revisiting the Tanner episode. Her cellphone buzzed. She pulled it from her jacket, walked to the porch for better reception. After three minutes she rang off, returning with a hard smile on her face as she shot McCoy a thumbs-up.

"I messengered the mushroom to a buddy in forensics. Tanner's chicken stew contained a fungus called a fool's mushroom."

McCoy winced. "*Amanita verna*. Deadly poisonous. A few bites would start messing up the head and tearing down the machinery. Think Brother Tanner's recipe came from the Borgia family cookbook?"

I thought back to fungi noted on my hikes. In under a week I'd seen perhaps fifty different varieties. "Does this happen often?" I asked McCoy. "Mushroom poisoning?"

"It's a problem."

"There's another possible explanation," Cherry said, shaking her third packet of sugar into her cup of coffee. "Brother Tanner was purposely eating poison mushrooms to prove he was touched by Grace, safe under the watchful eye of God. It's the creed of the snake handlers. Taking up serpents to test one's faith. Cousin Zeke had been getting stranger over the years, more insistent on proofs of faith."

McCoy said, "Two choices, then: Zeke got careless or tempted fate."

I said, "There's a third. Tanner's part of the other killings. The geocache murders."

Cherry shook her head. "It hurts to agree with Krenkler, but nothing ties Tanner's case to the others. He wasn't tortured. Nothing appeared on the geocache website."

"He looked a lot like a man in torture," I argued. "Especially those last few minutes. Something feels related to the others."

"Can you expand on that logically," Cherry asked, "or are you using your psychic powers?"

I thought a moment, shrugged, let it go. "What's your plan for the day?" I asked, changing the topic.

"Sonny Burton's visitation is today. The Feds want me there in case our killer pays his respects."

"The Feds are attending?"

"I actually convinced Krenkler they'd be too conspicuous in person. There's a junk shop a block and a half away. They'll park behind it and we'll use radio."

"Radio? So they'd never know if we added another pair of eyes to the mix, right?"

Cherry and I walked from the lodge together. The sun was high and warm, the air rich with the scent of pine and last year's leaves turning into humus, intoxicating and almost dizzying in its gentle fecundity.

"Do you want me along?" I asked. "Burton's visitation?"

"Very much, Ryder."

"If I recall, it wasn't all that long ago you were telling me to take a hike."

"That's when I thought you were a hot dog with an attitude."

"You don't think that any more?"

She smiled, coy and warm at the same time, a wonderful combination. Both eyes seemed to focus on mine. I felt my knees tremble.

"A little," she said. "But you're improving daily."

We stopped at her cruiser and I looked into her eyes. It was a moment with the chance of turning either beautiful or awkward, so I chopped it off, spinning toward my truck while my legs still functioned.

"I've got to change into a dress," she called to my back. "How about I come get you in an hour."

I winked as I climbed into my truck. "Done."

I started the engine, drove past Cherry. She held up her hand, *wait*. I stopped.

"One more thing just came to mind. We talked about Charpentier? I'm thinking if he's as perceptive as McCoy says, he might be another useful set of eyes. Think you could stop by his place and feel him out?"

My heart froze in my chest. "You want Charpentier at the visitation?"

"The man's a head doc, right? Given that we can use all the professional input we can, and the Feds won't be overly near . . ."

"Charpentier's an odd duck," I said, trying to keep from stammering. "But I'll ask."

# 20

I returned to the cabin, slipped into dark slacks and blazer and drove to Jeremy's. Though it was ten a.m., Jeremy was in pajamas, sky-blue with white piping, like we'd worn as children. His feet were in brown leather slippers and he was opening mail with a pearl-handled dagger.

I said, "You know, of course, that a man named Sonny Burton was the first killing."

"It was all over my police scanner. Fascinating methodology, no?"

"Burton's visitation starts in an hour. Cherry wants you along."

The knife fell to the floor. "WHAT?"

"Don't worry, you can make up a story about you having the flu or something. I want you to meet her. It's the perfect chance to brand the image of a benign professor into Cherry's head. Do it now and here, where you control the setting."

"Why does your little screech owl want me at the visitation?"

"McCoy told her you're a brilliant psychologist. It's your fault for talking psychobabble like you're the Freud and Jung Traveling Circus."

"I refuse to hide my light under a barrel," he sniffed.

"Cherry will be here in fifteen minutes," I instructed my brother. "Get into costume."

I was waiting on the porch when Cherry rolled up. She was in the first dress I'd seen her wear, a dark amethyst that highlighted her slender waist and compact hips. The demure décolletage nonetheless displayed a half-circle of warm cream ringed with small dark stones. Her knee-bottom hem hinted at curvaceous calves flowing into slender, defined ankles.

"You look ready for a Parisian runway," I said.

She shook her head like I was twitting her. "The dress cost twelve bucks at a second-hand store in Jackson. I spent a day with a needle and thread getting it to fit halfway right."

"I don't think I could take all the way right."

I saw her neck color slightly. "So is the Doc in or out?" she asked, changing the subject as she stepped to the porch.

"He has a malaise and won't be able to attend," I said, expecting Jeremy was eavesdropping behind the door.

Her face fell. "At least you tried. What's bothering the guy?"

The door opened at my back. My brother appeared in loose jeans and a sweatshirt emblazoned with the logo of the Edmonton Oilers hockey team.

"*Mon Dieu,*" my brother crooned, brushing past my introductions as if I were invisible, striding directly to Cherry. "You are the loveliest woman I've seen since arriving here!" Jeremy took Cherry's hand and bowed to kiss her fingertips. "You shame the angels, my dear."

Cherry's face turned red. Her mouth moved, but no words came out.

"I just explained that you're under the weather, Dr Charpentier," I said.

He shook his head, angry at himself. "I have a condition called IBS. It comes and goes. Today it seems particularly vexatious."

Cherry regained her voice. "My aunt has IBS," she said. "I understand why you need to remain here, Dr Charpentier."

"You're too kind. Before you go, Detective Cherry, please grace my home for a few moments. I get so few visitors, and none so beautiful."

Cherry stepped into the living room, eyes wide at the sophisticated decor. Jeremy followed, pretending to masturbate over her derriere while grinning lasciviously at me.

Eight minutes later – minutes my brother had jam-packed with dissertations on plant genetics, the nutritive components of honey, the geology of the area, and a speculative foray into the sexual psyche of Jack the Ripper – Cherry pulled out of the hollow to the main road and aimed toward the Mountain Parkway.

"Damn, Ryder, is Charpentier bright or what? I wish he felt better."

"You said your aunt had IBS? What's it mean?"

"Irritable Bowel Syndrome. It manifests a lot of ways, like cramps, diarrhea, constipation, flatulence. Some days you can't get too far from a toilet." Cherry shook her head in sympathy.

"Ugh," I said, inwardly complimenting my brother on a masterful choice of affliction.

"I'll drop you off at the church," Cherry said, as we pulled off the Parkway. "Then I'll see the Feds in their hideaway and get my mic in place. We can saunter into Burton's visitation like . . ." I saw Cherry's eyes rivet on the rear-view mirror. "Damn!"

"What?"

A roaring engine followed by a horn blast. Cherry veered toward the berm. A vehicle blew by, a blue panel van marked *A-1 Air Conditioning Service*. Seconds later it was out of sight.

"Must be one helluva AC problem," Cherry said.

After three minutes, I saw the church in the distance. Cherry pulled between a pair of church buses.

"Wait here," she said. "I'll get mic'd up. The we'll go hunting bad guys."

I stepped out just as a blue work van swooped to our

bumper. The *A-1 Air Conditioning* van. The side door slid open. Agent Gloria Krenkler was sitting in a jump seat in what I recognized as a surveillance vehicle.

"Why, Detective Ryder," Krenkler said, as though we were old friends. "I didn't know you were a fan of visitations. Why don't you jump in here and we can talk."

Feeling like a kid with his hand in the cookie jar, I climbed inside the surveillance van, Cherry behind me.

"My compliments to whoever pimped your ride," I said.

Krenkler folded a piece of Juicy Fruit and fed it between her teeth. "I didn't think it would arrive in time. But now we can see everything. Just like we saw you two on the road. Care to explain, Detective Cherry?"

"Explain what?"

"Why you invited Ryder to our show?"

Cherry canted her head, as if the question seemed bizarre. "I thought you'd want him along, Agent Krenkler."

"Why on earth would I want such a thing?"

Cherry ticked off reasons on her fingers. "One, I have doubled our surveillance range; two, added high-level experience and, three, put another layer of protection and safety in place should we encounter an armed killer. May I ask your specific objections to my considerations, Agent Krenkler?"

Krenkler's attendant agents snuck looks at her. I saw a slow smolder behind the eyes before Krenkler's face went blank. She nodded to the older agent in the front passenger seat, a mini-mic ready to pin inside Cherry's collar.

"Hook her up, Agent Rourke."

"Ryder, too?"

"I don't think I need to hear him."

Cherry and I stepped into the church lot two minutes later. Banks of flowers flanked the coffin. Cherry nodded to people, shaking hands or gathering someone in an embrace. She introduced me without reason, a good friend or perhaps a beau. I nodded that I was going outside to take a look around, mouthed *back in five*.

I leaned against a sycamore and studied rugged back-country types smoking and looking uncomfortable in collared shirts and clip-on ties. Bar buddies of Burton, I figured, none appearing particularly malevolent. I watched an ancient woman in a blue dress make unsteady progress toward the men, marking her passage with quivering thumps of cane and talking to herself as she went. She broke into the men's conversation, speaking to each in turn. They nodded and spoke back respectfully, holding their cigarettes behind their backs, like kids caught smoking on a schoolground.

I avoided looking the two hundred feet to the blue van at the far edge of the lot, figuring Krenkler had field glasses to her tight little eyes.

"Lose your love-muffin already, Carson?"

My head snapped to the smiling face of my brother. His dark suit was as fitted to his frame as a Vogue model, his smile radiating joyful warmth. Blue had been the perfect choice of shirt, highlighting his robin's-egg eyes. His cologne recalled smoked sherry served with fresh-picked limes.

"Jeremy? What are you—"

"You were right. If I pretend to be on the side of the angels for an hour or so, I can return home with Miss Cherry convinced of my stellar citizenship. You didn't tell me she was such a sugary little cupcake, Carson. What's keeping you from opening her legs and closing the deal?"

"The FBI's here, Jeremy," I hissed through closed lips. "They're watching."

He froze. "What? Where?"

"At the far end of the lot. Don't look, just shake my hand like we barely know one another."

We shook hands as Jeremy backpedaled to a semi-stranger's distance. "Perhaps I should leave," he said through a frozen smile.

"They'll ask who you are and why you left without visiting dear ol' Sonny."

We walked to the church. I didn't see Cherry, but figured she'd slipped out one of the side doors or the back, checking the gatherings there. I took my turn at viewing. A haphazard photo display of the deceased sat on a table beside the coffin, thirty or forty shots. Sonny Burton had a square, ruddy face and wide forehead, his hair waxed thick and combed back in curly waves. Burton was aware of the camera in most shots, meeting the lens with a grin, perfect teeth flashing as his broad, square hands pulled people to his side. Sonny Burton was a happy man, to judge by the beaming face, like life was an Italian bakery and he got born with a sweet tooth in every socket.

Jeremy appeared at my side. We were alone at the front of the church. "My, my," he said, glancing at the photographs. "There's an unhappy fellow."

"Unhappy?" I side-mouthed. "Are we looking at the same guy?"

"Learn to isolate, Carson. Cover the white teeth. Cut away the happy eye crinkles and brow furrows. Strip off the upturned lips."

My brother positioned his hands over an eight by ten shot, blotting out as much face as possible. Only the eyes were left, Burton staring between my brother's fingers like a man peering from a bunker.

"Jesus," I gasped. "I see hate."

My brother removed his hands, leaving the full-face shot of a happy man. I stared like seeing a palimpsest, a Bosch nightmare hidden beneath a Thomas Cole landscape. "The eyes are five per cent of the total, Carson. Burton had the other ninety-five trained to mimic happiness. Practiced from early on in life, it can be completely convincing."

My brother tapped a photo taken at a birthday party. Burton's arm circling the shoulders of a gangly, small-framed teen boy with liquid, feminine eyes. A cone-shaped party hat perched atop his head. He was grinning through braces.

Burton's palms were touching the boy's body, fingers pressing wrinkles into the fabric of his white shirt. I mentally walled off sections of face, isolating Burton in the slitted bunker. It was like another sense had been turned on. I smelled lust rising from the photograph.

"Burton looks aroused," I whispered.

"What a fast learner you are," my brother said.

We moved up to view the deceased himself. There was nothing to learn there but the skill of the cosmetologist. Burton looked as airbrushed as a centerfold, his heavy hands crossed over the chest where last week a truck had rested. I figured a pillow or air bladder beneath the black suit had been the mortician's restoration of Burton's ribcage to pre-truck standards.

We hustled toward the front door just as Cherry was entering, nearly bumping heads.

"Dr Charpentier?" she said, surprised at seeing my brother.

"I began feeling better," Jeremy said. "I thought I'd accept your invitation."

"Thank you for coming," Cherry said.

Jeremy nodded and glided outside, hands in his pockets and walking slowly, a man innocent of everything in the world, even care. Cherry went out to check cars for non-local license tags. I sat in a middle pew and watched a fast-thinning crowd drift in and out for several minutes. The visitation was nearly over.

A slight man in his early forties caught my eye. He stood a dozen feet from Burton's casket, holding a box of flowers, roses perhaps, the box long and slender. His choice of flowers seemed out of place at a funeral, but he didn't look overly sophisticated. His thin and sallow face looked nervous, and I put him among the people unsettled by ceremonies of the dead. In that, we shared the same feeling.

My scan was broken as the elderly woman from outside passed by, still mumbling to herself, unsteady with the cane. When she glanced at the man something seemed to click behind her bifocals and she turned for further study. He seemed to feel the woman's stare and looked away, clutching his flower box tighter. The woman pursed her lips in thought, then turned and muttered from the church, leaving only stragglers in the room.

I heard the man's footsteps cross the room to the casket. I looked up to see him studying Burton. I could only see a portion of the man's face and noted a nervous tic twitching his cheek. Had it just started?

The man stood still as stone. When he moved it was to untie the bow on the box of flowers. The bow fell to the floor. Followed by the lid.

Not flowers in the box, but a baseball bat. The man lifted the bat like a sledgehammer and brought it down on the corpse's face. A hideous *chunking* sound. Face powder exploded into the air like pink smoke. The bat came down again, this time the head blew apart, pink clots of gelatinous goo flying through the air. I heard screaming and running at my back.

The bat was lifting for a third shot when I got there, diving at the guy. He jumped aside, swinging the bat after me, catching me behind the ear. I went sprawling to the floor. My dizzy attempts to push to my feet resulted in a slow-motion breaststroke. The man was six feet away, still hammering. More cold goo splattered my face. A table leg below the casket broke under the onslaught and the coffin tumbled, spilling Burton to the floor beside me. His face was a puddle, a single eye floating in the middle. An inflated bladder had been provided to give volume to the deceased's chest, but it was damaged in the attack.

I watched in horror as Sonny Burton, now a Cyclops, stared at me, his chest deflating with a rubbery, blubbering hiss.

# 21

I was too unsteady to stand. The knot behind my ear was a beaut. Cherry lashed together a bag of ice from the church's fridge and held it to my head. Jeremy stood to the side, arms crossed, concern on his face. Krenkler crouched in front of me, face filling my vision.

"Who was it?" she snapped. "What did you see?"

"I, uh—" trying to get words to fit in my mouth.

"Come on, Ryder, spit it out."

"He had, uhm, slight build, brown hair and eyes, I think. Cheap gray sport coat over . . . gray flannel slacks. Brown shoes like Hush Puppies." I felt a wave of nausea and rode it out.

"I was out back grabbing a smoke," a man said to Cherry. "The guy went in the woods. Not even running, just walking fast."

Krenkler turned to her adjutants. "Get on it!"

I tried to stand but Cherry's hands kept my shoulders down. "How about you wait right here and we'll go take a look."

Krenkler stood to follow Cherry, stopped. She narrowed her eyes at my brother.

"What's your name?"

"Dr Auguste Charpentier, at your service."

"You don't leave until we've had a chance to talk, you hear me?"

"*Certainement.*"

Cherry was back in minutes, Krenkler and the boys at her heels. I raised an eyebrow in question.

"It's just a strip of trees behind the church, a four-acre wood lot for the family a block east. A block west is a failed restaurant. I figure our batter parked there, walked over, had his inning, zipped back to his vehicle. No one saw a thing. How's your head?"

"He could have slammed a home run into my skull. But he didn't. He bunted."

"He tried to murder you," Krenkler scoffed. "You got lucky."

I looked through a cloudy recollection. "I'm sure he choked up on the bat and thunked me pretty lightly, all things considered."

Krenkler shook her head like I was an idiot. I heard an ambulance in the distance. "Your ride's on its way, Ryder," Krenkler said. "Consider yourself lucky it's not a hearse."

I felt a wave of nausea and bent forward. Krenkler turned

the eyes to my brother, scoping him from hair-part to Florsheims. She didn't look happy with the results.

"Let's you and me go over here and talk, Doc. I'm interested in hearing your story."

I arrived at the nearby hospital in minutes. The small institution was backed up, and after a cursory inspection to make sure I wasn't about to die on the floor, I was left sprawling in the waiting room, watching the clock and sucking coffee.

Jeremy arrived twenty minutes later, dropped off by a Woslee cop.

"What happened with Krenkler?" I whispered. "What'd you tell her?"

"I'm a retired psychologist who specialized in dysfunctional psychology. Thus it made sense for you and Miz Cherry to have invited me along."

I relaxed a half-degree. My fear had been Krenkler's running some form of check on Jeremy while he sat before her.

"No in-depth questions?"

"I gave her all my fictional accomplishments, then begged to be put on the case as a consultant. Said I'd be by her side night and day, all for free."

"What!"

He grinned. "It got the intended results: She couldn't push me out the door fast enough. The Krenklers of the world don't want consultants, Carson. It means sharing the spotlight."

146

My noggin finally got X-rayed and pronounced solid. Cherry had arranged for an off-duty ambulance driver to return us to the hollow, where we arrived at half-past eight in the evening. On the way back, Jeremy had ceaselessly grilled me on every aspect of Sonny Burton's abuse and the perpetrator, prying from my aching head pictures I hadn't recalled earlier: the bat-wielder's curious gait toward the corpse, halting, like a man walking a plank. I recalled the tic in his cheek and the ferocity of his attack on Burton's face, as if the batter's very life depended on destroying the visage.

Jeremy coaxed the memories from me with a quiet hypnotist's voice, pausing as he absorbed the information, analysing. We stepped from the vehicle, thanked our driver, watched the taillights flee from the dark and quiet hollow. I turned to walk the last section to my cabin, to soak in the peace before falling into bed. I paused before my brother closed the door to his cabin, turned to him in the twilight.

"The man with the bat, Jeremy," I said. "He's the killer we're after, right?"

"No, Carson," my brother answered. "He's simply an opportunist."

Sometime in the wee hours, my battered head woke me up. Or maybe it was the picture in my mind, a snippet: the elderly woman who passed by the attacker. She didn't do a double-take, it was more like a take and a quarter, but I'd forgotten to mention it to anyone. I wrote it down so it wouldn't slip my mind, and in the morning called Cherry about it.

"Tell me again what the woman looked like," Cherry said.

I gave my description. "You know anyone like that?"

"Miss Ida Minton," Cherry said. "She's an institution, the librarian at the high school for something like eight hundred years. She retired when I was a sophomore."

"What you gonna do?"

"Got an hour to spare?"

# 22

Miss Ida Minton lived in a small retirement home near Campton. Her room was pin-neat and smelled of lilacs and baby powder. She wore a pink polyester pantsuit and a thick white sweater, blue slippers on her feet.

*"Miss Ida goes in and out,"* Cherry had warned, referring to the elderly lady's memory. *"Sometimes she remembers the tiniest details, the next minute she forgets where she is."*

I wavered on a loose-legged chair, fearful of its solidity, as Cherry asked the retired librarian about her seeming recognition of our mad batter.

"Who?" Miss Minton said.

I leaned closer. "I noted you looked twice at a gentleman at the church, Miss Ida," I said, recounting the description as best I could.

"I don't recall. What day was that?"

"Yesterday, Miss Ida," Cherry said, taking the woman's fragile hand. "At Sonny Burton's visitation."

The woman paused, frowned. "I remember Sonny Burton. He didn't like to read. A lost cause." She looked at Cherry. "Wasn't there some sort of commotion later? At the visitation?"

"Yes, ma'am. And Mr Ryder is asking about that. And another gentleman you might have recognized." She repeated my description.

Nothing. Then a light seemed to dawn behind the woman's glasses. "Didn't I see a student named Willie Taithering from maybe twenty-two or -three years back?"

"I don't know, Miss Ida," Cherry said. "Did you?"

She paused, tapping her chin with a quivering digit. "Or was that later, at the grocery?"

Cherry looked at me. I closed my eyes. "The church, Miss Ida," Cherry said.

But Miss Ida was drifting fast. "I wanted some fresh peaches from the store, but they were all hard as stones. I brought them home and put them in a paper bag. Would you like some peaches, children?"

"Thank you, Miss Ida," Cherry said. "But we have to go."

We walked to the door. Miss Ida's eyes were bright as diamonds. She waved.

"Come and see me anytime, Laura. You were always a very good reader."

*   *   *

150

Cherry returned me to the cabin. Mix-up and I hiked in the woods for an hour and a half. I discovered a house-sized boulder in the creekbed and practiced several climbing moves until missing a hold and falling a dozen feet, into sand, luckily, only then recalling Gary's admonition that *Those who climb alone, die alone.* I brushed off my clothes and returned to the cabin.

Cherry was parked in the drive, reading through case materials.

"Is this where you're hiding from Krenkler?" I asked.

"I stopped by the FBI's digs earlier. They were all swarming like bees and Krenkler made me feel like some kid trying to play with the grown-ups."

"Condescending?"

"She did everything but pat my head and tell me to run along. So I did."

"Did you mention Miss Ida?"

Cherry laughed without mirth. "Tell Krenkler my lead is a name from twenty years back from a ninety-year-old woman who only occasionally remembers who I am?"

"I see your point."

"Didn't keep me from searching on my own. I went to the school, cross-checked between twenty-year-old records and the state phone directory. There's a William J. Taithering living in Augusta, up on the Ohio River, about an hour away. You up for a ride? Charpentier's going along. I stopped and asked. He said he feels healthy and would love some fresh air."

"He wants to go?"

"He seems fascinated by the case."

I drove on the way up, Cherry on the phone, checking with various local bureaus. Jeremy sat in back, seemingly deep in professorial thought. Cherry discovered that Taithering had lived at the same address for fifteen years, was unmarried, a self-employed accountant and notary public, and had no police record.

"I got the background from Bob Murray," she said. "Bob used to be a Statie, retired last year as a part-time deputy with the Augusta force. He says once a year – June twenty-third – the Augusta cops get called to a local bar after Taithering drinks himself into a stupor. It's like a ritual. They drive him home and make sure he gets inside safely."

William Taithering didn't sound like a corpse-basher, but did seem a man with a problem or two.

We found Taithering's house, a small bungalow in a 1950s subdivision. A four-year-old Prius sat in the drive. A sign on the door said *W.P. Taithering, CPA/Notary*. It was a tiny sign, as if a larger version might constitute braggadacio.

"I'll call for local back-up," Cherry said on our second drive-by recon. "Get a couple cars and an ambulance here. I'll have the ambulance stay down the block."

"Why all the drama, Miss *Cherie*?" Jeremy asked.

"If Taithering's the guy who tore into Burton's dead body with a ball bat, he might come out with guns blazing."

Jeremy frowned. "Why would a man who already killed

and tortured a victim – slowly and ritualistically, with time to perform every gruesome need – risk his reputation to publicly inflict destruction on the dead man?"

"Maybe the killer needed more."

"I suspect Mr Burton's killer got all he needed in the woods."

Cherry looked unconvinced. She drove on, passing Taithering's house. I saw her head whip to the side as she stood on the brakes.

"I see a guy out back, burning trash or something. It could be evidence."

She jammed the wheel hard, spun in the street, thundered into Taithering's drive. "Cover me, Ryder," she yelled, sprinting around the side of the house. I scrambled out, smelling smoke in the air.

"Police!" I heard Cherry yell. "Drop the pages and keep your hands away from your body."

I rounded the corner to the back yard as a man turned, confusion in his face. He was standing beside a rusty burn-barrel, feeding sheets of paper into a fire. I ran to the barrel and kicked it over, sending a few singed pages rolling over the grass.

"William Taithering?" Cherry said.

"That's me," Taithering said, voice flat, hands held out like bird wings.

"Is this the guy from the church, Ryder?"

When I nodded, Cherry pulled her cuffs from beneath her jacket. "William Taithering, you're under arrest for—"

153

From nowhere, Jeremy was between Cherry and Taithering. He held up his hand to cut Cherry off.

"It's rather warm out here," my brother said pleasantly, like we were a foursome on a golf course, ready to go club-housing for cocktails. "How about stepping inside where things are cooler, folks?"

And then my brother had his arm around Taithering and was guiding him toward the patio door. Cherry stared, open-mouthed, cuffs dangling in her hand.

# 23

We reconvened in Taithering's living room. Cherry and I did a quick search of the furniture and closet to assure ourselves no Uzis were planted. Taithering sat on a chair dragged in from the dining room.

The man was thirty-four and looked a decade older. Part of it was his carriage, holding himself close and hunched over, like a frail elder walking on ice. His eyes were tight and lined, the kind of eyes I got when a case kept me awake for days. His mouse-brown hair was speckled with gray. Taithering was staring at the floor and seemed numb. His hands shook and he held them in his lap to staunch the motion.

Cherry pulled a chair in front of Taithering as I stood to the side and Jeremy relaxed on the couch. "Let's start with Sonny Burton," she said. "Is that all right, Mr Taithering?"

He nodded, not meeting her eyes.

"Tell me about what happened," Cherry said. "From the beginning. Why did you put Sonny Burton under the truck?"

Taithering's eyes went wide. "What? NO! I didn't do that."

"You didn't lower a truck on to Burton's chest?"

"No!"

"You didn't kill Sonny Burton?"

"NO!"

"What about Tandee Powers?"

Taithering stared at Cherry. I swear his short hair was standing on end. "WHAT ARE YOU TALKING ABOUT?"

"Mr Taithering, you need to calm down and answer my—"

My brother was suddenly standing beside Cherry, his hand in the pockets of his jacket.

"I believe this might be a propitious time for us to trade places for a minute or two, Miss Cherry."

Cherry looked up, surprised. "Uh, I—"

My brother was smiling gently, his words so perfectly weighted they offered no option of refusal. It was a strange and potent effect that seemed to border on hypnosis, a master manipulator's skill honed over decades. Jeremy looked to Cherry and me.

"Could you folks please give us a few minutes together? Alone? I think it would be most helpful here."

Cherry shot me a glance. I nodded toward the kitchen and we retreated out of sight.

"What's Charpentier doing, you think?" Cherry asked, perplexed.

"I expect he's gaining Taithering's confidence and getting a read on the man's mental state," I approximated. It's said that Alcoholics Anonymous works because the only person capable of reaching an alcoholic is someone with the same affliction. I suspected my brother was meeting William Taithering in some strange land of dysfunction, trading images and symbols incomprehensible to the normal mind.

Called back ten minutes later, we found Jeremy standing behind the sitting Taithering, hands resting on the man's shoulders. Taithering looked alternately ready to flee or burst into tears.

"William would like to speak with you, Miss Cherie," my brother said. His eyes and voice said *go easy*.

Cherry got the message, positioning her chair not in the confrontational front and center, but canted to the side, conversational. "Tell us about Sonny Burton, William," she said. "Explain yesterday. Take all the time you need."

Taithering's face screwed up in misery. "Every . . . day . . . he . . ." The man's mouth made several missteps, chokes and swallows. He tried again.

"E- Every day for twenty years he . . . Burton . . . was in me. I'd wake up and he was there. I'd take a breath and feel him stealing part of it. I could feel him squirming inside me."

"You were in Burton's truck, right, William?" Jeremy said, his voice as soft as cotton. "Things happened there. Started there."

"He p-pushed INSIDE ME. He got stuck there and

I couldn't g-get him out. I moved away. But he stayed in me. I went to college. But he stayed in me. I been in Augusta for years but he was always on top of me with his fingers in my hair and his tongue in my . . . I tried BUT I COULDN'T GET HIM OUT OF ME."

"Easy, William," Jeremy said. "You've thought about yesterday a long time, haven't you?"

Taithering thrust out a forceful jaw. "I got FREE of him. For the first time ever. I took his face out of mine. I took HIM out of ME."

"But Sonny Burton was dead, Mr Taithering," Cherry said.

"HE WAS STILL ALIVE INSIDE ME."

Taithering began weeping uncontrollably. I felt claustrophobic and went to the back yard. I retrieved a sheaf of photos only touched on the edges by fire. I stared a long time and returned to the house.

Cherry was in the kitchen. I heard a toilet flush and my brother came down the hall from the bathroom and joined us. Taithering was still weeping, and I took it they were giving space to his grief. I set the rescued photos on the cheap table.

"What was Taithering burning?" Cherry asked.

"Pictures from his youth." I tapped the top photograph. It was similar to a photo I'd seen earlier at the visitation: Sonny Burton with his hands around a gangly boy with a shy smile and braces on his teeth: William Taithering in his early teens. The other photos were nearly the same:

Burton hanging on Taithering, smiling at him, touching him. Some had other kids in the background, others didn't. In one photo, both Taithering and Burton were in swim trunks, standing at the edge of a pool, the grinning, thirtyish Burton seemingly a picture of happy camp-counselor innocence behind Taithering, Burton's outlined penis nestling in the small of Taithering's back.

Cherry looked ill. She turned to my brother. "It still doesn't make sense: Burton was nothing but dead meat. How do you get revenge on dead meat?"

"Whether Burton was alive or dead is meaningless. He was a strand of symbols inside a coffin. Mr Taithering, fueled by years of agony and imagined retributions, came to vanquish the symbols."

"Surely the photographs were symbols, Dr Charpentier? Taithering didn't burn the pictures until now. Why?"

"He couldn't destroy them, Detective Cherie. As long as Burton was inside Taithering, Burton had control over these pictures. They didn't belong to Taithering because Taithering didn't belong to himself."

"That makes no sense," Cherry said.

"It makes perfect sense if your life is the singular arc of events and memories that comprise William Taithering. Yesterday, after years of belonging to Sonny Burton, William Taithering employed a power ritual created in his subconscious and gave himself back to William Taithering."

Cherry shot a glance at the weeping man.

"It seems a shame to arrest him, but . . ."

Jeremy frowned. "One day of freedom after twenty years in the bleakest of prisons, Taithering goes to jail? Does that seem just, Detective?"

"I truly don't want to hurt him any more, Doctor. But he's broken laws."

"Such as?"

"Creating a public disturbance. Abuse of a corpse. He did it to himself, Doctor. He chose to go to the visitation."

"He had to go, Detective Cherie," my brother argued. "It was his only chance to confront his tormentor and escape his past."

"Only chance?" Cherry said. "Here's a grisly what-if, Doctor: why not wait until Sonny Burton was buried? Taithering could have dug him up and beaten him like a gong all night long."

"A very intelligent question," my brother said. "But to unearth Burton in the dark would have been the coward's path. Taithering's salvation demanded three primal elements: personal risk to Taithering, Burton's metaphoric humiliation by the loss of his face, and a public viewing of that humiliation. Even if William Taithering didn't realize that, his subconscious did."

"Danger, destruction, display?" Cherry shuddered and looked to me. "You studied psychology, Ryder. You agree with this?"

In truth they were not connections I would have made

so quickly. But when it came to sailing through the dark waters of the human mind, my brother was an Odysseus. I nodded the affirmative.

"Let me talk to Taithering by myself," Cherry said.

"This is truly insane," Cherry said as we drove back to Woslee County, Taithering still home in Augusta. "If Krenkler finds out, she'll tear me apart. My superiors will have no choice but to pull me from my position and . . . jeez, I don't even want to know."

"William Taithering was telling you the truth," Jeremy said.

Cherry nodded. "Burton was a mentor, a big-brother type, supposedly providing a role model. What Burton provided was increasing amounts of liquor and pornography. His bonding culminated on the floor of the snack truck during a weekend camping trip. The date, as you might expect, was June 23rd. The confused kid let Burton have his way for a couple of months, until Burton found another fish, I imagine."

"Taithering never told anyone in authority?" I asked.

"You know how it works. Burton convinced Taithering that he initiated the relationship. Plus it would have gotten to Taithering's parents, very religious folk who . . ."

"Who would never look at their son the same way again," I said.

"That's what used to happen to raped women," Cherry said, her voice simultaneously sad and angry.

"You're doing the right thing," I assured Cherry.

"Would you do the same thing, Ryder? Take that kind of—"

I heard Cherry gasp. I looked down the road. A quarter-mile ahead and coming at us like a flying rage were two black cruisers with grille lights blazing and sirens blasting.

"Get off the road," I said.

"Where?" Cherry said.

"There," I pointed. "A farm lane."

Cherry whipped off the road, skidding on to the lane. She pulled ahead and we turned to watch as the two cruisers howled past. We saw Krenkler in the lead cruiser. And then they were over a hill and gone.

"Is it what it appears?" Jeremy said.

Cherry nodded. "Yes, Doctor. The Feds have discovered William Taithering."

# 24

We returned to the road and drove for several miles before anyone spoke, Cherry taking the honor.

"What happens when Taithering mentions the cop who let him go?" she whispered. "Me."

"He won't mention our visit," Jeremy said. "I suspect that, given Mr Taithering's mental state, he'll . . ." Jeremy paused, settled back in the seat. "Never mind."

A hushed and pensive Cherry drove back to Woslee, turning down into the hollow to drop Jeremy off, then to my place where I picked up a lonely Mr Mix-up and followed Cherry to the ECKLE office. Whatever was happening in Augusta would get back to her soon enough.

The hour hand swept slowly and the sun dropped in the sky. There was a field behind the office and I walked its perimeter with my dog. He seemed to have absorbed my tension, padding at my side rather than bounding madly through the furrows of earth. Twice I saw Cherry wandering outside her small dank office, as if needing sunlight to clear the shadows left by William Taithering's tale of menace and grief at the hands of Sonny Burton.

I wasn't convinced we'd done the right thing in not bringing Taithering back to Woslee. But that was part of the potency of my brother: he had with spellbinding wizardry created a scene where we had bonded with Taithering, a sort of reverse Stockholm syndrome.

I kicked a clod of dirt, sending Mix-up racing after broken clumps of earth. I turned back toward the highway, saw Cherry waving frantically from the door of her trailer office.

News had arrived.

I was running by the time I got to her, Mix-up churning at my heels. Cherry's face was blank.

"You heard something?" I asked, climbing the metal steps, stepping into the trailer.

"Taithering's dead."

"What happened?" I blurted. "How?"

She laughed without humor. "Krenkler put everyone on her team and the Woslee PD to calling florists shops in an expanding radius."

"The flower box Taithering brought."

"Had to come from somewhere, right? The calls crept outward, county by county. Someone at a florist shop in Augusta recalled selling a single rose to a man named William Taithering. It stuck in her mind because he asked for a larger-sized box to hold a single flower."

"The Feds raced up there on that info alone?"

Cherry waved her hand, *wait*. "Taithering's purchase seemed odd, so they looked closer at his most recent credit-card purchases. He'd been at a sporting-goods shop two days ago. Guess what he bought?"

My head drooped. "A ball bat."

"They also found that, an hour before the attack, Taithering purchased fuel and antacids at a gas station eight miles north of the church."

I remembered my phone conversation with John Morgenstern. He'd said Krenkler was thorough. I hadn't expected her to be fast. I didn't like the woman, and because of it had underestimated her.

"Anything else?"

"Here's where it gets a little sketchy. I called my buddy again, the ex-cop from the area. Seems Krenkler radioed the locals that she was coming, making it sound like a visit from the Queen. The Augusta cops were to put all their resources at her fingertips. Except the sheriff up there isn't Roy Beale. The guy has a backbone. Plus he knew Taithering – the guy did his taxes – and he wanted a pow-wow to see what the Feds had on Taithering. If it looked solid, the sheriff himself was planning on visiting Taithering, letting his people handle the take-down and trying for peaceful."

"That didn't sit well with Krenkler, I take it?"

"Long story short: the Feds bypassed the locals and surrounded Taithering's house. Krenkler did the bullhorn bit for a few minutes, then they tossed in the flash-bangs and tear gas and stormed the place."

"Taithering?"

"His body was swinging from a joist in the basement. He'd hanged himself with a loop of electrical wire. By the way, there was another loop on the joist beside the first one: broken clothes line."

I saw the picture, felt my heart fall away.

"Yep," Cherry said, seeing my stricken face. "The tragic little man even screwed up his first suicide attempt. The cheap rope broke, so he had to cut the cord off a lawn edger."

Cherry looked at me and her eyes were wet. I wanted to hold her and tell her nothing was her fault. That the sad and broken man named William Taithering had his fate sealed two decades ago in a snack truck parked outside a youth camp. That there was only one person responsible for the tragedy of Taithering's life, and that was the grinning and malevolent beast known as Sonny Burton. I wanted to go with Donna Cherry to a place where everything was still and quiet and we could share the feeling of another human heart inches away.

But a voice called between the hearts and said I was using the sorrow of another to gain a momentary pleasure. That it was my way, part of my condition.

I told Cherry I hoped to see her soon and retreated without looking back.

# 25

I took Mix-up to the cabin, then reluctantly returned to Jeremy's. It was full night and a gibbous moon blazed above. I knocked and entered. The electric lights were out, a smattering of white tapers lighting the downstairs, my brother's favorite form of illumination. I had long ago recognized that candlelight best approximated the darting shadows and darkened recesses of my brother's head. Nothing was quite real nor visible in the round.

Jeremy was sitting in a chair in the corner, in deep shadow. He wore his gardening outfit, white shirt and dark Levis, with the long white gardener's jacket that reached to his knees.

"Taithering's dead," he said.

I nodded.

"Tell me how it happened," Jeremy's voice was a ragged whisper, sorrow or anger or a mixture of both. I recounted the story. It took under a minute. My brother stood and walked to the nearest candle, on a tabletop. He stooped to blow it out, as if there was too much light in the room.

"Why did Taithering kill himself, Jeremy?" I asked. "Was it shame?"

"William didn't make it all the way to redemption, Carson."

"But that's what he did with the beating: danger, destruction, display. A symbolic way of gaining the upper hand. That's what you said."

Jeremy continued to the next candle, on a counter between the living space and the kitchen. He snuffed it dead between spit-wet fingertips, moved down the counter and extinguished another.

"I said it's what William started. He wasn't finished. Taithering saw himself as insignificant, Carson. A man without significance can't judge whether his private symbolism holds the potency to shatter the past. Even though he'd handled everything in his ritual correctly, the presence of risk, the destruction of the face, the public display, Taithering was lacking the final element."

Jeremy walked to the fourth and fifth candles, on a shelf beside the stairs. Blew them dead. The only lit candle was the shivering taper on the table at my feet. Jeremy stepped back into the shadows. Outside, in the forest dark, barred owls were calling one another through the trees.

"What the hell element was left?" I asked.

"The validation of a higher authority."

"Are you talking about God?"

"I'm talking about judgment from a guide who knows the forest, Carson." He held his hand out into the light, thumb to the side like an emperor. He turned it down, then up.

My brother's remarks were typically cryptic, and anger welled in my gut, at my brother and at myself. Yet again I was asking a mentally ill man for insights into the mental conditions of my fellow humans, again sucked into a world where image and symbol thudded together like blind whales in a black sea.

I stood, shaking my head. The past twenty-four hours had been nightmarish.

"I'm going back to Mobile," I said.

"What?"

"I'm going home, Jeremy. I'm packing tomorrow, leaving the following morning."

A long pause. "I bought you more time, Carson."

"Ask for your money back, Jeremy. I'm gone."

For the second time in the evening, I retreated from another human being, this time gladly. Back at the cabin I showered off the day and started to gather my belongings, but weariness overcame me like a wave and I fell asleep on the couch, a pile of clothes and a dog at my felt.

Morning brought the rude awakening of a siren outside my window. I bounced up to the window, saw Cherry behind the window of another cruiser, same color and vintage, like the Kentucky State Police had cornered the market on dark Crown Vics. Mix-up and I stumbled to the porch as Cherry cut the siren. I stared through hazy eyes and pushed hair from my face.

"Jeez, what now?"

"Sorry about the wake-up," Cherry said, stepping from the cruiser. "Something's happened and I thought you should know," she said. "Zeke Tanner's gone missing."

My mind's-eye showed me two medics leaning back from a corpse, putting away the cardiac paddles.

"Gone? Uh, isn't he dead?"

"The state's forensics people were sending transport this morning, taking him from the funeral home to the morgue in Frankfort. When the funeral director went to prepare the body for the trip, it was gone. A window got busted for entry."

I shook my head; weirdness piled on weirdness. Cherry said, "Right now I'm running up to the funeral parlor to get a statement." She nodded toward the passenger seat. "You in?"

"I'm planning to head back home. I'm packing today and leaving tomorrow."

She looked stunned, caught it fast. "You're booking in the middle of the battle?"

"This isn't my war, Cherry."

She pushed a half-smile to her face and shot a thumbs-up. "Gotcha. I understand. I'd do the same thing." The smile started to waver.

"Maybe I could use a break from packing," I said.

\* \* \*

The owner and director of the funeral establishment was Harold Caldwell, a portly man in his fifties with a fleshy chin-wattle bobbing above blue tie and white shirt. Though the parlor air seemed as cool as the storage units, he was sweating as I re-questioned him about the lost body. Caldwell was one of those folks who, when rattled, find security in detail.

"What time did you notice Mr Tanner's disappearance, Mr Caldwell?"

"Like I told Detective Cherry, I always stop at McDonald's for breakfast, carry-out, coffee, two Egg McMuffins and a—"

"Time?"

"Six fifteen. I came early to prepare the papers for the transport. There are seven forms to fill out, the one for—"

"Who was the last person here last night?"

"Wendell Nockle. He's the janitor, or I guess today they're called maintenance staff or—"

"Nockle left when?"

"He always leaves at seven thirty. Blanche's Diner closes at eight. They always save Wendell a piece of pie. Apple. Or banana cream. Or cherry. I don't mean you, Detective Cherry, I mean cherry like in the pie filling—"

I dismissed Caldwell before he started in on the fifteen-bean soup.

"You come up with anything?" I asked Cherry, the detective, not the filling.

"The parking lot's in back. It's not well lit, nor openly

171

visible from the street. The perp could park back there, grab the corpse, drive away. All without arousing attention. It's flat-out dead around here after eight at night, nothing to do."

I studied the surroundings from the parlor parking lot, saw the backs of a couple warehouses, an antique store, a used-car lot. But less than the distance of a football field, I saw the rear of a small trailer park. There were a lot of windows faced this way.

Stanton was in the county adjoining Woslee and Cherry had a far better relationship with the cops than with Beale. Three uniformed patrolmen were happy to go door to door in the park, asking if anyone happened to be watching the parking lot behind them last night. They got a hit: a man named Gable Paltry.

Mr Paltry was a sallow and skinny man in his mid-sixties with a brown theme – brown eyes, brown teeth, thinning brown hair, brown scrofulous patches on his cheeks. His sleeveless T-shirt was stained with something brown, as were his pants. His shoes were brown. He was dipping snuff or chewing tobacco, and when we entered his living room he spat a thick glob of something brown into a paper cup.

"I'll deal with Mr Charm," I whispered to Cherry.

"I owe you one," she said.

The guy looked sad when Cherry claimed she needed to make a call and peeled away. I pulled a chair close as possible without getting into the splash zone, pulled out my notepad.

"I saw a semi-rig," Paltry wheezed, looking past me, hoping for another shot of Cherry. "It was red, old. Silver trailer. Sometimes drivers pull off the highway and use the lot to snooze. I saw me a big RV pull in there and stop. Stayed maybe ten minutes. Light color. Had bikes and crap roped to the back. A barbecue grill tied up top, too."

A vacationer, I figured, checking a map or grabbing a quick snack and a few minutes of respite from the night-time drive. Like the semi driver, probably.

"Anyone else?"

"Yeah. A couple parked back there, man and woman. It was maybe one in the a.m. She had red hair, but I couldn't see much of the guy. They were there a half-hour or so and never got out of the car that I saw."

I looked over the distance to the funeral parlor. Imagined it at night.

"You said she was a redhead, Mr Paltry?"

"Kinda long hair. Had on one of those tight tops. Halter top, pink. She was on the side facing me, passenger. She had a pretty decent set of—"

"What power are your binoculars?" I asked innocuously.

"What? I wasn't spying on no one."

The blast of red to his face confirmed my diagnosis. I figured Mr Paltry had been hoping to see a little action. A darkened parking lot just off the highway seemed the perfect venue for a fast pullover for high school kids with dates, or older types who can't take the date home because the spouse would object.

It might have even been Paltry's hobby: see a vehicle in the back lot and run for the binocs hoping for suggestive head bobbing or – joy of joys – a drunked-up couple that stumbles from the car and does it on the hood.

I gave him my squarest chin and most stentorian voice, the image I employ – infrequently – when receiving commendations from professional and civic groups.

"I encourage citizens' watch groups to use the best equipment possible to assist in the fight against crime, sir. People should always pay attention to strangers in the area."

Paltry puffed out his sunken chest, held up a finger, meaning *back in a second,* and padded into the next room, returning with a stubby black tube mounted on a tripod, stroking it like a kitten.

"Here's my baby, a Bushnell spotter's scope. See a gnat at a hunnert paces."

I pretended to admire the instrument. "And you say the couple never got out of the car?"

"I had to pee a time or two while I was watching. It takes me a while cuz I've got the prostrate. And sometimes I couldn't see them but figured it was because, ah, they was, uh . . ."

"Engaged in seditious acts of horizontal alliance," I said. "Flagrant concupiscent involvement." I took his scrawny claw and shook it. "God bless citizens like you, sir."

He puffed out his chest even further. "One time I even saw a buncha Mexicans being sneaked down the highway. I called the cops."

"Really, sir?"

"They was in a farm truck fulla dried cob corn. It was night and I was looking for, uh, things like you said. The driver got out and lifted a tarp on back. The corn started moving and three Mexicans stood up. They were eating and drinking some stuff when the cops rolled up."

I flicked a *well-done* salute and walked away. Stopped. Something moved in my mind, but I didn't see what it was, just that a thought had been ignited somewhere. I frowned its direction, saw Mexicans pushing from corn. *Farm. Hidden. Farms have tractors and . . . hay.*

I pulled my phone and called Harry Nautilus, my partner back in Mobile.

"I think I know how Bobby Lee Crayline got away," I said.

"That was over six months ago, Carson. It took you this long to figure it out?"

"I'm not missing your humor, Harry. Odd, I know. The farmer's name was something like Oakes. That's it, Farley Oakes . . ."

"You think that really happened?" Harry Nautilus said after I'd laid out my thoughts.

"If it went down as I suspect, there are two possible reasons: coercion or a willing accomplice. Either way, the best approach assumes willingness."

"He just drove away?" Harry confirmed. "The farmer?"

"It was dumb, but everyone got so busy with the dead guards and chasing a motorcycle with Crayline aboard that . . . well, it just happened."

"I'll see if I can't get Babe Ellis and Sandhill in on this," Harry said. "Could be fun. How's the vacation?"

"Right now I'm helping look for a corpse that walked away from a funeral home."

"Aren't there more vacation-type things to do? Are there no pretty women in the area?"

"There's one. I'm helping her look for—"

"—a corpse that escaped from a funeral home. Gotcha."

Cherry was leaning against her vehicle when I walked up. "Anything?" she said, face hopeful.

"Thanks to the old letch, I might have figured out how a psychotic named Bobby Lee Crayline escaped while being transported to prison."

"How does that help us here?"

"It doesn't. And neither did anything else."

We got back on the road and were on the Mountain Highway just east of Stanton when Cherry pulled out a notepad, studied it, exited down a ramp.

"Where we going?" I asked.

"Quick trip to tie up a loose end. I want to see if anyone's home at the house on the lane leading to Tandee Powers's death scene. The creek. No one was home the day we checked."

I recalled the small house. It was probably too far from the road for an occupant to have heard anything.

"You said you knew the occupant?"

"An elderly lady. Hell, for all I know, she passed. Like

I said, she was in her eighties. This'll take a few minutes, then I'll get you back to your packing."

Looking over at Cherry I had a moment of doubt. But staying here would mean being sucked deeper into the black hole of my brother's mind.

"I've got to get on that," I affirmed. "I want to be Mobile-bound at daybreak."

# 26

We wound down roads growing tighter and tighter. Turned on to the long slender band of crumbling asphalt that ended at the creek where Crayline had left Tandee Powers's body floating in the water. We both knew nothing would come of the trip, but it was one of those investigative motions that had to be made, a box checked off.

"This is the only house on the road back," Cherry said, slowing at a bend. "Let me see if the lady's home."

It was the small and rickety frame dwelling with a big silver propane tank at its side and the maples filled with birdhouses. A single rocking chair sat on the porch. As we pulled in the drive I thought I saw a motion at a window curtain, as though the occupant had heard us a mile back.

"Wait in the car," Cherry said. "Some folks live deep

in the woods because they fear, or don't particularly care for, people. Strangers, especially."

I did aghast. "Are you telling me I'm strange?"

"Sit, cowboy."

I waited as Cherry knocked on the door. It occurred to me to put on a big yellow happy face so as not to threaten whoever, but I figured Cherry kept the happy face in the trunk with the bullhorn.

The front door opened. Cherry spoke for several minutes. I couldn't hear her words, only her tone, like a traveler bringing news to an isolated settlement. I figured Cherry's accent – which I was beginning to view as "richly textured" instead of "grating" – permanently marked her as a member of the mountain tribe, a powerful asset in a culture where outsiders had always been viewed with suspicion, generally for good reason.

Cherry walked back to the car, told me to come to the house. She stayed tight to my side as we approached, a hand over my shoulder. She'd never been so close or touched me, and I realized her nearness symbolized sanction. Cherry was giving me her approval so that Miz Bascomb could see that I was safe, a man who brought neither shadow nor harm.

Leona Bascomb was a tiny woman with bottle-thick glasses and few teeth remaining in a head that had seen at least eighty years of life. Her gray hair was full and fell past her waist. She wore a faded gingham dress under a starched white apron. Her brown and gnarled hands seemed constructed entirely of knuckles.

The room was Spartan in furnishing: a rocking chair, a small sofa, a pair of TV trays beside the furniture. It was the walls that drew my eyes. They were covered with sheets of cheap simple paper, the kind run through copiers. Each sheet displayed colors arranged in a variety of ways. Some colors were hard and disparate shapes, others merged and flowed. Many pages recalled works by Kandinsky, others Chagall.

There were at least a hundred such paintings taped to the walls. It took a moment to catch my breath, startled by the surprise.

"Your walls are covered with beauty, Miz Bascomb," I said.

"They're my birds," she replied.

"Birds?"

She looked embarrassed. "I know they don't look a bit like birds, an' I cain't he'p it. Whenever I tried to draw a bird like a pitchur, it didn't look right. I couldn't see birds real good anyway cuz my eyes was always on the low side. So I started drawin' how they sound."

I studied the walls again and began to see the music, the rhythmic bursts of color. The shading of notes gliding into others, or tapering off as a trill must have tapered into the air. One compelling picture displayed a three-color arc: blue, becoming a sideways, bottom-weighted crescent of purple, transmuting into a wavering series of lines, blue again. The background was coal black, providing a stillness behind the color, the sense of a night sky. I'd heard those colors recently.

"This one," I said, pointing to the picture. "It's a whip-poor-will, right?"

Cherry's eyes turned to me with surprise. Miss Bascomb stared through the thick lenses, canting her head as if bringing me into focus. She walked to me, took my hand in hers. Her hand felt like driftwood.

"You're the first person to ever see one right," she said, leading me past the walls like at a gallery opening, pointing out towhees, starlings, robins, crows – a nervous jitter of black and yellow – martins, several varieties of thrushes and finches, bluebirds, cardinals, willets, grebes, plovers, and dozens more. When the tour was finished, a smiling Leona Bascomb went to fetch tea and cookies.

"How did you do that, Ryder?" Cherry whispered when the bird artist had retreated to her tiny kitchen, clattering dishes. "How did you know those splotches were a whip-poor-will?"

"I couldn't imagine it being anything else."

When Miz Bascomb returned, Cherry steered her into our questions. I sipped tea and nibbled a sugar cookie, happy to be out of the limelight.

"I wasn't here that morning the poor woman's body got found," Miz Bascomb said to Cherry. "The health service came by real early and took me to the clinic for my six-month look-see. I'm good, praise God."

"You mentioned hearing a car the night before?"

"It was almost midnight. I was up, puttering. Cain't never sleep no more, just doze. I heard a car out on the road. Sounded big. I can tell by the sounds of the motors.

I cain't see hardly none any more, but God gave me ears as good as they git."

"Is that common, Miz Bascomb, nighttime traffic on the road?" Cherry asked.

"Any traffic ain't real common. Nothing back there but the ol' logging camp. In the daytime, local kids sometimes go back there in summer to splash around. But most of 'em goes to the divin' rock over in the Red River. Water's deeper and there's other kids to show off for. I did the same myself, when I was a girl."

"So the vehicle on the road caught your ear?" Cherry asked.

"I was waiting for it to come back out. It did, 'bout two hours later."

"The same vehicle?"

"No way to tell that perzactky. Same kind of one, to tell by the sound."

Cherry made some notes in her pad. "So a vehicle went in around midnight, came out around two. Possibly the same vehicle."

The old woman nodded.

Cherry looked at me. It fit the timeline, given what we'd learned from the lab about time of death. Tandee Powers was probably taken from her home around eleven, driven past Leona Bascomb's house, then another desolate mile to the creek. She'd been dressed in a sexually suggestive manner, dragged into the water, tortured by being pulled under and then released back to the surface. This could have gone on for an hour and a half. Perhaps longer.

182

"No other vehicles went back down the road after that?" Cherry asked.

The birdsong artist frowned, trying to discern a memory. "I drowsed off around four in the morning. Something popped my eyes open just afore six. I'm purty sure it was a car, but I was sorta drifty. It seemed like it was going west toward east, like driving away."

Cherry looked at me and shook her head. *Not the car.* It didn't fit the timeline, the sun rising by six. It was the midnight ride that carried Tandee Powers to her death.

We stood and bid our farewells, Miz Bascomb seeming loathe to see me go, offering more tea and cookies, or dinner. I again complimented her work as we withdrew toward the door. I paused, turned, a sudden thought lighting my head.

"One more thing, Miz Bascomb," I said. "The sound the earlier vehicle made. Do you think you could draw it for me?"

A smile crossed her face, as though the challenge was amusing.

"Why not? Lemme git my workings."

Leona Bascomb walked to a cabinet, withdrew a sheet of paper and a box of bright pastel crayons.

"I got a daughter lives up in Louisville sends me my colors from an art store," she said, sitting in the rocker and placing the sheet on the TV tray. She thought for a full minute and I saw her lips move as the sounds replayed in her head. Her ancient fingers whisked over the colors, selected.

The gnarled hands began drawing.

Two minutes later she handed me the paper. I saw a vibrating line that ran a few inches in yellow, turned green, jumped into blue and stayed the same until running off the edge of the page. I peeked out the window and confirmed the bridge that had slowed Cherry's vehicle three hundred feet away. After crossing the bridge the vehicle would have accelerated to the speed the potholed road could bear, twenty-five or thirty miles per hour. The colors in Miz Bascomb's drawing shifted abruptly, as the sounds must have changed.

"A standard transmission," I said. "I see it shifting."

Cherry stared at me.

# 27

Cherry dropped me at my cabin. We climbed out, stood on separate sides of the car. "Well, Ryder, it looks like this is it," Cherry said over the hood, her smile strained. "I'm sorry your vacation turned into work. And for the record, I truly wasn't the person who called you."

"I believe you," I said.

"Thanks for all your help. And your company. I just wish that we'd had the time to—"

I turned to the cabin. Something was missing. Mix-up was nowhere to be seen.

"You all right, Ryder?"

"Mix-up. Where is he? Mix-up!" I yelled into the trees. "Yo . . . Mr Mix-up. Come here, boy!"

Nothing. I turned to Cherry. "This is strange. He never goes far."

She clapped her hands, yelled, "Here Mix-up!" I joined

in and we walked up and down the drive, calling. I told Cherry I was heading into the woods and I'd let her know when he came back. I whistled, clapped, banged a wooden spoon on his metal food bowl, playing his favorite music. I hiked a mile up the creek, a mile down, yelling and banging until my hand hurt and my voice was a painful rasp.

No rustling in the underbrush. No happy bay as he raced to my side. Nothing.

I drove the nearby roads, stopping to speak to everyone I saw outside. Giving them my cell number in case they saw him.

*"What's your dog look like, mister?"*

*"Like nothing you've ever seen. And a lot of it."*

I saw a barrel-bodied guy wearing overalls and a ZZ Top beard sitting on his porch and cleaning a shotgun. I stopped, told him my story and passed him my number. "You know there are b'ars in the woods, don't you?" he said, spitting tobacco juice over the porch rail.

I nodded. "But bears are few and far between, right?"

He thought for a moment. "E'yup. It almost ain't never b'ars that get lost dogs . . ."

*Thank God*, my mind said.

"They usually get tore apart by coyotes," the guy finished.

I added the aspect of heart-pounding frenzy to my search and continued another hour, passing out my number like a religious zealot jamming tracts into people's hands. My breath stopped at a mound of fur at the side of the road, started again when I saw it was a deer carcass. Several times I wondered if passers-by thought me a crazy man, parked beside the road, yelling into the woods while beating a bowl with a wooden spoon. I didn't care.

After two hours of nothing, I returned to the cabin, passing Jeremy's home. Though I figured I'd said my goodbyes, I had to check.

"You're still here?" he said when he answered the door, seeming to stifle a yawn.

"My dog's gone. You haven't seen him, have you?"

He wrinkled up his nose. "Not in two days. The smelly cur was on my porch. I was going to set out poison, but figured that would set you off."

I stared at him.

"You're still leaving, right?" he asked, looking like I was keeping him from a task.

"My dog's here, Jeremy. He's lost."

"A dog's going to keep you from leaving?"

"I have to find him."

My brother looked perplexed, as if I was talking Gaelic. "But didn't you say the thing cost you something like ten dollars?"

Mix-up had been a deal. The shelter folks were so happy to have him saved from Death Row they dropped the adoption fee. My sole cost was an annual license.

"Five," I corrected.

He looked thoughtful. "Five bucks for a hundred-plus pounds of dog? Maybe I should start shopping at the pound. How do the things taste, Carson?"

I jammed my hands in my pocket to keep from punching out my brother's teeth and walked away.

Mix-up hadn't returned to the cabin. All I heard when listening into the woods were bands of rabid coyotes. Like most Americans under the age of forty, the prospect of traveling without connectivity was too daunting to consider, and I'd packed my laptop. In common with most pet owners, I had more shots of my dog than I could count – his first bath, his first swim in the Gulf, his first steak dinner. It took fifteen minutes to lash together a DOG MISSING poster complete with photos, basic description, and my phone number. I also added a reward, a hundred bucks at first, but the coyotes started howling in my head again and I upgraded to five hundred.

I climbed into the truck and rushed to the local library to print canine wanted posters, dropping them off at any venue with human traffic, gas stations, restaurants. I taped them to phone poles, bulletin boards at trailheads, the message boards used by rock climbers.

My travels took me past the Woslee County Police Department. I gritted my teeth and turned back, telling the person at the desk I wanted to speak with whoever was in charge, hoping for Caudill, but knew by the way my luck had been running it would be Beale.

"The Sherf's on the phone," the young woman at the desk said, pausing in the filing of her nails. "He says for you to hold your water 'til he gits done."

I turned to the photo wall ubiquitous at cop shops,

the parade of past leaders. There were five: a mustachioed fellow who had been sheriff until 1947, a hollow-eyed and cadaverous-looking fellow who had the position until 1967, and square-jawed man who'd started in 1967 and held the position until six years ago. The names beneath the last two photos were Earl Gaines Beale and Roy Stimple Beale, granddaddy and daddy, respectively, to the current holder of the title.

McCoy had described the earlier Beales as stubborn and humorless men from a time when rules were pliable, with enemies punished, friends rewarded, and the position paying so poorly it was almost expected that illegalities – moonshining and so forth – would be overlooked if an envelope of the correct thickness moved beneath a table.

Indeed, I saw nothing akin to humor in either pair of Bealean eyes, nor anything resembling stern-jawed integrity. They looked more like members of Ike Clanton's gang than Eliot Ness's crew.

The desk phone buzzed. I heard a burp and Beale Junior's voice.

*"Ryder still there, Louella?"*

"Yup, Sherf."

A pause. *"Send him on back, I guess."*

I nodded thanks to Louella, pushed through the door to the rear, found Beale leaning back in his chair with his feet on a desk holding no visible sign of activity save for the lone *Hustler* half-tucked under a local newspaper. In one hand was a cigarette, in the other a bottle of Ale-8-One, a regional soft drink consumed like water by seemingly everyone in Eastern Kentucky. His eyes were bloodshot and I wondered if he'd spiked the drink.

"You're not up in Augusta, Sheriff?" I said by way of greeting.

"Ain't my party, Ryder. What am I gonna do that the FBI can't?"

"You never knew William Taithering? You're both about the same age, from the same county."

"I used to see him around when I was in school. He was one a them geeky types, always looked like if you slapped your hands hard, he'd jump outta his shoes. You never know who's gonna turn into a serial killer, right?"

"That's what Agent Krenkler thinks? That Taithering's the killer?"

"You don't?"

I shrugged, not wanting to debate psychology with someone who would spell it with an S in front. Beale yawned, showing teeth that saw more repair than maintenance. "Guess it don't really matter. Looks like the FBI nailed it where Cherry couldn't. Be nice to have some peace an' quiet around here again."

It suddenly occurred to Beale that I wasn't usually standing in front of him.

"Why you here, Ryder?"

I held up a sheaf of posters. "My dog's lost. I hoped you could distribute posters to the guys on patrol, have them keep an eye out."

Beale sucked in smoke and waved the poster away. "We got more to do than look for a lost dog, Ryder."

"There's a five-hundred-dollar reward, Sheriff."

Beale's eyes widened. He rocked forward in his chair, hand waving the *gimme* motion.

I went from Beale's office to Cherry's. Her desk was antithetical to Beale's, a visual cacophony of files, folders, and photos.

"I made these up," I said, handing over a dozen posters. "If you're out, could you please—"

"I'll put 'em all over the place. Give me all you have and I'll take care of it."

I gratefully handed her the stack. When I looked down at her desk, I saw it was covered with her handwritten notes and photos of Burton and Powers and the man in the shack.

"You're pondering the cases?" I said.

She frowned, tossed her pen atop the mound of papers. "I've been thinking . . ."

"And?"

"What if Taithering really is the killer? Or was. What if Charpentier was wrong with all that academic symbol and metaphor hoo-hah, and Taithering was another Manson or Gein or . . ."

"You mean someone more like the Zodiac Killer," I said, lapsing into my detective persona. "The Zodiac left cryptic messages." I went to the whiteboard and picked up a red marker, scrawled the odd geocache sign on the clean white surface.

"How does that relate to Taithering?" I asked.

"I don't know . . . yet."

Cherry crossed the room to the board and wiped the symbol away. I figured she hated the damn thing. She hopped atop the small conference table and pulled her feet beneath her long legs, sitting cross-legged. She fixed me with the right eye.

"Do you ever think we were wrong, Charpentier was wrong . . . Taithering was the killer?"

"Yes," I admitted.

She nodded toward the paperwork jungle on her desk. "I'm revisiting Tandee Powers and Burton. Soldering-iron Man's still a cipher, but he's wired into this somehow, no pun intended. I want to see if Powers ever crossed paths with Burton."

"You sharing anything with Krenkler?"

The eyes darkened. "As much as she shares with me. At least until I find something solid."

"She still using you as a messenger service?"

"No. Sometimes she has me make copies."

I thanked her for distributing the posters, and turned to carry on the search for my lost dog. I felt Cherry's eyes inspecting my back as I left.

"Good luck finding your doggy," she said quietly as the door closed between us.

# 28

The night brought little sleep, every sound causing me to sit up with the hope my companion had found his way home. Either that or I heard ravenous and red-eyed hell-hounds pursing my gentle giant of a dog.

Morning arrived with a siren's call, literally, a long keening howl at seven a.m. I stumbled out to the porch, saw Cherry stepping from her vehicle. I saw her mouth move but heard nothing until she reached inside to kill the screamer.

"Sorry I'm becoming your alarm clock," she said. "But a new entry on the geocache site arrived minutes ago."

"It wasn't Taithering," I said, feeling like someone had kicked me in the gut.

Cherry sighed. "Doesn't look that way. The coordinates are close to Rock Bridge."

I'd hiked that trail my second day here. Rock Bridge trail inscribed a mile-long circle down into the Gorge to the trail's namesake, a natural stone arch over Swift Camp Creek. It was basically a dilettante's trail, the Park Service having poured a slender asphalt band most of the distance, winding through rhododendron tunnels and past towering hemlocks ringed with ferns. Though paved, the trail was no cakewalk, owing to the steep angle in and out of the valley.

Cherry looked past me toward the cabin, saw no happy mound of mutt. "Your dog back?"

I shook my head. "No."

"Look on the bright side. He's probably found a girl-friend and they're doing something that doesn't involve you, at least for a day or two. So come with me, Ryder. We've come this far together."

"What about the Feds?"

"Krenkler's in Washington. Some kind of meeting not related to here. Her people are still in Augusta. Krenkler was so convinced Taithering was the killer she set up a command post there. The Feds are tearing Taithering's house apart for evidence. They sent his computer to the forensic lab in Washington, that type of thing. I alerted her to the new geocache entry. She didn't sound happy, and she's heading this way on the red-eye."

I startled internally, fearing the Feds finding my brother's fingerprints in Taithering's home. Then I recalled that, save to pat Taithering in camaraderie or consolation, my

194

brother's hands had never left his pockets. Always a step ahead.

"So we won't have to deal with Feds at the site?" I asked.

"Not for a while, at least."

I looked down: wrinkled shirt, Levis, bare feet. "I don't suppose I have time for a shower? Before we head to Rock Bridge?"

She hid the smile poorly. "You got time for shoes. That's it."

In a minute I was inside the SUV and pulling on a fresh shirt and my hiking boots. Cherry turned and headed out of the hollow, passing my brother's home.

"No stopping for Charpentier?" I asked.

She shifted to low and angled up the hill. "I'll be frank, Ryder. The guy's got more smarts in his pinky than I do in my entire brain. He knows things about the insides of people I'll never see . . ." She clammed up and concentrated on driving.

"There's a *but* in there," I prompted.

"But the more I think about it, the more the guy weirds me out. It's like he knows too much about how people work . . . does that make sense? It makes me nervous when he looks at me. It's like he's studying thoughts I haven't had yet. If we find anything that needs shrink action, then we'll come calling on the Doc."

*Nice alarm system, Cherry*, I thought, pulling on my seat belt for another whirlwind adventure in driving.

When we arrived, Beale had closed off the road, Caudill and another county cop manning the block. Caudill waved me through, then turned to stop one of the ubiquitous RVs from pulling on to Rock Bridge Road. I wondered what Caudill would tell the tourists.

*We've got a madman killing folks right and left. Have you considered Yosemite?*

We drove to the trailhead and found McCoy pulling a backpack from the gate of his vehicle. Beale was pacing and tapping his holster, trying to appear in command. When he saw me, his dark eyes went a shade darker, but he didn't complain aloud.

"Christ in a hammock, where you been, Cherry?" Beale bellowed. "I ain't got all day."

"Let me go first, Sheriff," McCoy said, shouldering into his pack. "There are things I need to see."

"Like what?"

"Spiders."

Beale, confused, jumped in behind McCoy. Cherry and I fell in after that. We descended a long series of wood and rock steps into the valley, jogging toward the co-ordinates on the geocache site. Every hundred feet or so McCoy stopped to peer into trailside vegetation.

"Almost there," McCoy yelled, studying his GPS as we ran alongside Swift Camp Creek and passed Creation Falls. "The coordinates are at Rock Bridge."

We picked up speed, Beale now stumbling and puffing two hundred feet back, years of biscuits and gravy taking their toll.

"Oh, lord," I heard McCoy say.

Rock Bridge was at the far end of a miniature plain,

a flat and open acre scoured by seasonal floodwaters. The top of the rock arch was fifteen feet above the slow, green water, the bottom about ten feet from the surface.

Zeke Tanner's naked body was hanging in the space between the arch and the water, ankles lashed together with rope, arms dangling down, as if frozen in the process of diving. He was twisting in the breeze and as the body swirled toward us I saw a rough zigzagging of tattoos from his pubis to his sternum. They looked like black lightning bolts.

The sight froze me in my tracks. Cherry was half the distance closer, her hand cupping her mouth in horror.

"What's with the tattoos?" I said.

Cherry turned, her face ashen. "They're not tattoos, Ryder. They're stitches."

It was late morning when Harry Nautilus and Conner Sandhill met Sheriff Babe Ellis at a Dairy Queen in west-central Alabama, climbing into Ellis's county-cop cruiser, unmarked. All three men gazed longingly at the window posters of caloric treats offered by the DQ. "Eve didn't tempt Adam with an apple," Nautilus said. "It had to have been a banana split."

Ellis, six foot six, almost three hundred pounds, patted his belly, a soft roll over his belt. "Tell me about temptation."

"Tell me again why we're here," Conner Sandhill said, tugging at his thick black mustache. Like Nautilus and Ellis he was well over six feet tall. "Some sudden impulse of Ryder's, right?"

197

Nautilus nodded. "Carson's pretty sure he doped out Bobby Lee Crayline's escape method, wants us to put the screws to a guy named Farley Oakes."

"How'd Carson figure it out?" Ellis asked, still gazing wistfully at the poster of the banana split.

"He says he got the idea from Mexicans and corn. Don't ask."

"Where the hell is Ryder?" Sandhill snorted. "I haven't seen him in weeks."

"Vacationing in Kentucky," Nautilus said.

"But he's still thinking about a six-month-old case not even in his jurisdiction?" Ellis chuckled.

Nautilus shook his head. "You know Carson. Can't let anything go."

"Ryder's probably spent thirty years investigating why the Tooth Fairy doesn't visit any more," Sandhill said. He turned to Ellis. "You said you had a rap sheet on Oakes?"

Babe Ellis passed Nautilus and Sandhill copies. The men studied the crimes. There wasn't much, but it was telling. Ellis put the blue Crown Vic in gear.

Farley Oakes lived in a small frame house a couple hundred feet back from the road. It needed paint. There was a work truck on blocks in the front yard. The barn was a hundred feet beyond, a small corral to the side. A rusting green tractor nosed from the barn *like sniffing out visitors*. Nautilus counted two *No Trespassing* signs, three *Private Property – Keep Out* signs. Mr Oakes seemed a tad fearful of outsiders.

"How you want to work it?" Ellis asked.

"I'll lead," Sandhill said. "But I need you to be an irritant, Harry."

Nautilus grinned. "It's the sand in the oyster that gives us pearls."

"Lawd," Ellis sighed. "You guys stay up nights working on the routine?"

They pulled to a stop at the end of the rutted drive. Ellis pointed to a bright red Dodge Ram pickup parked in the side yard. It glittered with chrome.

"There's about forty thousand bucks' worth of truck. Looks a little out of place, don't you think?"

"Let's hit it and git it," Nautilus said, opening his door.

Ellis looked at the property, then at the house. "You guys handle the inside stuff. I'm gonna go look for a place to take a leak, right?" He grinned and disappeared around the side of the house, heading for the barn and moving mouse-quiet for a man so large.

Nautilus and Sandhill were a dozen paces from the door when it banged open, Oakes framed in the doorway, wearing an angry look and holding a shotgun. He glowered at Nautilus.

"Git off my property, whoever you are."

Nautilus held up his badge. "I'm Detective Harry Nautilus, Mr Oakes. My partner, Detective Carson Ryder, was at the prison-van situation – remember him? This is Detective Sandhill."

"Oh my goodness," the man said as he digested the

information. "I'm sorry. I thought you was insurance salesmen."

The weapon was quickly tucked behind the door.

"We're flummoxed by the killings, Mr Oakes. We'd like to ask a few more questions. Just to see if anything's jogged in your memory over the past few months."

Oakes shrugged, tapped his forehead. "I cain't think of anything. I been trying."

"May we come in for a couple minutes, run some questions by? It won't take long."

"Hang on a sec. I got to tidy up a few things."

He disappeared behind the door. It reopened three minutes later, Oakes gesturing them inside.

The tight space was cluttered with magazines, unwashed clothes, a dining-room table strewn with a disassembled alternator, the pieces interspersed with plates, dried food clotted to them, cigarette butts studding the food. Nautilus shot a look at the magazines: *Handgun Digest, Modern Weapons, Southern Partisan.* The only clean place was a computer desk in the corner, a large monitor behind a keyboard. Hanging above the desk was a Confederate battle flag.

"I ain't as neat as I should be, but then if any of you fellas are single, you know we're all pretty sloppy."

*Time to put the sand in the oyster,* Nautilus thought. He smiled benignly.

"I'm single, Mr Oakes," he lectured, a ghost of condescension in his voice. "I keep things neat by setting aside fifteen minutes daily for putting things in their proper place. Just amazing at what that fifteen minutes can do, if you put your mind to it."

"Mebbe I'll give that a try," Oakes said, voice tighter. "Fifteen minutes, you say?"

Nautilus looked around Oakes's home. Frowned.

"Here, maybe more like an hour."

Oakes's eyes flashed. He turned away and shunted aside a pile of clothes on the couch. "You can sit here, you want."

Nautilus studied the ragged couch like it was infested with lice. "I think I'll stand, thank you."

"Do what you want," Oakes grunted.

Sandhill leaned against the wall, arms crossed. "You know, Mr Oakes, that a man named Bobby Lee Crayline escaped from the van that day. You said just before you got to the scene you heard motorcycles moving away."

"That's what I told the cops."

Sandhill stepped close, his broad body all Oakes could see. "Crayline was a member of the Aryan Conquest. It's like a prison club for white guys only. You ever heard of that particular organization?"

The farmer scratched his temple with a yellowed nail. Shrugged at Sandhill.

"Can't say as I have."

"It's figured that a person or persons unknown drove by the van on motorcycles," Sandhill said, "blew off the driver's head with a shotgun. The van crashed and the fuel tank ruptured. They would have worked fast to get Crayline out and on a bike, haul his ass away. Was that what you heard?"

"I was hauling hay bales with my tractor. It's loud. I just barely heard them bikes over it. Then I seen the smoke and run over fast."

"And you found?"

"The front window was busted on the van and the guy on the passenger side was crawling out of the fire. I pulled the guy away. That's when the cop came up, the Ryder fella."

Sandhill doodled in his notebook. "Tell me, Mr Oakes, was the—"

"Where's that black guy?" Oakes said, suddenly aware that Nautilus was no longer in the room.

"In the john, maybe. Tell me, Mr Oakes, was the back door open on the van?"

But Oakes was heading around the corner to the kitchen, looking for Nautilus. "Hey, you there, come on out here. There ain't nothin' back there."

"I was just taking a tour, Mr Oakes," Nautilus said, standing in front of an ancient, shuddering refrigerator. "I haven't been in many farmhouses. Just seeing how you people live."

Nautilus emphasized the words *you people*.

"What people you talking about?" Oakes said.

Nautilus did wide-eyed innocence. "Just you people, you know? Agrarians."

Oakes's eyes went dark. "I'll tell you how my people live, Mister Detective. We live out here in the clean and open air. Not all piled up together. We live righteous, God-fearing lives and—"

"The door on the van, Mr Oakes," Sandhill interrupted. "Was it open?"

Oakes spun. "How'm I supposed to remember that? There was a crash and a fire and I was busy tryin' to save a man's life and—"

"Details, Mr Oakes," Nautilus interrupted, stepping closer to Oakes. "Sometimes at a crime scene there are details that people remember after time has gone by." He spoke as though trying to make a slow child understand a simple concept. "It's like they suddenly see the scene with more clarity. Clarity means—"

"I goddamn know what the hell clarity means."

"You were pulling a trailer full of hay bales?" Sandhill asked, his turn to take a step closer to the farmer.

"I just goddamn said so."

"Where did you get the bales, Mr Oakes?" Sandhill asked. "And where were you taking them?"

"Get the bales?" Oakes slapped his forehead. "It's a farm! Don't you know nothing? I think it's time for you two to—"

"Were you feeding animals? Taking the bales to a feeding station?"

But Oakes was looking from side to side, Nautilus no longer in sight.

"Where the hell has it gone now?" Oakes spat, angling his head to peer into the kitchen. Sandhill stepped aside, revealing Nautilus sitting at Oakes's desk. Nautilus looked up, two dog-eared paperbacks in his hand.

"I'm right here, Mr Oakes. I was just admiring some

of the books you enjoy. *The Protocols of the Elders of Zion, The Confessions of Nat Turner.* Are you aware scholars have found both to be of spurious origin? Spurious means—"

Oakes snatched the books from Nautilus's hand.

"I'll read whatever I goddamn want. It's a free country – least it used to be. And I think it's time for you to get your snooping black ass out of here."

Nautilus shot Sandhill a *get-ready* nod and the pair shuffled to the door. Oakes stood in the center of his living room with his arms crossed, framed by yellow newspaper clippings, rotted food, broken machinery and a deceased flag. Nautilus paused and turned.

"I checked your past, Mr Oakes. You and four buddies harassed two black women you thought were lesbians, punched one of them. A couple years later you burned a six-foot cross in the front yard of—"

Oakes jutted his chin. "I stand up for my own."

Sandhill opened the door. Nautilus winked at him; *time to shuck the oyster.* He walked to the threshold. Paused as if something had just become clear in his head. He turned to the farmer.

"I know that you were part of the escape plan, Mr Oakes. The bales on your trailer were a shell. The shooter wasn't on a motorcycle, but on the road, maybe holding up his hand like he needed help. The van stopped, the shooter went to work. Bobby Lee Crayline and the shooter slipped into the space in the bales, and you dropped more bales in place to close them off. You answered all the questions, then hopped on your tractor and pulled away." A hint of a smile crossed his lips. "How'd I do?"

Oakes's eyes shifted from Nautilus to Sandhill and back again. "Prove it," he spat, his chest puffed in defiance. But Nautilus saw fear in the man's eyes and heard the quiver in his voice.

"We always do," Nautilus said, stepping outside, talking over his shoulder as he and Sandhill went down the rickety stairs. "Be a lot better for you if you tell us now, Mr Oakes. A judge will knock years off your sentence for telling the truth. By the way, we already know about that other nasty stuff you did. Everything."

Sandhill *tsk-tsk*ed. "We've been watching you for some time, Farley. You've been a bad boy."

With these people, Nautilus and Sandhill knew, there was always other stuff. It made them natural paranoids.

"Wh-at stuff?" Oakes said, voice cracking. "What are you lying about now?"

As if cued by Cecil B. DeMille, Babe Ellis appeared from the side of the house, grinning like a delighted goblin.

"WHO THE FUCK ARE YOU?" Oakes railed at Ellis. "WHAT WERE YOU DOING BACK THERE!"

Ellis didn't look at Oakes. He smiled broadly at his fellow cops and brandished a pudgy yellow envelope with the word EVIDENCE stamped over both sides.

"I ASKED WHAT YOU GOT THERE?" Oakes screeched. He sounded like a terrified child.

Nautilus high-fived Ellis, as if he had a major crime-breaking find in the envelope instead of his own handkerchief. The men walked to the car, laughing as though every wish they'd ever made had just been granted in triplicate.

*Come on, come on . . .* Nautilus thought.

"I didn't have any fucking choice," Oakes whined to their backs, defeat in his voice. "Bobby Lee said I had to do it."

# 29

Tanner's body went straight to the state morgue in Frankfort. Cherry arranged to have the body put atop the post-mortem list, going from transport to autopsy. We ate a light breakfast to give the transport a head start, then drove the ninety minutes to Frankfort, the state capital. McCoy returned to the scene to see if he could make any further reconstructions using his woodsman's knowledge.

"It's unreal," Cherry said as we zoomed down the ramp from I-64 to Frankfort, "the perp carried Tanner's body almost a half-mile. He went down steps, up and down the trail, pulled it to the top of the arch. Oh yeah, he was also carrying a big coil of rope. You know the kind of strength that would take?"

I shook my head in disbelief. I was fit and relatively strong and would have crapped out halfway down the trail. If it was one person, he was built like Mike Tyson in his prime.

The attending pathologist was a man named Vernon Krogan, late fifties, close-cropped gray hair, wide blue eyes incapable of surprise. I knew Doc Krogan, his species anyway, closing in on retirement after a lifetime disassembling bodies, many of them victims of hideous and violent crimes. He'd performed the autopsy as if tearing down a carburetor, not interested in philosophical aspects of the device – carburetors have neither philosophy nor theology – but only in such things as carbon accumulation and surface pitting.

The autopsy complete, the body was covered by a drape. Cherry and I stood to the side of the table as Krogan pulled off his mask. The room smelled of death and disinfectant and I'd smell it for days. I used to think the smell was on my clothes, my skin, but realized it had gotten trapped in my head.

"The corpse had been slit open," Krogan said, removing his mask. "I'd figure a gutting knife, like hunters use on deer. Hang them upside down, slit the belly, let the innards fall out."

Cherry grimaced. "Tanner's guts were gone?"

"A crude job, intestines slashed out, cut top and bottom. A lung had been left behind. But mostly everything got yanked out."

Cherry was having trouble grasping the news. "Tanner was emptied out and sewed back up?" she said. "That's what you're saying?"

Krogan pulled off his paper lab gown and jammed it into a receptacle. "Sewed is an imprecise term. Someone punched holes in the opened flaps of flesh, lashed the pieces closed with black boot laces."

"Why sew him back up?" Cherry asked.

"To keep the stuffing from falling out, of course."

"Stuffing?" Cherry said.

Krogan paused. "Oh . . . No one told you? Several of my colleagues came back to take a look."

"Told us what? Look at what?"

"The emptied abdominal area was packed with a brown substance before being stitched closed."

"What kind of substance?"

Krogan snapped off his gloves and dropped them in the receptacle. "We're doing tests, but everything points to horse manure."

"Tanner was packed with horseshit?" Cherry said, eyes wide.

Krogan regarded Cherry with a look combining curiosity and amusement.

"So far you've sent us a man with a soldering iron in his lower bowel, a drowned woman dressed like a hooker, a man crushed by a snack van, and a corpse packed with horsepoop. What do you have going on over there in Woslee County, Detective Cherry? Sure seems like a corker."

# 30

"Tanner was full of shit," Cherry said when we were pulling away from of Frankfort's city limits and roaring on to Highway 64, heading east to Woslee. "Nothing real academic in that symbol."

"Hard to ignore," I acknowledged. "It also suggests Tanner was purposefully poisoned. But how did the stew get on his stove?"

Cherry thought in silence for eight miles, until we pulled on to the Mountain Parkway. "I got it!" she yelled, smacking the steering wheel with her palm. "Remember the three by five card I found, *Bless you Brother for your constant inspiration*?"

"The card in his kitchen," I nodded, remembering the seemingly inconsequential find.

"I expect half of what Zeke Tanner ate came from his flock. Folks lacking money to drop in the collection plate make it up with food or services. All the killer needed to do was cook up a tasty-looking bowl of death, leave it on Tanner's front steps when he was out, the note as the clincher. It would have happened all the time, totally normal, except this time Tanner sat down to his last meal."

I mulled over Cherry's words. "Something's bothering me," I said. "Tanner was poisoned by our killer, right?"

She nodded. "He used the geocache site to crow to the world. Or whoever was looking."

"But the killer jammed a tool inside John Doe, presumably waiting to enjoy the show from hell. He knelt a foot from Burton's head and slowly cranked down the snack truck. He stood a dozen feet from Tandee Powers as he bobbed her under water with the rope and pulley . . ."

It took a couple seconds, but Cherry got it. "There was no personal involvement with Tanner," she said. "The killer wasn't in on his victim's final breath."

"Something went wrong with the killer's plans," I said. "The guy on the bush-hog showing up, maybe. Tanner was sick or hallucinating and got freaked out by the guy, went amok with the gun. How far is it to Tanner's church?"

"Twenty minutes," Cherry said, now thinking parallel to me. "I'll have McCoy meet us there. This is his kind of thing."

Lee McCoy was parked near Tanner's shattered church when we arrived. The ranger listened quietly as Cherry confirmed that Tanner appeared not a random bit of mayhem as initially thought, but our fourth serial victim.

"Horse manure?" McCoy said. "Doesn't that say . . ."

I nodded. "Brother Tanner was full of shit. Someone wasn't buying Tanner's status as a holy man, Lee."

"We thought Brother Tanner was nuts," Cherry said. "We didn't know the problem was part of the bigger picture. Thing is, in all the other cases, the killer was in on the death."

McCoy had a fast mind. "You're thinking someone was watching?" he asked.

I nodded. "Nearby and waiting for the mushrooms to take effect, perhaps. Hoping to step in and do nasty, up-close things to the poisoned man, stuff like he did to Burton and Powers. Actions with a personal symbolism."

Cherry jumped in. "Best-laid plans gone awry."

McCoy jogged to the fence line behind Tanner's house trailer and studied angles of sight, peering into pines and hemlocks ringed with honeysuckle. After several minutes of studying the land, he inspected the barbed-wire fence separating Tanner's land from the dense national forest property in the rear. He studied the wire as he walked, the same curious look he'd given to the trees along the Rock Bridge trail.

"Wire's been cut here," he said, pointing to an opening forty feet from Tanner's back door. Cherry leaned close, studied the truncated wires between two solid posts.

"Cut recent," she said. "Not a touch of rust."

McCoy passed through the broken wire and into the woods. I was looking down for footprints or disheveled branches, McCoy looking up, broad brown hand porched over eyes crinkling against the sunlight.

"There," he said after we'd walked two dozen feet. I looked up and saw a black-and-green metal assemblage resembling a chair attached to the tree about thirty feet up.

"A deer stand," I said.

"Portable and camouflaged," McCoy said. "The killer climbs the tree, snaps the stand in place, sits in comfort and watches Tanner's place. He notes Tanner's patterns, leaves a pot of toxic stew and waits a bit longer. Hoping he can go inside and have – what did you call it, Carson – his symbolic moments?"

"Jesus," Cherry said, sighting between the tree and Tanner's trailer, two hundred feet away. "The guy could have been watching the whole Tanner meltdown from here."

I climbed the tree. The stand was positioned to reconnoiter the multi-windowed rear of Tanner's trailer. A man with good binoculars could watch like his nose was pressed to the glass.

I retrieved the stand, hoping we could pull prints, figuring we wouldn't, given the extreme care our perp had shown so far. McCoy pushed further down the trail as Cherry and I combed the ground beneath the tree for evidence, finding nothing.

"Got a trail back here," McCoy yelled after a few

minutes. We followed his voice to a hard dirt path half obscured by undergrowth.

"Looks rugged," I said. "Could you ride it on a dirt bike?"

"Somebody has recently," he said, pointing to a tire scraping in the gray dust. "If it was me, I'd ride to the Forest Service firebreak a quarter-mile north. Then it's an easy ten-minute run to a real road. This guy had it figured out."

McCoy's phone rang. He snapped it open, spoke for several minutes, questioning his caller about times of day, from the sound of things. He asked the caller to verify the official time of sunrise. Waited. Nodded when the information arrived and turned back to Cherry and me.

"The spiders have spoken, folks. And they're saying something interesting. Let's re-group back at the park, where I can put together a little show and tell."

# 31

We met at the office in the lodge. Cherry had called Beale, protocol, and he'd grumblingly assented to an appearance. He brought Caudill along, presumably to do the remembering if anything important was said.

"You're doing this without the FBI?" Beale grunted when he entered. "That's gonna piss off Krenkler."

"They'll be apprised of everything going on, Roy. And you can tell them anything we leave out, right?"

The barb zoomed by Beale, who nodded and broke wind as he sat. Inside the room it was the five of us and, for about a minute, a female ranger in her early twenties who entered to hand McCoy a file holding slender strips of paper and a few other pages. McCoy studied the information as he and the young ranger spoke quietly in a corner. When she turned to leave McCoy patted her shoulder and said, "Great job." The kid practically floated out the room on a cloud of euphoria.

"Can we get some goddamn coffee in here?" Beale bayed.

"The waitresses only work in the restaurant, Roy," McCoy said quietly, turning from his task to pull his wallet. "But if you run over there I'll buy the coffee. Donuts, too."

Beale's eyes darkened in dilemma: be the coffee gopher or miss out on a freebie. He snatched up McCoy's twenty and waddled out the door.

McCoy finished his calculations and looked up. "The road into Rock Bridge trail? Eight vehicles went down it after seven p.m. yesterday. Five before eight p.m. One was between eight and nine, just barely dark. Here's the two I think we're interested in: one vehicle headed toward the trailhead just past midnight, exited at half-past two. The second vehicle entered at bit before five a.m. and left at six-ten."

I stared at McCoy as if he'd conjured polka-dot elephants as the table's centerpiece. "How the hell do you know that, Lee?"

He dangled the slender scrolls that resembled calculator paper. I saw printing, numbers and times. "Ever see a pair of skinny hoses crossing the road and attached to a box to the side? Traffic counters. We have several throughout the park, including one on that final stretch of Rock Bridge Road leading to the trailhead. They count entering and exiting vehicles."

Cherry looked up. "You're saying . . .?"

"I'm saying the vehicle crossing the counter at midnight was carrying the body. The perpetrator took it down the trail to the arch, strung it from the bridge."

"The other vehicle," I said, confused by the timeline, "the one that crossed the counter hose near five a.m., why don't you think it was our man?"

"The killer had to haul the body to the bridge, then create the suspension system. That meant getting in the water, running rope under the bridge, climbing back atop the arch and setting the knots. Then hiking back out. Had to take at least two hours."

"What about the later entry?" Cherry asked.

McCoy leaned forward. "A strange story by itself. Someone went to Rock Bridge a bit after five in the morning."

"Whoa," I said, holding up a hand, my alarm bell ringing. "That's supposition, Lee. All your counter registered was a vehicle on the road. You can't conclude that the person in the vehicle got out and hiked to Rock Bridge."

"Maybe it was a benign civilian who drove to the trailhead," Cherry said, weighing in on my side. "An insomniac who couldn't sleep. Or an alky having a pre-dawn eye-opener. Believe me, I see a lot of that. The mystery early visitor left without ever setting foot down the trail. He or she might never have gotten out of their car."

"That's not what the spiders tell me," McCoy said.

I said, "Pardon me?"

"We're all hikers here. We've all been the first person

down a trail at daybreak, right? What do you do about every hundred feet?" McCoy used his hands to make a swimming motion in front of his face.

"Push away spider webs," I said, getting the clue. "I always use a walking stick or fishing pole to knock them down."

"There should have been cross-trail webs on the way to Rock Bridge. The spiders are industrious critters with plenty of time to string webs after the killer was gone. But I didn't find a single strand . . . all the way to the bridge. Our five o'clock visitor went all the way to the body, knocking aside the webs."

"It jives with Miz Bascomb," I said. "She heard a vehicle on the road a few hours after the killer drowned Tandee Powers. The vehicle with the stick shift."

McCoy cleared his throat. His brow was knit in frown, his chin perched on tented fingertips. "It's interesting to me that the killer is gone before two or three a.m., but nothing appears on the geocache site until hours later, after daybreak. That seems to jive more with the appearance of the second person."

"You think the killer's not entering the symbol and data on the site?" Cherry said, shaking her head. "The mystery visitor is?"

"The timing suggests it," McCoy said.

"It's a reach," Cherry said. "But I'm at the point where reaching is progress. The question is – if it's true – why?"

I saw Judd Caudill's hand quiver on the table. It lifted two inches, fell to the table, a kid in class wanting to raise his hand, but frightened he'll get laughed at for his answer.

"What is it, Judd?" I asked. "Speak up."

"I was, uh, thinking. My cousin is the county representative for the state environment agency. He checks new installations of septic tanks and goes in after the tanks have been installed to see if they're done right . . ." He paused, still unsure of himself.

"Go on, Judd," I said. "We need every idea we can get."

"Uh, well, I was just thinking . . . what if the later person is like a killing inspector or something?"

Beale had entered during Caudill's appraisal, bags in hand and confectioner's sugar smearing his face. He started laughing uncontrollably.

Caudill shrunk down in his seat. I wrote *Killing Inspector?* in my notebook and underscored it twice.

# 32

It was four in the afternoon when we left the meeting, heads spinning. We were standing in the lodge parking lot looking over the steep cliffs and mulling the new information when Harry called.

"You were dead on, Carson," he said, after giving me a brief rundown of the action. "You should have seen Oakes's face when Babe came strutting out from the back of the house, grinning like he owned the mortgage on Oakes's soul."

"The perils of a guilty conscience," I said, buoyed by Harry's sprawling and cheerful voice. "How Oakes get enlisted?"

"A couple ex-cons showed up a week before Crayline was brought to the Institute for hypnosis. Hardcore Aryan types, the kind of assholes who think Bobby Lee Crayline's something to aspire to. They brought a carrot and stick.

The carrot was fifty grand if Oakes bought in. The stick was, Don't help Bobby Lee, and he'll take it real hard."

"Fifty grand is nothing compared to being on Crayline's shit list," I said.

"Like you figured, Carson, the hay bales were the hiding place. Oakes drove away from the madness, brought Bobby Lee to the farm, hid him in a dug-out dirt hole under the house. The space was about the size of a coffin. Get this: Crayline stayed there seven weeks."

"*Seven weeks?*"

"When the roadblocks were taken down and everybody thought Crayline was five states away, he slipped out."

I tried to imagine the willpower it would take to stay almost motionless for one week, unable to stretch, starving, bitten by insects, voiding yourself, all in a casket-sized hole in the ground.

I said, "Crayline say anything to Oakes before he booked?"

"Oakes asked Bobby what he planned to do with his new freedom. Bobby Lee said he was going to kill history, Carson. His exact words."

"Kill history?"

"You got any idea what that means, bro?"

"Nope, brother. And I don't want to."

Harry had a call on the second line and I reluctantly let him get back to business. I walked to Cherry. She looked at me expectantly.

"You were smiling during the call. Good news about Mix-up?"

"Just some input on a case far from here, the one I referred to earlier." I felt my shoulders slump, like someone was letting the air out of my body.

Cherry studied my face. "I know just what you need, Ryder. A fix. Just like what I need. Good thing my dealer is about a minute away."

She drove down the steep hill. Instead of pulling to the highway she continued straight a quarter mile, ending up at an acre of asphalt, a parking lot. To the left was a wooden cottage with a sign saying SKYLIFT TICKET OFFICE – SOUVENIR SHOP. Towering beside it was a huge and horizontal steel wheel. The slow-spinning wheel was running cables to a rocky peak about a half-mile distant. Suspended from the lift's cables were red park benches, basically, some heading up, others returning from the top. Most were empty, the lateness of the hour, I figured.

I swallowed hard and followed Cherry into the cottage, saw racks of souvenir T-shirts, caps, postcards. A smiling man stood behind a cash register. He was in his sixties, round-faced and pot-bellied, wearing a Natural Bridge cap that looked fresh from a rack.

"This is Bob Quint," Cherry said, nodding to the capped man. "He's my dealer."

"Been a while since you've had a fix, Donna," the guy said. "At least on my watch."

"Twenty-seven days. No wonder I've been such a bitch." She rummaged in her purse for some bills. "I need to get a ticket for my friend here."

"You don't need a ticket?" I asked.

222

"Donna has a lifetime pass," Bob said, winking at Cherry. "Something we worked out a few years back."

Ticket secured, Cherry yanked me out the door like a toy wagon. "We need to get on before anyone else shows up."

"Why?"

She ignored my question, tugging me out to the platform where a teenager took our tickets. A bench coming down the mountain swirled in a circle, came around and we jumped aboard. The kid dropped a heavy restraining bar across our laps and *whoosh*, up and away we went.

At first we skimmed the ground, no higher than twenty feet, following a path rising toward the mountain, a hundred-foot-wide swath cleared of trees, looking like a golf fairway. To the sides the trees were thick and dark. A small creek ran at the woodsy edge to my right. We passed beside a huge boulder. Previous riders had pitched coins atop it for fun. The surface glittered. I wondered if I could jump to it and make my escape.

"What was that about a lifetime pass?" I asked Cherry.

"It's a long story," she said, watching a cardinal in a nearby tree, a dot of red in the green.

"Edit," I said.

"Bob and his wife Cindy own the lift, not the state, which receives a cut of the proceeds from passengers and the concessions. The skylift cost a helluva lot. When the previous owners wanted to retire, Bob put together financing from several places but was still two hundred grand short. He made a naïve decision."

"Borrowed from a shady source?"

She nodded. "The interest jumped from manageable to oppressive in six months. It looked like the lender might grab the lift, which was the plan all along. I renegotiated the deal with the lender, grabbing his attention by offering ten-plus."

"Per cent interest?"

"Years in prison."

The ground began to fall away. Suddenly we were fifty feet up. Eighty. A hundred. I cleared my throat and checked the firmness of the restraining bar. We passed one of the cable supports. I wondered when it had last been maintained.

"You look nervous, Ryder. Don't you have the hots for rock climbing?"

"I'm fine," I said, forcing a yawn. "I imagine a skylift gets inspected at regular intervals, right?"

Cherry patted my arm. "It's steel. The supports are rooted in bedrock. But you feel safer hanging your life off a tiny bolt fifty feet up. Is that sweat on your forehead?"

I mumbled something. She laughed. "You know what's going on here?" she said.

I looked past my dangling shoes. The ground had dropped away another twenty feet.

"What?"

"It's control. You're in control when you climb. You have no control over the lift. That's it, right?"

I didn't answer, afraid my voice would squeak. I looked ahead. The lifting cables ceased paralleling the ground and rocketed up the vertical cliff face. How could they be so steep and not rip from the upper supports on weight alone?

Cherry spun to check the benches behind us. Empty. There was no one coming down, either. We were alone on the lift.

She said, "This is way against the rules, but . . ."

Cherry pushed the restraining bar up and over our heads. We now sat unrestrained on a slender bench dangling above a rocky chasm. And rising. Cherry crossed her legs and pointed to the ground, growing more distant every second.

"Look at the world, Ryder," she said. "What's it doing?"

No way I was looking down. "I don't know. Rotating?"

"It's falling away."

A gust of wind made the bench quiver and I grabbed the edge of the seat. Cherry smiled serenely and put her hands behind her head.

The lift took us higher than most surrounding mountains, providing a panoramic view of miles of rugged, rumpled green. Cherry sighed, the good kind, where fresh air replaces bad thoughts, tight muscles unfurl and, for her at least, the world falls away.

Reaching the peak, I jumped off to feel the joy of solid ground pushing back against my feet. It was a short walk to Natural Bridge, the park's namesake, a magnificent natural arch carved over millennia by wind and rain, twenty feet wide, a hundred long, flat on top. We stood near the edge and scanned the mountaintops.

"I can't figure out how it works," Cherry said.

"How what works?"

"When the world starts to drive me nuts – like the past three weeks – I jump on the skylift and it's truly as if the world falls away. I'm above it all, at least for a while. I feel better. Cleaner. You studied psychology. Does that seem crazy?"

"What do you mean?"

"The skylift's just a glorified carnival ride that lifts me a few hundred feet. Nothing's changed. But it makes me feel different, better. Why is that?"

"You surrender yourself to the metaphor," I said. "Making the journey a symbol for escape, being above it all. If you've prepared yourself to believe strongly enough – to trust the metaphor – your subconscious allows it to happen."

"I needed someone to tell me that. Thank you."

She smiled and turned to the view. I wanted to hold her hand. Not in any romantic fashion, but to verify the presence of another human being standing beside me in the sky. But when I opened my hand and moved it toward hers, I felt a thrill rise in the pit of my belly and realized that perhaps there could have been a passing touch of romance in my heart.

And then a following wave of folks from the lift – two dozen German tourists – came down the trail chattering and taking pictures. The spell was broken and we returned to the world below.

# 33

"Here's my plan," Cherry said as we climbed into her ride. "The FBI's back in the picture tomorrow and I'll be running errands for Dark Lady Krenkler. I'm going to drop you by your cabin so you can check on your doggie. Then we're going to my place for supper."

"I don't know if I should—"

"The hell with the world, Carson. I want to stay up in the sky a while. Have supper with me."

She'd never used my first name. I can't explain it, but at that moment I would have jumped headlong from the nearest cliff had she asked.

"The sky it is," I said.

Mix-up wasn't at the cabin, but I hadn't expected it. Cherry gave me directions to her place and boogied. I showered away the day and changed into a fresh white cotton shirt, barely used cords, brand spanking new socks.

I put out fresh food for Mix-up and changed the water. When I looked into the woods and felt my gut begin to hollow out, I took a few deep breaths and thought of Cherry beside me in the sky where she had felt free, at least for a few minutes.

When I drove off for her home, directions in my lap, I passed my brother's home. He was on the porch and reading a newspaper. He didn't look up.

I twice passed the drive to Cherry's house and would have taken a three-fer if I hadn't finally swerved into the gravel drive I'd initially thought an ATV trail. Unruly vegetation bordered the lane, as though Cherry enjoyed making visitors brush shoulders with nature. I followed the track several hundred feet, stopping in a graveled parking strip at the rear of a two-story log cabin with a steep metal roof of green. I pulled next to Cherry's cruiser, beside it her muddy and jacked-high Jeep.

"Come on 'round front," I heard Cherry's voice yell.

My heels found limestone slabs forming a walkway to the front of the cabin, passing a massive stone chimney set against square-cut logs chinked with gray caulk. Looking ahead, I faced a breathtaking mountain panorama of verdant forest studded with massive rock cliffs and outcroppings. The impression was of rock-hulled ships pressing their bows from beneath the green.

I turned the corner to find Cherry above on the cabin's broad porch, drifting lazily in a swing, one hand on the chain. Music fell from the open windows, a woman singer with a plaintive voice singing a rock song rooted in madrigal. Cherry wore a dress, white and simple, the neckline square and open, the hem at her knees. The effect was limited by a ball cap touting Ruger firearms, but it still took a second to start breathing again.

"How about a cool brew for a warm day?" she asked.

"Sweet idea."

She padded inside, her feet bare, her sandals beneath the swing. I returned to inspecting the view. The cliff's edge was directly before Cherry's porch, twenty feet of scruffy grass ending in a dozen feet of dark sandstone. Beyond lay only air.

I crept as near the edge as my skittish heart allowed, looking far down into dense treetops parted by a slender thread of creek. Adjoining cliffs rose from the valley, sheer cuts of sandstone between hillsides angled just enough to hold vegetation. I found myself holding my breath as if underwater, not knowing why.

"Watch that first step, Ryder," Cherry's voice called from behind me. "The second one doesn't show up for four hundred feet."

I returned to the porch, where Cherry was setting down a tray with sandwiches and bottles of beer. "I was sure I had some duckling à l'orange left over from yesterday," she winked. "But all I found was sandwich stuff."

"You really ought to put a barrier at the edge of the cliff," I suggested, picking up a half-pound of roast beef and cheddar on rye. "A fence or a rock wall or something."

"I know where the edge is," she said. "And a fence would block my view."

"It's a helluva view. I'll give you that. And a real fer-sure log cabin." I tapped my knuckles on the door frame, as solid as concrete.

"Built thirty-three years ago by Horace Cherry, my uncle on my father's side. My father passed away when I was seven. Horace never had kids, and always took a shine to me. When he died, three years back, he left the place to me, knowing I loved being here as much as he did."

"Do you have any siblings?"

"I have a lot of relatives, but I was an only child." She smiled wistfully. "I'm the last Cherry on the tree."

"Everyone around here seems someone's kin in some way."

"When there's only a few dozen families who inhabit a three-county area for the first hundred years after a place gets settled, everyone's kin to everyone's kin, in some way or another. That's changing, but not as fast as everywhere else. A writer once called Appalachia the most foreign of American cultures."

"Foreign?" I said. "Isn't it Scots-Irish, mainly?"

"And English, and plenty of Germans. Yeoman farmers, back in the old countries, people who knew farming and animal husbandry and pulling food from land that blunted plows and busted the spirits of lesser folk. It's not foreign because the people are so different from the rest of the country, but because they're similar

230

to the way they always were. They're only foreign in time."

I took a bite of my sandwich. "Are you foreign in time?"

"I grew up with people who have never been out of the mountains, never will. Not even as far as Lexington. There are more of them than you'd think. I've been to college, spent a few months traveling abroad. Even been to New-freakin'-York and Los Angeles. I like big cities. But I love it here, too. So I guess I'm sort of suspended between two worlds. Come on inside, Carson. Let me give you the tour."

I followed her into her home, basically the floor plan of my cabin back at Road's End, just fifty per cent larger. There was a living area with vaulted ceiling, a half-loft above, a door at the end leading into an upper bedroom.

The wall open to the high ceiling on the fireplace end of the living area had been plastered or dry-walled and painted a creamy white. Ditto the wall beside the stairs to the loft. The seamless white formed the background for dozens of items from photographs through old advertising posters to antique tools. A tan and red-banded hat of straw centered the collection. Arranging a sizeable number of items on a surface is difficult – it's composition – but Cherry had an eye for balance.

I studied the tools, odd assemblages of wood and leather and metal. A couple of them looked cruel, almost threatening. "I've never seen tools like these before," I said. "What are they?"

She padded over and stood at my side, beer bottle in hand. "I have no idea. They were in Uncle Horace's shed. I suppose they have something to do with horses. The hat's his, too; he wore it everywhere. Here's my favorite picture—"

She pointed to a photo of a pretty young girl, eight or nine, standing beside a barrel-chested man with waxed dark hair. He was wearing a cream-colored suit, dark bolo tie, and the same tan hat hanging on the wall. He was grinning like he'd just won the lottery.

"Uncle Horace and you?" I asked.

"Yep. That's Uncle Horace in most of the shots."

I studied another photo, Horace Cherry bedecked in an ice-cream suit with cocked and jaunty hat riding his crown. His smile seemed radiant and boundless, the young Donna Cherry at his side looking heartbreakingly innocent.

"He always wore the suit, right?" I asked, knowing it was a uniform.

"With the hat atop his crown everywhere he went. He was a dandy. It was funny."

Something in the photo started to make me uneasy. Something in the eyes perhaps. Or maybe it was the age of the photo, a darkening of the shadows.

"Hey, I've got an idea." Cherry crouched to reach into a low cabinet, pulling out a squat brown bottle. I tried not to notice the way her dress hugged her body. She shook back her hair and studied the bottle's yellowed label as she stood. I saw her nipples buzzing against the fabric of her dress like anxious bees. I wanted them to carry honey to my tongue.

"It's some kind of special cognac," she said. "A gift from Uncle Horace years ago. He said to have a sip on special occasions. Want a tipple to celebrate your first skylift ride? All in all, you liked the trip, right?"

"It was wonderful," I lied, feeling a smile rise to my lips as I moved a half-step closer to Donna Cherry. My knees loose with the promise of honey, I started to reach for her hand.

And stopped. Froze with my hand suspended in mid-air. I couldn't tell if the hand was part of the me I knew as me or the priapic rogue my brother kept telling me was me. Was it me interested in Cherry or was it he, the broken me? From nowhere my brother's mocking voice rose unbidden in my head.

*"Part of your childhood damage manifests in a shy roguish charm you use to warm yourself with temporary lovers, Carson . . ."*

I realized he'd said those things knowing I'd hear them at moments like this. I'd forgotten how consuming was his need to affect others from a distance. To keep a tight chain.

"Wait here a second," I told Cherry.

"Uh, Carson, did I say something?"

"You're fine. I'll be right back."

I walked outside, close to the edge of the precipice, where I crouched and found a round chunk of sandstone. I mentally mapped my position, turned to the general

233

direction of the hollow, trying to aim my eyes directly at my brother's cabin, visualizing him sitting on the porch. I side-armed the stone high and away in his direction and closed my eyes. I pictured the rock traveling five or so miles, falling from the sky like a meteorite and smacking my brother dead-center in his forehead, knocking him backwards in his chair, newspaper fluttering down on his startled face.

"Keep your hands outta my head, Brother," I said, backing my symbolic missile with the most potent digital icon in American culture.

When I stepped back inside I felt fifty pounds lighter, like a leaden yoke had melted from my shoulders. "Pour the cognac," I said, stepping to Cherry and no longer wondering who was talking.

She lifted a perplexed eyebrow. "Are you all right?"

"I had a simple ritual to perform. Like an exorcism."

"Uh, do you always—"

I pressed my finger to her lips, stilling them. The sensation of warmth was exquisite. "My own small skylift ritual. I had something bothering me, but it fell away." I withdrew my finger, reluctantly.

"When you put it in those terms, I think I understand." She lifted her glass. "Shall we drink to solving the case?"

"No," I corrected. "Let's drink to us."

We clicked glasses. The cognac was dizzying in my head, distilled manna aged in oak and leather. We next raised our glasses to the tan hat of our cognac-giving benefactor, Horace T. Cherry, staring dark-eyed from the photo centering the wall of pictures and weird objects. We set the glasses on the table and sat on the couch, almost touching. I'm sure I heard her bees buzzing.

My cellphone rasped from my pocket. I rolled my eyes and answered.

"This is Heywood Williams," an elderly male voice said, loud, like a guy with hearing problems. "I'm manager of the Pumpkin Patch Campground. We got a dog running loose around here matches the description on a poster one of the Woslee cops dropped off."

"The dog's a big guy?" I asked. "Kinda odd-looking?"

"I guess. Odd looks different to different people. Big ol' boy. Friendly."

I took the address, clear on the other side of the Gorge. I'd already had several calls, able to figure out it wasn't Mix-up by questioning the caller. But this call had promise.

"I heard," Cherry said as I dropped the phone back in my pocket. "Go, Carson. I hope it's Mix-up. But even if it isn't, I'm still hopeful, right?"

She stood on her toes and gave me a millisecond's kiss on my lips, more dizzying by far than the cognac.

# 34

The Pumpkin Patch Campground was twenty minutes distant. I drove past the campground sign, pumpkin-shaped and promising hookups, fire pits and a dumping station. Mr Williams was reading a newspaper in a folding chair beside a small wooden kiosk where guests checked in. He was somewhere in his seventies, wearing a pumpkin-colored porkpie hat and Bermuda shorts.

"I'm sorry," Williams said sheepishly. "The dog belonged to a group of campers. I hadn't seen it when they checked in."

He pointed to a bright recreational vehicle across a small park area. The family – husband, wife, three smallish kids – were still setting up, the husband on the roof of the vehicle passing lawn chairs down to the wife as a huge shaggy dog with some resemblance to Mix-up frisked at the wife's ankles.

Williams was a chatty guy and since he'd made a valiant effort on my behalf, I kept him company for a few minutes, talking about the weather and his work.

"We got twenty sites for RVs," he related proudly. "Full hookups. And another dozen sites for tent campers."

"Must keep you busy."

"Busy enough. People drive in, stay a night or two, head off to another place. Easy to do when you're driving a box filled with all the comforts of home."

I saw a big recreational vehicle that had recently pulled in for the night; hooked to the towbar behind it was a Mazda compact.

"Do many people pull cars with them?" I asked, killing time.

"Sure. So they can move around locally with less gas. If a big RV is like planting your house anywhere you want, having a car is like bringing your garage along as well."

"Are there many RV campgrounds in the area?"

"Depends what you mean. There's maybe five or six real near the Gorge. Add another thirty miles to the circle and you get a bunch more. Plus some folks have acreage set up to hold a few RVs to make a little pin money."

I studied nearby RVs, saw three more with towing packages. It hit me that the set-up was the perfect mobile hideaway, especially with props like bikes and boats and fishing rods. A recreational vehicle could be moved from campsite to campsite, hard to track. They offered a place to plot, to change disguise, to sneak in under cover of dark, tear a body apart, pack it with manure. There was also the image: recreational vehicles were the happy whales of the road, friendly and benign, filled with cheery families and retired couples. Mad killers drove rusty vans and dark, low-slung sedans with obsidian windows.

I recalled the words of Gable Paltry, the scruffy old voyeur who scanned the parking lot behind the funeral home where Tanner's body had been stolen.

*"I saw me a big a RV pull in . . . Stayed maybe ten minutes. Light color. Had bikes and crap roped to the back. A barbecue grill tied up top, too."*

I asked Williams if I could wander the campground and, sauntering from site to site, I looked at the bright machines, seeing families and children and several RVs with no one around, owners out hiking or kayaking the river or sightseeing.

When I left Pumpkin Patch, my mind was fixated on the possibility of RVs as hideouts – not just this case, but for future reference. I passed another such campground and pulled in to take a look. That led to a third such place, the Haunted Hollow Campground. The campground was up by Frenchburg, high on the northwest side of the Gorge area. The murders and bulk of the investigation had occurred on the eastern side.

I parked near the entrance and wandered past the twenty or so sites. The lot, thick with trees, was tucked back in a verdant hollow – haunted, presumably – with a small creek singing merrily alongside. It didn't seem a place where a killer would tuck down and think murderous thoughts.

I scanned RV after RV, seeing occupants, or swimsuits drying on a line, or hearing voices from inside, doors open wide to accept the cooling air of dusk. At the end of the road was a huge cream-colored RV resembling a vacation on wheels, bikes parked against the rear wheel, man's, woman's, a couple kid's bikes. Two short recreational kayaks were strapped atop the vehicle, plus a plane-sized inner tube for playing in the water. The tips of fishing rods pressed against a back window. The shades were drawn and no one seemed inside.

I wandered to the rear and saw the requisite bumper stickers: *Smoky Mountains, Everglades National Park, the Ozarks,* a dozen or so. The stickers looked new and I wondered if the vehicle's owner or owners were recent retirees.

The vehicle had both a tow bar and a rack holding a Kawasaki dirt bike, a big one. The distance from the ground to the rack was twenty or so inches and I figured it took a couple people to grunt the motorcycle into the rack. Or one strong one.

Turning away, a motion at a rear window caught my eye, a curtain shifting perhaps. Or a motion behind it. I stared for several seconds and saw nothing, recalling a classic bumper sticker admonition:

*Don't Come Knockin' When This Van's A-rockin'.*

Hoping my nosy wanderings hadn't disturbed anyone's merrymaking, I retreated to my car, shooting backwards glances at the RV and wondering if my imagination was running past the red line.

I started back to my cabin, but being cloistered with my thoughts seemed claustrophobic so, for a few minutes at least, I drove where the roads led me, restless, thinking that maybe if I gave Mix-up a little more time, he'd be at the cabin when I returned, nose-nudging his food bowl my way as though nothing had happened.

Dusk was thickening and I saw headlights behind me, but they dissolved into the distance. I drove westward, windows down, as night fell deep into the valleys. The road straightened for a moment and I saw the headlights again, closer, the vehicle moving at speed. To my left I saw a Forest Service road and pulled from the main road, wanting to find a bit of calm before returning to the cabin.

I heard a slow rumble through the mountains as I stepped from my truck and stretched my back. It was distant thunder, the promised front approaching. But for now the moonlight was bright enough to light the trail.

I started walking, right away stepping into a spider web. I brushed it from my face, recalling McCoy's observation regarding a second traveler on the Rock Bridge trail. I was a half-mile down the trail when I heard a car door close somewhere to my right. My parking area was behind me, the other vehicle at another trail access; kids, I figured, kissing or sipping beer in the dark.

Two minutes later I heard a limb stepped on, the sound from my side quadrant. I gauged the distance as two or three hundred feet.

After a few seconds, I heard a second footfall. Then, a third.

I nearly called out a plaintive *Hello*, but stopped myself. If I could hear their footfalls, surely the other person had heard mine. It seemed odd that in the hundreds of square miles of the local forest, two people had chosen this section as a nighttime venue.

The night bloomed darker and I looked above to see a cloud covering the white face of the moon. The cloud sifted free and moonlight blazed so white as to feel hot on my neck. To my right I heard an odd sound, like tape being stripped from a roll.

I was craning my ear that direction when a bullet slapped a tree four feet to my right. I dove to the ground, heart racing.

At first, no sound. Then a voice in the dark.

"Here coppie, coppie, coppie," it crooned, as if calling a dog, a high and metal-raspy voice. Another pop. The bullet sizzled past my ear.

The voice was unforgettable. I'd heard it once at a brief prison interview, once at a hypnosis session turned sour: Bobby Lee Crayline.

*Bobby Lee Crayline?*

For one horrible second it occurred that speaking of

him recently, figuring out his escape in Alabama, had worked black magic, that I had conjured him into my life like a demon from hell.

I breathed away the irrational and started running low, tough enough when the moon was out, impossible when clouds passed between us. My feet snagged roots and vines, stumbled over rocks. I stepped on limbs that cracked like firecrackers, ran headlong into low branches.

*Why is Crayline here?* my mind kept saying. *Why is he trying to kill me?*

The clouds released the moon and I was spotlit on the trail. Another shot from Crayline. A rifle that sounded somehow blunted and dull.

"Here, coppie, coppie, coppie . . ."

The forest went black. I crouched and waited for the moon to light the path. It blazed and I moved forward, staying low, the trail a maze of shadows. I heard Crayline angling behind me. I had left my weapon tucked in a closet in the cabin. Sweat dripped from my forehead, my heart seemed to engulf my chest. I could find no avenue to set an ambush.

The moon poked through again. The trail veered into rhododendron and all I saw was rock and more rock, rising into the night sky until it disappeared into black. I had no escape route left. I had come to the end of a hollow, a box canyon.

I heard laughter at my back, a hundred feet? Less? Bobby Lee Crayline was moving with caution, tree to tree. Safe in the cover of the hemlocks and pines, he had only to slowly advance until I was in his sights.

I was in the point of a V, with nowhere to go. Nowhere at all.

*Up*, said a voice in my head. *There's nothing left but up.*

# 35

I craned my head back as the moon shone through a wisp of cloud. Four stories above me in the sandstone I saw a hueco – Spanish for "hole" – a depression eroded into the cliff face, common in the sandstone cliffs. I heard a trampled branch, a crunch in the black air. Crayline had moved one tree closer. He was silent now, fully focused on gliding in for the kill.

I looked back to the cliff face. There was cover of a dozen feet of rhododendron before I'd be lit bright on the sandstone. Sweat stinging my eyes, I hid my shoes under leaves and leapt on to the rock, hand grabbing upward at a small shelf. I missed, tumbling to the ground. My clothes were binding me and I stripped to skivvies and pulled off my socks. I hid the clothes with my shoes.

I leapt again and made the jump, fingers holding. I pulled, straining, until my scrambling toes found purchase.

A dull pop and I heard lead splat against the cliff a dozen feet away. Crayline was guessing at my position, firing blind into the point of the V. The moon broke through the clouds and the world turned spotlight white for twenty seconds. I saw a vertical crack, used it to pull ten feet higher, leaves tickling at my back. I emerged above the rhododendron, now an easy target on the cliff face.

The moon disappeared and I recognized the impossibility of my task. The only way to see hand and footholds was in the moonlight. But the same light displayed me like I was centering a snow-white screen at a movie theater.

The moon filtered through a thin cloud and I saw a handhold two feet above me. My feet scrabbled, found purchase. I brought my right foot to the tiny outcrop now holding my hand. With my foot secured, I slipped my hand away, slapped it upward. My face pressed into the stone. Even my breath was an enemy, inflating my chest, pushing my center of balance back an inch or so. I heard Crayline move another tree closer, the sound now as much below as behind. I prayed his upward view was cluttered by limbs or brush.

I saw another hold four feet up and three laterally, a handhold no larger than a pack of cigarettes. An impossible move, almost, the edge of my limits.

The world went black, a thick cloud rolling over the moon. *Come back!* my mind screamed at the moon. *I need you!*

I froze against the sandstone, heart pounding in pitch-black. I heard a gnome in my head: Gary, my rock-climbing instructor. *Make the move before you make the move,* he constantly lectured, promoting visual and physical visualization. I pictured the rock's surface, the small holds I needed to catch, felt how it would feel to make the move.

I launched myself upward, exploding like a coiled spring, scrabbling for something only seen in my mind, feeling nothing, then . . .

My right index and forefinger fell atop a one-inch outcrop, left toe on a tiny shelf, the rest of me stretched tight between hand and foot.

Another shot from Crayline, a dull pop aimed into the rhododendron below. The moon returned. To my right, waist-level, I saw a small stone rumple that might hold a foot. My fingers burned, shivered, muscles filling with lactic acid, strength dying away. I checked the position of the rumple, brought my leg up . . . easy, easy . . . Visualize as the moon tucked under cloud. See the move and . . . *Got it!* I pulled upward with every ounce of strength, sweat searing my eyes.

"Here, coppie, coppie, coppie . . ."

Crayline returned to the taunt, trying to spook me into making a move, but still looking for me at ground level. He was almost to the cliff. I tried to pull up another few inches for stability but my toehold crumbled into dust, my foot kicking wildly. My body canted sideways, falling, hands flailing uselessly, slapping at the rock, *falling, goddammit it's over why now falling* . . .

My fingers slammed something pushing from the rock. A metal circle. I grabbed. My fingers howled in pain, but held.

*It was a bolt. A freaking BOLT!*

I'd found a regular climbing route, a path pioneered up the cliff. The rock had been drilled, bolts jammed in to hold safety ropes affixed to harnesses.

I had no rope. No harness. No chalk to enhance my grip. But I was on a pre-built route. The moon blazed again, white light now revealing the series of bolts above me, tiny lighthouses in the rock. I tried to recall everything Gary had taught me. Every move. Every technique.

The moon fled. I dangled one-handed from the bolt for several seconds until my feet found holds. My hands patted rock above, knowing the metal circles were there, waiting. I found one and grunted upward, crossing my body length through the dark in seconds.

Moon. I looked up and saw the dark hueco just feet above me, beside a cleft in the rock. I heard a muffled pop and the stone inches beside me splintered. Seen! I held my scream of terror and pulled for the hueco like a man swimming vertically, waiting for the second shot.

I tumbled into the hueco seconds later. Below me I heard cursing and the sound of stripping tape. I realized Crayline was using a soft-drink silencer – an empty plastic bottle duct-taped over the weapon's muzzle – to blunt the shot's sound. A fresh bottle had to be taped on for each shot.

Crayline knew an open gunshot could carry for miles. But the semi-silenced shots sounded numb and inconclusive, liable to be mistaken for a falling branch if noticed at all. He probably had a backpack full of bottles.

Another pop. The bullet whanged off the roof of the hueco, buried in the dust three inches from my knee. I rolled against the rear of the hole and tucked fetus-tight. "HELP!" I yelled into the night, hoping the cavity performed like a giant megaphone. "HELP! CALL THE POLICE!"

I heard my words echo back to me, no idea if they were carrying a hundred feet or a thousand yards.

"HELLLLLLP!"

I screamed for two more minutes, until I saw a flash-light through the trees, moving quickly away. Crayline had decided it wasn't worth the risk. I watched his light diminish until I knew I was out of range. I crawled into the crevice at the side of the hueco, wormed the final dozen feet to the ridge and circled toward my truck.

Rain had started when I found it an hour later, shoeless and limping from countless stumbles, listening into the dark before I approached. I tried my phone, but recalled the nearest cell tower was miles away and this section of the forest was a dead zone.

I fired up the engine but kept the lights off, snapping them on only when shadows indicated I might be nearing a precipice. I was afraid Crayline was lurking in the trees. I continued several miles until the service road intersected two-lane. I was still deep in the backcountry, but felt safer using headlights and speed. The rain escalated as I tapped a phone button, finding no reception. I flicked on the dome light and checked between the map and the road. Cherry's home was about three miles away.

I saw headlamps ahead on the highway. They shifted to dim as I cut mine back. Then they blazed bright and blinding between my wipers. I held my hand in front of my eyes to cut the glare. The vehicle passed by, a high-sprung mini-pickup painted with camouflage blacks and greens.

A hunter's truck.

I looked in the rear-view and saw the scarlet lights of braking. I knew in my gut it was Crayline. My eyes returned from the rear-view to see a tight curve ahead. I braked too hard, skidding from the road into a shallow ditch, wheel spinning in my hand until I grabbed tight, losing valuable seconds. Crayline roared up and banged my bumper, pushing me ahead. I downshifted, slid through a bend, straightened.

He was on me in an instant, another ramming. I heard a gunshot as my side window crumbled away. I braked hard for a switchback, rain sweeping my face. Crayline's lights seemed in my back seat.

"History's getting fixed," he roared incomprehensibly. "You ain't stopping it."

I ran another blind curve, Crayline cutting low and trying to clip me into a spin. I watched him miss by inches, screaming out his window between shots. Rain blew into my eyes like a gale. I downshifted and gained a few feet. Somewhere ahead was the turn-off to Cherry's home. Crayline was on my bumper.

Our combined lights showed a lane between trees. I jammed on the brakes, cut sideways and slid off the road a hundred feet before Cherry's drive. I clipped a tree, fought for control, made the turn on to the lane to Cherry's house.

Crayline was behind me seconds later. I blinked away rain and saw the lights of Cherry's house, the tree-studded yard, the drive appearing to continue beyond the cabin.

Crayline was closing fast. A shot screamed off the cab.

I roared past Cherry's house, waited a millisecond beyond hope, downshifted to second. The truck slowed with a jolt but without brake lights. I aimed into a tree, hit a glancing blow. The air bag exploded. I shoved it aside as Crayline roared past, probably wild with glee at seeing my wrecked truck.

But there would be no stopping and no coming back for Bobby Lee Crayline. I pictured his hideous grin freezing as he looked ahead and saw nothing but air.

Crayline jumped on the brakes. His taillights were horizontal for a split second, then arced inexorably into the valley. I pushed from my truck as the door opened on Cherry's cabin, I saw a shotgun muzzle sniffing over the threshold.

"It's OK," I yelled. "It's me."

She stepped outside, wearing an outsized T-shirt and little more. It seemed appropriate, given that I was standing in her yard solely in sodden boxers.

"Sweet Jesus, Ryder. What's going on?"

I waved her to follow me to the edge of the cliff. We stared into the valley. Forty stories below the trees were orange with the gasoline-fueled glow of Bobby Lee Crayline's funeral pyre.

# 36

Eight thirty a.m. found Cherry and me at the largest of the pair of park cabins the Feds used as their Woslee field HQ. Krenkler had arrived, her hair even brighter and stiffer than I remembered, the out-curling side points like she'd honed them in a pencil sharpener. She was on her cell and sending her harried agents to and fro solely with irate glances and fingersnaps.

She jabbed her fingers toward where we should sit: the dining-room table. Krenkler finished her call, popped a stick of gum between her scarlet lips and gave me her best cross-examination stare as she strode over.

"You knew this guy, Ryder. You interviewed him in the Alabama State Prison. You were at the mental institute when he escaped. He died trying to kill you. That's three too many coincidences for me. What's the story?"

Questions I'd been asking myself for hours. I rubbed my face with my hands.

"I'm flummoxed. Utterly mystified. There's nothing I ever did to Crayline to piss him off. He probably had grudges against half the people in his life, but he picked—"

"You. He wanted you here."

"There's no reason for it. I was never anything to him."

Krenkler had big hands with several shiny rings aboard. She set the hands on the table beside me and leaned close. "You sure it was a woman's voice that called you to the guy with the tool up his pooper?"

I said, "It sounded like a woman's voice." And it had, that being the gender my brother was imitating.

"You're absolutely sure?"

"Yes," I said, frazzled and sore and feeling like I was still clinging fifty feet in the air with bullets slapping beside me. "Why?"

Krenkler stood and backed away, leaning against the knotty pine wall, her arms crossed. With her black pantsuit and flared lapels, she resembled a looming raven, only blonder.

"Ryder, can you think of any reason Robert Crayline would want to kill any of the three others he's killed here?"

I rubbed my face. "I don't have any idea what he'd have against . . ." I paused, hearing Crayline's words the day of his escape, right after the lawyer's hired goon had spat on Bobby Lee and called him a genetic moron.

"Don't go dumb on me Ryder," Krenkler said. "What is it?"

"Bobby Lee threatened a guy the day he escaped. Last name was Bridges. I don't recall the first name. Bridges was half-bright muscle, probably an occasional employee of Crayline's legal firm. Call Arthur Slezak, of Dunham, Krull and Slezak in Memphis. Ask Slezak if he's seen Bridges lately."

Krenkler frowned. "You think the guy with the tool up his tailpipe might be this Bridges?"

I thought back to the horror show in the reeking shack, saw the body wired to the bed. "The corpse's face was ruined," I said, "but the body size fits. Hard and fit. Crayline said he was going to fry Bridges's guts for supper."

I heard one of the agents at my back mutter *Holy shit*. Krenkler glared at the agent. "How about checking on this Bridges?" she snapped. "That too much to ask?"

In the past dozen hours I'd been to my cabin only long enough to put on clothes and note with despair I was still sans dog. I stood.

"Where you think you're going, Ryder?" Krenkler growled.

"I'm going to shower and go to bed for a couple hours," I said quietly. "Anyone thinking different better be ready to use their gun."

Cherry said she'd drop me off, my truck still at her home until photos and reconstructions were made, but Krenkler wasn't through grilling her on local developments.

Now would come the reconstruction: why Crayline had selected Woslee County as his killing field. Cherry didn't look happy at the prospect of continuing the tête-à-tête with Krenkler, but it was part of the job. I was ferried back by Agent Rourke. He seemed the most human of the robots on Krenkler's team.

"How is it, working with Agent Krenkler?" I asked him.

"I retire in two months," he said, not turning his eyes from the road. "Ask me then."

"Gotcha," I said.

He dropped me at my front door. I had hoped whatever forces propel the universe had put my night's ordeal in the book and, checking the account to date, decided I might deserve the return of my dog.

The budgeting was not in my favor.

I showered and changed and, still charged with adrenalin residue, lost my need to sleep. I downed two power bars and made coffee strong as the bolts I'd clung to on the cliff face. I added a tot of Maker's Mark, going out to the porch to sit and think.

Crayline had been at the Alabama Institute for Aberrational Behavior, the first time during my brother's tenure. That in itself didn't mean a whole lot. Though the Institute housed seventy or eighty full-time patients, another hundred or so criminals might rotate through on an annual basis, there for a few days or weeks of evaluation or study. Plus there were levels of security, different wings – "wards" in the semi-hospital parlance used at the Institute. Since Crayline had been there as a transient, a person for temporary study, he might not have had access to the general population which included my brother.

But I had to know, just for my own knowing. I called Dr Wainwright at the Institute, gave her a brief overview of the situation with Bobby Lee Crayline, and asked for records of his stay. Wainwright was apologetic.

"Those records are just for staff, Detective. And not even the general, non-medical staff. Only the doctors are allowed to view the records."

"It could be important," I said.

"I'm very sorry. There are certain notes and observations made that could be subject to privacy issues."

"It wasn't that long ago, Doctor, you begged me to come to the Institute to help stop Bobby Lee Crayline's hypnosis. I came running. Afterwards, you said you owed me big-time and if there was anything you could ever do to—"

"I remember," Wainwright said.

"In my book that was a promise. I'm here to collect."

A long pause. She said, "Let me close the door to my office."

I started taking notes as Wainwright looked through Crayline's records, but after a couple minutes I flung the notes to the floor of the porch, too angry to write. My voice was even as I thanked Wainwright and told her she'd closed the account.

I hobbled toward my brother's cabin, fists clenched as tight as my jaw.

# 37

I stood on Jeremy's porch and willed myself calm. If he saw my anger he'd shut me out or disappear into the forest. I had to appear serene. The door was unlocked and I entered.

"Jeremy," I called, stepping over the threshold. "Where are you?"

"Upstairs, in my office," he yelled, joy in his voice. "Come watch me make money, Brother. The blustering drunkard is starting the day on a binge."

I took the steps two at a time, strode the hall to his open office door. He was at his desk, wearing a dark pinstriped suit, pink shirt, tightly knotted tie. It seemed odd until I realized he was in his business mindset. He had his gentleman gardener garb, his button-down business dress, his retired academic outfit, his rugged outdoorsman wear . . . he affected the uniform necessary to fully complete each personality.

"What are you doing here?" I said.

He spun in his chair. The screens on his desk danced with charts and graphs and crawls of stock symbols. "The Chinese Ministry of Economics issued a report calling for increased spending on infrastructure. The drunkard is puking gold . . . I've got a heavy position in an Asian copper-mining company that jumped eight points in an hour on the Hang Seng Index. I'm about to—"

"NO! What the hell is going on here?" I said, flailing my arms, meaning *here*, the locale, the region.

He regarded me warily before turning back to the monitor. "Whatever kind of question is that, Carson? It's vague. What are you talking about?"

I crossed the room in a half-heartbeat, grabbed the back of his chair and spun him to face me. My voice was a constricted hiss. "I'm talking about Bobby Lee Crayline. He just tried to kill me. He's dead, thankfully."

The surprise in my brother's eyes turned to evasion, which in Jeremy was less a tactic than an emotion. He switched into acting mode, moving up-angled eyes back and forth, as if searching a catalogue of names in his head.

"I'm sorry, Carson. I have no idea who you're talking about."

"You know exactly who Bobby Lee Crayline is," I said, sick of his games. "You got into the heads of everyone who came near you at the Institute. You needed to know what made them tick and how they could be of use to you."

"That's so cynical. I never had any real contact with the man."

"STOP LYING!" I roared. From nowhere my hands were around my brother's throat, lifting him from the chair, spinning him into the wall. "Did you know the staff at the Institute keep round-the-clock track of who the inmates talk to, relate to, spend their time with? It's an interaction study to see who pairs up, weak with weak or weak with strong . . . and who appears to be using who."

"It's *whom*," my brother snarled. "And it's disgusting."

"From the moment Crayline walked in the door, you started circling him. Nodding the first day, speaking in passing the second, eating together on day three. Five days later you two were bonded like Siamese twins. Crayline started his mornings in the community room, waiting for your dramatic daily entrance. The staff read the body language, Jeremy. You were the Alpha in the relationship. Big nasty dangerous Bobby Lee Crayline treated you like some kind of wizard king."

"A pack of lies from a den of spies."

"You know what else was recorded, Jeremy?"

"My bowel movements, from the sounds of it."

I wrenched him tighter to the wall. "You and Bobby Lee Crayline sitting alone in a corner of the ward, Crayline sobbing on the couch as you patted his back and whispered in his ear. People like Crayline don't cry like babies, Jeremy. What was all that about?"

Jeremy pushed my chest, hard. It broke my grip,

sending me backwards. "All right," he said, holding up his hands in surrender. "I remember Bobby. He had things clanging together inside him, issues."

"Everyone there has issues!" I snapped. "They define issues. What did you and Crayline talk about?"

"I told Bobby things about my past. My experiences touched something inside him. He seemed fascinated at how I'd overcome my history. My abuse."

"You told him how it ended?" I said. Jeremy had disemboweled our father and strung bits of him in the trees.

My brother smiled and stabbed his hand in the air, as though plunging a knife deep into tissue. "Not an end, Carson. A beginning." He canted his head, regarding me with curiosity. "Helluva day, wasn't it, Carson? The day the cops came to tell us we were free?"

*. . . police at the door telling my mother her husband had been found in a nearby woods, lashed to a tree, disemboweled while still alive, his innards spread across the ground and into the surrounding trees as if a terrible ritual had been performed.*

I said, "I'll remember it forever."

"Do you remember the knife I used, Carson? You do, don't you? Father's old hunting knife, the one he'd gotten from his father? Hidden in the back of his top desk drawer?"

*I felt the knife in my hand as if I'd held it yesterday. Razor sharp. Hickory handle, an eight-inch stainless-steel blade with a curve like a gentle smile.*

259

"Of course," I said. "I know the knife. Why is this important to—"

"Did I ever tell you why I selected it?"

"I don't know. I guess it was close and wouldn't be missed."

My brother shook his head like I was wasting his time. "Don't be a simpleton, Carson. It was Daddy's beloved knife. I needed to do something very important with it. But first, I needed to perform a magic trick: I had to move the knife from his alliance to mine."

My brother's voice had dropped into a soft monotone and I again felt him leading me into the chaos of his mental landscape. "You're talking about befriending wood and metal?" I scoffed.

"I'm talking about a power akin to magic, Carson. Gaining power over the past. I started by opening the drawer to get the knife used to seeing me. Later, I took it on visits to my room where it learned to trust me. After I'd made the knife mine, I put it above the ceiling tiles. Beside the light above my bed."

"Jeremy, this is completely insa—"

"SHUT UP! Whenever Father entered my room, he walked beneath the knife. I visualized fingers of blood-red light reaching from the knife to Daddy dear. It felt delicious. By the time I used the knife, Carson, I had granted it power unheard of by Excalibur: the power to cut me free of my past."

I shook my head. Excalibur, befriending knives, transforming time through delusions . . . Talking to my brother was like being locked in a revolving door and thrown into a maelstrom. I walked to the window, finding the reality my brother was attempting to dissolve. Reality was the amber sunlight filtering through the trees and dappling the garden. Reality was the red wheelbarrow, the weathered shed, the hoe against the fencepost. Reality was the finches pecking at the feeder, the bees criss-crossing above the hives.

My brother's voice broke into my thoughts. "You don't believe me? You came into possession of father's magical knife, Carson. You discovered it behind a brick in the storm cellar, right? Where it had been waiting for you."

"It was just a knife, Jeremy," I sighed, keeping my eyes outside, looking at the real. "It was always just wood and metal."

*hidden behind a loose brick, rolled in a strip of velvet, the blade mottled with dark stains*

"Really? What did you do with the knife, Carson?" he asked. "What happened?"

"You know that, Jeremy. I threw it away."

"Oh? Just tossed it in the trashcan? Or perhaps flung it out into a field?"

"I threw it in the Gulf, Jeremy."

"So the knife went into the sea," he purred. "Interesting. Where in the sea, Carson? Where exactly?"

*at the mouth of Mobile Bay, or perhaps throat*

"It's not important."

"Come on, O brother mine," he said. "Tell big brother about the knife."

"I was on the Dauphin Island ferry. I threw the knife overboard. No big deal."

*waiting far out on the waters and knowing the sea floor was littered with the carcasses of broken ships and doomed men*

"Ah. In the channel where the Battle of Fort Morgan occurred. Seems a heroic place to drop a sad old knife, Brother. Down to the depths where the bones of the valiant dead rattle and cry."

*the knife concealed in my belt, shirt overhanging, my thumb sliding over the edge of the blade as I looked side to side, no one watching*

"Yes," I admitted.

"How did you feel when it sunk beneath the waves?"

*the knife moving in a see-saw motion in the current, as if cutting away bonds, a final glint of light slicing from the blade and then covered forever by green and flowing water . . .*

"Free," I said, closing my eyes, amazed at how swiftly I'd been manipulated.

Jeremy walked over and stood beside me at the window, surprising me by laying a reassuring arm around my shoulders, pulling me tight. "The people Bobby Lee wants to kill are already dead, Carson. That was the terrible clanging in Bobby Lee's head: He needed to kill people he thought had wronged him, but they were already in the ground. I have no idea who they were, Brother, God's truth. But you can't kill someone twice, right?"

"You've not seen Crayline since the Institute?" I asked.

A half-beat pause. "Not a blink's worth. He was at the Institute two months, Carson. It's like you said, I got to know him because I wanted to get in his head. Everyone needs a hobby."

"So you haven't . . ."

Jeremy squeezed my shoulder. "Haven't spoken a word to Bobby in years. I'm happy he's dead, Carson. I expect he's happy he's dead, too."

The room seemed to close in and I could take no more of the darkness inside my brother's home. I turned and exited the cabin, shaking loose from Jeremy's spell, letting the sun burn his words away. It felt like escaping a darkly enchanted castle, where fierce dreams whirled and fought in the charged air. I breathed deeply, wondering how I'd again let his words pull me into his obsessions.

Walking back to my cabin I heard tires crunching gravel at my back, turned to see Krenkler in a dark sedan piloted by one of her drones. I turned as the car pulled beside me, Krenkler looking out through the window and folding a stick of gum into her mouth.

"If you think you got your beauty sleep, Ryder, think again. You look terrible."

"Always a pleasure to see you, Agent Krenkler. Might I ask the reason for the delight of your company?"

"There's a 2008 Fleetwood Discovery in the Haunted Hollow Campground, empty and locked. The campground manager ID'd a pic of Crayline as the owner. Now that we know who to show photos of, we're finding out Mr Bobby Lee C stayed at every campground in the area, two days here, three there. He kept moving. You nailed his hideout."

"I stumbled on to it."

"That's a big shiny box he was driving. Expensive. He made good money, I figure, as the one-time head honcho of SFL."

"XFL – Extreme Fight League."

"Whatever. We're more interested in his current history. Like why did he spend his money living in an RV and killing people? And did he do it other places?"

"Damn good question." Fifty-four per cent of all murders went unsolved. A small percentage were serial killings, madmen – and occasionally women – skulking in the dark and taking lives. It was very possible Woslee County wasn't the first place Crayline visited. Or perhaps it was his shake-down cruise. I wondered if that was why he'd alerted the Bureau, his maniacal ego figuring if he could kill with the Feds around, he could kill anyone, anywhere.

Krenkler continued: "Did you know Crayline is under suspicion of gunning down three people in his home county in Alabama? Someone shot them four years ago, a rage shooting, the bodies riddled like Swiss cheese."

I nodded. Krenkler said, "I take it you also know why Crayline went to prison the last time?"

"He abducted the only guy who ever beat him in a fight."

"Mad Dog Stone. How's that for a name? Crayline

tossed the poor schnook in a pit and fed him garbage. Guess ol' Bobby Lee Crayline hated to lose. But he lost to you, Ryder."

"Is there a point here, Agent Krenkler?"

"I also wanted to tell you Soldering-iron Man was Charles Bridges, the guy who pissed off Crayline at the Alabama crazy hospital. Like you said, Mr Bridges did occasional work for Dunham, Krull and Slezak."

"You spoke to Slezak?"

Krenkler's nose wrinkled. "I spoke to him personally. It reminded me of what it must be like to talk to a grease pit."

"Good description," I said, meaning it.

"Thank you. One more thing you might like to know. Something we dug up from a long time ago back in ol' Alabammy. Ever hear of the Marshmallow test?"

I saw a mind picture: a bespectacled experimenter holding a bag of marshmallows while talking to a child sitting at a small desk.

"The Bing Nursery School studies at Stanford," I affirmed, wondering what the hell it had to do with Bobby Lee Crayline. "Young kids were offered treats, like candy or marshmallows. An experimenter gave them a choice: eat one marshmallow right then, or wait for the experimenter to leave the room and return fifteen minutes later. If they waited the full time, they got two marshmallows."

"An experiment in patience?" Krenkler asked. "Or maybe self-control? Most kids popped the treat straight away, right?"

"What's truly being observed is the child's ability to reason," I corrected. "To create a situation where they can out-think their own need for immediate gratification to gain the larger reward. Some did it by covering their eyes, or looking away, or singing, or playing games with their fingers. What does this have to do with Crayline?"

Krenkler consulted some notes on her lap. "Back in the early eighties a psych class at Alabama U. replicated the test with children in the rural Talladega Mountains. One of the test cases was Crayline. I guess Crayline's screwed-up parents heard the test paid a stipend, used the kid to make a few bucks."

I pictured a skinny, poorly nourished Bobby Lee diving on the treat like a hawk on a sparrow, jamming it down his gullet with unwashed hands. "I take it Bobby Lee devoured the marshmallow and maybe the experimenter's hand?"

"Listen to this, Ryder: when the experimenter told Crayline one marshmallow now or two in fifteen minutes, the kid looked up and asked, 'How many do I get if I sit here until tomorrow?'"

"What?"

"The researchers put Bobby Lee to the test with a dozen marshmallows. Not all night, of course. But three hours."

"Crayline waited *three hours* to pounce on the candy?" It was unheard of.

"The kids are observed through a one-way mirror, naturally. When the experimenter left the room, Crayline closed his eyes and didn't move a muscle for three hours."

"Jesus."

"The prof said he'd never seen anything like it. They might have let the test continue, but little Bobby was starting to spook them."

I pictured Bobby Lee Crayline sitting motionless at the table, the delicious reward an arm's length away. It seemed to defy everything I knew of the man.

Krenkler continued. "So either Crayline has enormous willpower and self-control . . ." she let the words hang, waiting for my conclusion.

"Or he could invent an interior world so lavish that time meant nothing. When he stepped inside himself, time stopped."

"How's that for weird?" Krenkler asked. "Anyway, thought you'd like to know."

I couldn't tell whether Krenkler actually thought I should know that tidbit about Crayline, or she just wanted to display the FBI's power to dig. Like maybe I'd made contributions to the case, but she wanted me to know that the Bureau was on top, nonetheless.

Did it matter?

The sedan kicked gravel and spun away. I stiff-legged my way back to the cabin, made fruitless calls to the local animal shelters, and finally went to bed.

# 38

I awoke at four in the afternoon and called Cherry, asked what she was up to now that the threat of Bobby Lee Crayline had blown past like a hurricane. The destruction had been severe, but all that remained was the mopping up.

"Krenkler's got me studying Crayline's backstory," she said. "Still trying to find the connection between him and the victims, other than Charles Bridges."

"Where you going to start?"

"By thawing a couple of steaks."

"Excuse me?"

"I also have some potatoes the size of footballs. Two, to be exact. Know anyone with an appetite?"

It was unsettling to re-visit Cherry's drive and see Crayline's tire impressions in the grass, two straight lines that disappeared off the cliff. I saw the tree that had stopped me dead, peeling off my front fender. My truck looked disheveled, but ran fine, a trouper.

Cherry met me on the porch.

"Nice to see you arrived fully dressed. And without company. You hungry?"

I was ravenous. I followed her into her home. We polished off a beer and ate soon thereafter, planks of rare meat and fluffy Idahos with butter, sour cream and crumbled bacon troweled within. In twenty minutes I filled a six-month cholesterol quota.

We headed into the living room, the windows wide. The rain that had bedeviled me last night was paying penance by freshening the grass and trees and filling the air with a gentle balm of chlorophyll.

"I've got to do a little homework yet today, Carson," she said. "If I can keep feeding Krenkler information, I figure she'll book back to Washington. I think with the threat gone, her thrill's gone."

She pulled a canvas bag from beneath the swing, shaking a clattering handful of DVD boxes to a small table. I saw slick photos and graphics and titles like *XFL Championship III: The Battle in Seattle*, and *XFL Highlights: Blood in the Cage*.

"From a video store in Winchester," Cherry said. "I don't know jackshit about Crayline. So I wanna see him moving. Hear his voice. I want to look at the audience. You think that's strange?"

"I understand completely." It was the way I worked: suck up detail like the mother of all vacuum cleaners and learn the quarry on a cellular level. Though Cherry's perp was dead, his history was a living entity, and she could follow it like a trail if she was diligent or lucky or usually – I'd found from experience – a combination of both.

We watched six of the seven bouts Cherry had rented, taped after Crayline became one of XFL's rising stars, a man who deserved his own specials. He won them all in brutal fashion. And even when hit hard – punched, kicked, pummeled – he always roared back as if pain were fuel. Or maybe pain was just a passing sensation, like mild hunger, or the errant thought of a long-dead acquaintance.

His countenance was always one of anger – deep, visceral, frightening. The only time we saw anything bordering on happiness was when Crayline was with a guy who looked like a body builder with a hefty jewelry and Armani suit allowance. Twice we saw Crayline wrap the guy in a bear hug after winning a match.

"You catch who the suit with the steroid shoulders is?" I asked.

"Mickey Prince, the owner of the XFL. The P.T. Barnum of extreme sports or whatever. Likes cameras, being in *People Magazine*, stuff like that. Big shoulders. Bigger mouth."

Cherry reached to the floor and picked up the final DVD, tossed it to me.

Emblazoned over the cover were the words, *XFL World Championship XII: River of Blood*.

It was the championship bout. The only fight Crayline ever lost.

Cherry fast-forwarded through announcer hype to the introduction of the fighters in the cage: Bobby Lee Crayline and Jessie "Mad Dog" Stone.

Stone was not a tall guy, five-ten or so, but he resembled a doctor's anatomical wall chart covered with a film of tanned and oiled flesh. His face was square and looked younger than the body somehow, even with cauliflower ears and a nose lowered and fattened by repeated breaks.

The clang of a bell. Stone and Crayline circled, firing jabs, attempting kicks, measuring one another. Crayline dumped a couple hard shots in Stone's direction, the blows dying on Stone's big forearm. Stone shot back, catching Crayline in the side of his head, causing him to go for the clinch. I saw Crayline grinning as he jabbered into Stone's ear, jumped back, firing a kick at Stone's head.

The bell pulled the fighters to their corners for mop-up and various instructions. Stone seemed to listen to his corner man; Crayline just aimed eagle eyes across the ring at Stone.

The next round started. Another clinch, Stone pressed against the cyclone fencing of the cage, Crayline's mouth running like a set of chattering toy teeth. In the background the crowd was in bloodlust, howling, screaming, waving fists. Men built like XFL fighters stood beside guys looking like they lived on lard fondue.

"What an audience," Cherry said. "These people would have loved the Roman Coliseum."

A flurry of blows. Stone feinted left, dodged right. Stepped forward with an uppercut, his cleanest shot of the match. It knocked Crayline two steps backward and allowed Stone the straight-arm punch that set Crayline on his ass. Crayline tipped over, his mouth spitting red foam across the mat. The camera zoomed in tight to adore the spectacle.

When the referee called the fight in Stone's favor the crowd, predictably, went rabid. Stone's people came into the cage, wrapped him in a robe. Crayline was below the raised cage, being led away by handlers, wiping his face with a towel. He paused to again hug Mickey Prince.

"Wait," Cherry said. "Look at Crayline."

Cherry paused the machine on Crayline's face. He had turned back to look into the cage as Stone gave his victory speech. Crayline wore not the expected look of defeat, but a strange and smirking triumph, the oddest face I'd seen on a man beaten in a fight.

Almost six months from that day, Jessie Stone would be discovered in a deep-dug hole in a barn in West Virginia, imprisoned in filth and fed garbage, and only by good fortune rescued from death at the hands of Bobby Lee Crayline.

Was Bobby Lee Crayline already planning his revenge?

"We're out of tapes," Cherry said, punching off the player. "Which is good, because I'm sick of looking at

Bobby Lee Crayline, though I get the feeling he'll be much on my mind until this case gets put to bed."

She gathered the tapes and put them in a brown grocery bag, shoved the bag under the couch.

"There. Now I don't have to look at the damn things."

I checked my watch. Barely eight p.m.

"There's a lot of night left," I said. "What should we do now?"

"I'll pour us a cognac," she said quietly. "Seems that's where we left off last night."

I heard bees.

# 39

"You know what I can't get out of my thoughts?" I asked Cherry.

"I surely do," she replied. "Not that I mind."

The sun was rising and Cherry's home was redolent of fresh-brewed coffee. Her cup was on her bedside table, mine in my hand as I sat cross-legged, sipping and thinking.

I laughed. "Beyond that."

She pulled the sheet over her face in mock exasperation. "You're about to talk work, aren't you?"

"Sorry."

She popped out with a sigh. "Lay it on me. Uh, I mean continue."

"Bobby Lee never had a good word for anyone that I can discern. But he was hugging that Prince guy like a brother."

"And?"

"I wonder, did Bobby Lee ever have a confidant?"

"I can't imagine it."

I couldn't either. But I also knew that for a brief period in the Institute, Crayline had confided bits of his past to my brother and was even, at one point, moved to weeping. The public tends to view serial killers as freaks of nature, which is wrong. They're almost always freaks of nurture, or non-nurture, to be specific, coming from families and backgrounds so dysfunctional and often savage that the average person would find it hard to believe such treatment could be given an animal, much less a human being. Usually, the killers' humanity got destroyed along the way. They might hurt and kill with impunity, but sometimes, deep within, beat a morsel of heart that craved contact with reality.

"I think you ought to talk to this Prince guy," I told Cherry. "It's possible Crayline confided in him."

"Oh sure, Crayline told Prince he was going to kill people."

"Not that. But maybe something to help us unlock Crayline. I remember Slezak saying the XFL was operated out of Louisville. How far is that from here?"

"Two hours. This means I have to get dressed, right?"

"Not quite yet."

Before we committed to the trip, a friendly voice had called the organization, representing a company wanting to deliver Mickey Prince a case of steaks, the caller figuring

Prince got lots of yummy gifts from people wanting to cash in on his success.

"Prime filets frozen in dry ice, ma'am," the caller had claimed. "Will Mr Prince be in today to take them home? Or should we wait delivery to another day?"

"Mista Prince is in the oh-uh-fus until tomorra aft'noon," the receptionist had trilled in an accent thick enough to cause the caller to picture her in an ante-bellum dress and sunbonnet, sitting side-saddle in her chair. "He'll be dee-lighted. Mista Prince luuuves a good steak."

By ten thirty we were standing in the Louisville lobby of X-Ventures. The receptionist was not as pictured. "Did y'all have an appointment with Mr Prince?" the woman challenged, not calling up hoop skirts and bonnets. This Clydesdale-sturdy woman conjured images of Slavic prison guards named Ulga, only with nattier tailoring.

"Appointments are so gauche," I told Ulga, trying a lighthearted approach. "They impair spontaneity."

Humor was not her métier. "Mister Prince is a busy man. You must have an appointment."

"I understand. But inform Mr Prince that we're here, please. In case he finds an opening in his schedule."

"And exactly whom shall I say is calling?"

We showed our badges. Ulga made a phone call. She said nothing, just pointed us toward the back of the building, through the gym area. I suspected it was for effect, to show visitors this wasn't an accounting firm. It was obvious a re-location was in progress, large moving boxes stacked in corners, several of them with the THIS END UP arrow pointing at the floor.

We walked down a fenced-off corridor to the side. A round fight ring centered the gym, in it a compact black guy was chasing a towering white guy backwards with a series of snap kicks. We passed a man whose torso was blue with tattoos, punching a wall-mounted board wrapped with sisal rope. His knuckles looked like raw meat. Two guys with shaved heads and brick-muscled bodies stood beside the guy, bellowing, *Go! Go! Go!*

There were another dozen fighters either working on strength machines or pumping iron, huge stacks of weights clanking up and down. A couple more were in a corner doing sit-ups. The room reeked of sweat and liniment and socks rotting in lockers.

Cherry wrinkled her nose. "This place smells like where stink was invented."

A door opened in a windowed office at the far end. The man who stepped out resembled Sylvester Stallone, only re-decorated for the new millennium. His glossy black hair was carefully cut to make it look carelessly cut. Diamond studs brightened the ear lobes. Though slender of waist, Prince's shoulders looked wide enough to lay dinner settings for two, and I took it the CEO spent time aplenty in the gym. He wore a dazzling sky-blue suit and an embroidered silk shirt open to display a tanned and fluffy chest. The requisite gold chains nestled in the fluff.

"Let's not lead with Crayline's death," I side-mouthed.

"See how it works out. And if I get weird with accusations, play along."

"*Si, Jefe,*" Cherry mouthed.

The man walked up, hand out. "I'm Mickey Prince," he announced. It was unnecessary, as a large nameplate beside the door proclaimed his name in four-inch silverflake letters.

"We got a couple questions about a fighter, Mr Prince," I said. "No big deal."

"Hey, if Alberto Ventura beat up his girlfriend again, I don't want to hear. I'm sorry I signed his work papers. Send his sorry ass to the border and kick it back into Mexico."

"Don't know Ventura," I said, turning to eyeball the boxes. "Looks like you're moving."

"Vegas. Be gone in two weeks. Got four full floors on top of one of the biggest buildings on the strip. We're negotiating to buy the building."

I hoped there were good breezes high up on the new building. Maybe if they opened the windows the new place wouldn't smell like the old one.

Prince said, "OK, you're not here about Ventura, so lemme guess. Did Ironman Michaels bust up a hotel room again?"

Cherry said, "We're here about Bobby Lee Crayline, Mr Prince."

Prince's smile turned sour. "Bobby Lee never ever calls me. I always tell you guys I'll let you know if he tries to get in touch. Why keep bugging me?"

Prince was thinking we were asking if Crayline had been in touch. I imagine he got called monthly by the investigators in Alabama.

A big fighter who'd been kicking a bag a couple dozen feet away saw Prince's unhappiness and appeared beside us. His neck was tattooed and his face looked like a shark.

"Need any help, Mr Prince?"

Cherry whipped out her shield, held it to the shark. "Private conversation, sweet-ums. Beat it before I ask your name and check your priors."

The guy flared his nostrils as if breathing fire and slumped away. Prince nodded to the door at his back. "Let's take this to my office."

Which turned out to be a ponderous mahogany desk in a room cluttered with more boxes. He pulled a pair of folding chairs to the front of the desk, then sat in a black leather Herman Miller chair that looked as if it had been stripped from a jet fighter.

"You started out here?" Cherry asked. "In Louisville?"

"Over ten years back. The gym's gonna stay open, one of our franchise training spots. We're gonna have three dozen across the country by next year."

"Sounds like you make decent money," Cherry said.

"No," Prince smiled. "We make big money."

"Kinda big?" I asked. "Or kick-ass big?"

Prince leaned back in his sleek seat. "Last XFL bout on pay-per-view TV? We had one point seven million tune-ins at fifty bucks per. Plus we got magazines, posters,

T-shirts. Action figures are next. And I haven't even added in the arena revenue."

"What kind of audience do you have?" I asked.

"Guys hot for action. Young guys, mainly. The best demo out there."

"Demo like short for demonstration?" Cherry said, mystified by marketing-speak.

"Demo like demographic: age, income, education. There's also the psychographic . . . basically the mindset of the consumer. What he or she needs to feel fulfilled."

"Violence," Cherry speculated. "Men tearing one another apart."

"Action," Prince corrected. "The real stuff." He pointed through the window to the gym. In the round ring, two men were helping another man to his feet. Blood was dribbling from his mouth. The man who'd caused the leakage was leaning against the ropes, idly scratching his six-pack belly.

"This ain't sports entertainment, like pro wrestling. These fuckers go at it like pit bulls because (a) the money's good, and (b) they need to beat the shit outta another guy."

"Need to?" Cherry asked.

"A lotta those guys got hornets in their heads. Issues, you know? Fighting lets the hornets sting someone else for a while. I spend half my time trying to keep their fighting in the gym and in the ring, not a nightclub or alley."

"Why's the ring round?" I asked, not unaware that traditional square boxing rings were oxymoronic.

"No corners to hide in," Prince said. "The crowd likes to see fighters fight, not catch their breath in corner clinches."

I looked over the floor, every body chiseled down to muscle, not an ounce of flab. "These guys live in the gym, Mickey?"

"If they wanna make it in the XFL they'll be here ten hours a day, minimum. They pump up their bodies, I pump up the image, get them looking right, named right."

"Excuse me," Cherry said. "Named right?"

Prince smiled, leaned back in the chair, put crossed legs atop the table doubling as a desk, showed us the bottoms of his sleek, gunmetal-gray loafers.

"A kid walks in here with a name like Lester Doodle, we change that shit to something like Bruce Cartwright, a cross from Bruce Lee and the cowboys on that show *Bonanza*. Now that's a fighter's name."

"You didn't change Bobby Lee Crayline's name."

"It's a great name already. Right away, you got the Southern feel."

I shot Cherry a near-invisible nod. Her turn. "Bobby Lee's got new problems on top of the kidnapping and deadly escape, Mr Prince," Cherry said. "Seems like he's suspect numero uno in three murders in eastern Kentucky and another three in Alabama."

Prince closed his eyes, sighed, and shook his head. He looked honestly saddened but maybe he was a good actor. I waited several seconds and added the second punch, the pile driver.

"Ain't it a crying shame, Mickey?" I said. "A lot of people dead, all because of the escape you helped plan."

Prince's eyes snapped open. "What?"

"We know you hired Slezak, Dunham and Krull to get Bobby Lee brought to the Alabama Institute for Aberrational Behavior. Bobby Lee escaped on a trip financed by your company. Coincidence?"

Prince's feet pulled from the table and slapped the floor. The chair rocketed upright.

"I had NOTHING to do with—"

"You may want to call Mr Slezak," Cherry said. "This time to defend you on an Accomplice to Murder charge."

Prince looked shaken. He'd expected the standard questions about contacts from his former employee, not being linked to the executions of two prison guards. Not the kind of PR any growing empire needed.

He hustled to the windows, closed the blinds. "No way I tried to spring Bobby Lee," he said. "I was trying to help him. Both times I only wanted to help him. You gotta believe me."

I gave Prince my most piercing cop stare. "I believe you, Mick. That you wanted to help Bobby Lee. But now I want you to help me."

Prince looked confused. "With what?"

"Bobby Lee died yesterday. He drove off a cliff while trying to kill me. I'm kinda interested in finding out why."

# 40

"Let's start with the chronology, Mick," I told a more-chastened Mickey Prince. "Tell me about Bobby Lee's first incarceration. His six-month sentence."

"It was an accident. He killed a man in combat."

"Oh?" Cherry said. "I thought he killed a man in an entertainment event."

"People die in boxing. People die in football. People die in bicycle races, for crying out loud. Do they spend six months in prison?"

"Crayline didn't go to prison," I corrected. "Because of his history of violence, the judge sent him to the Alabama Institute for Aberrational Behavior for evaluation. They're prisoners in prison, Mickey. They're patients at the Institute, safe from each other and treated as humanely as their conditions permit. It's not close to prison."

"Yeah, you're right," Prince nodded. "I'll give you that."

Cherry said, "Then Bobby Lee got out and picked up where he'd left off: fighting. There were no problems with the audience because he'd killed a man?"

"Bobby became an even bigger star. Don't look at me like that. It's how things are."

"Let's move ahead, Mick," I said. "Bobby Lee fights for another couple years, winning every bout. Becomes a top XFL star, the champ. But then he loses a fight. It must have crushed him."

Prince shrugged. "No big deal. Jessie Stone was a damn good fighter, but Bobby was the best. Bobby would have won the next time. I woulda promoted it as a grudge match and everybody'd make even more money."

I pulled my feet from the table and went to lean against the wall beside Prince. I looked down on him while he had to crane his head up to talk to me. Control.

"Instead," I said, "Crayline suddenly quits and disappears. Six months later he kidnaps Stone and imprisons him in a pit, killing him through exposure and deprivation. Bobby Lee's sent to prison. But you pull political strings and get him returned to the Institute. You hire a high-caliber law firm—"

"I wanted Bobby to get real mental help," Prince said, actually sounding sincere. "I owed him, since he helped make me rich. Slezak wanted a shrink on Bobby Lee's case. Bobby Lee laughed and said, sure, try it out, figuring he'd never go under. Turns out hypnotizing Bobby Lee was easy as turning a light on and off. Dr Neddles pulled the story out in little pieces then put it together so it's

284

right in time. It's nasty shit. You really want to hear it all?"

"I think we can take it."

Prince started pacing, as though motion helped tell the story. He crossed and re-crossed the room as he spoke.

"Bobby Lee's daddy took off when he was five. His mama died of an OD a couple months later, at home. A relative stopped by one day, found Bobby Lee's mom on the couch half rotted away. They found the kid under the house, hiding in a root cellar."

"Lord," Cherry said.

"Bobby ended up with an aunt with mental problems and her husband. His uncle made a living staging cockfights and dogfights. The dogs lived in shit-filled cages. He starved the animals, beat them, zapped them with cattle prods."

"To make them better fighters," I said, my stomach going sour.

"Then one day . . ." Prince took a deep breath. "Then one day, the uncle wondered if an eleven-year-old kid could be made into a fighting dog."

I closed my eyes. Felt my guts turn over.

"To start with," Prince said, "the uncle made Bobby Lee live in a tiny dirt storm cellar. There was no light. Bobby pissed and shit in a washtub that got emptied maybe once a week. The uncle fed him scraps. Beat him to get him used to pain."

"Who the hell could an eleven-year-old fight?" Cherry asked, aghast.

"Other kids. Bobby never knew where they came from.

Once every couple months he'd be yanked out of the basement and trucked off, sometimes on the road for hours, to an old barn or abandoned mine tipple. Other kids would be there, fighters."

"Were there gloves? Rules?"

"The kids fought naked except for athletic cups to protect their balls. The fighters didn't have names, numbers were pinned to the cups. The kids were put in a long, narrow pit – they nicknamed it the grave – and beat the shit out of each other while the audience bet on the action."

"No kid said, I'm not doing it?" I asked.

Prince's eyes rose to mine, held. "You know what a breeder does to a dog that won't fight? Kids that didn't fight weren't ever seen again."

"How long did this go on?"

"Three years. Then the uncle welshed on a gambling debt. Got his throat slit one night. Bobby Lee was sent off to a group home. Later, of course, he showed up here. Looking to fight professionally. I gave him a spotlight. He made himself a star."

Prince fiddled with his chains. Cherry and I sat in stunned silence until a question crossed my mind. "The time he returned from his first trip to the Institute, Mickey. How was he during that period?"

"I was hoping he'd be calmer. But Bobby Lee seemed even angrier."

"Angry because he'd killed a man?" Cherry asked. "Self-anger?"

Prince looked drained, exposed. He sat heavily.

"Look, Detectives, I'm not a bright guy in math and geography and all that. I couldn't tell you where in the water Hawaii is, and I don't care. I know about people, like I can see through doors most people can't. It helps me understand my fighters and how to shape them according to what they need. With Bobby it was different. He got to be champ, but that wasn't what he needed. He needed something else. I'm not sure I can explain."

"Try," I said.

"I always needed to be rich," Prince said, almost like an apology. "It took time, but now I am. It feels good and makes me happy. But I think, what if God opened the clouds when I was poor and said, 'Mickey, I hate to tell you this, but no matter what you do, you're always gonna be poor as dirt.'" Prince raised his eyes to me. "That's the feeling I got from Bobby. Does that make any sense?"

"Like Bobby Lee Crayline knew something was to be forever denied him?" I said.

"Yeah. Exactly. Just like that."

Cherry aimed the big cruiser back toward Woslee County. We didn't know the Whys of the murders, but we were steadily discovering the Who of Bobby Lee Crayline. I pulled my ballcap down over my eyes, leaned back, and tried to dope-out what had been denied Bobby Lee, getting nowhere. Around Lexington Cherry broke my haze with a question.

"The kidnapping – how did Crayline get found out?"

"Pure luck," I yawned. "A surveying firm was determining the best route for a gas pipeline. One of the workers needed permission to survey a corner of the farm Crayline was renting. The worker ignored about a dozen *No Trespassing* signs, and walked the long drive to the house and barn. He was about to walk into sight when he saw Bobby Lee, buck naked except for a jockstrap, step into the barn. He watched Crayline pull some boards off a hole in the dirt floor and start yelling into it. The surveyor scooted and told his tale to the law. Why?"

"I was just thinking . . . Crayline was going to kill the guy he kidnapped. Was it revenge for beating him up in front of an audience, you think?"

"I think Crayline always needed to win, no matter what Prince said. Bobby Lee's driven to come out on top."

"So why didn't Crayline finish up where he left off? With the guy he left off on?"

I pulled my cellphone, rang the number for X-Ventures. Got through to Prince. He started with, "Please tell me you figured out I had nothing to do with Bobby Lee's escape or anything else."

I said, "You're dealing straight, Mick. But we got to thinking, what if Crayline wanted to pick up where he left off. With the Stone guy."

"Too late. Jessie Stone's somewhere in Ireland. He booked after Bobby Lee busted out. Maybe now he can come home."

I thanked Prince and rang off. Cherry shot me the questioning eye. I said, "It seems Jessie Stone retreated to the Emerald Isle to avoid seeing Bobby Lee again."

"Probably the smartest thing the guy ever did," Cherry said.

We crossed the Woslee County line at seven thirty p.m., putting at our backs a company that created fighting humans in much the way that Bobby Lee Crayline's uncle bred fighting dogs, though Prince did it with his fighters' consent and without deprivation and cruelty. There was a ready market for bloody combat, though the dog- and child-fights were hidden away in backcountry arenas while those who satisfied their bloodlust on national pay television made millions of dollars.

But at base, they seemed to me the same.

Cherry had been thinking along the same lines. "Prince reckoned people paid fifty bucks to watch two guys knock each other senseless in a cage," she said. "Did I hear that right?"

I nodded.

"And Crayline was an even bigger draw after knocking a guy dead in the ring?"

"Sure enough."

Cherry thought a long time. Shot me a glance. "You ever read any early human history, Ryder?"

"Some."

"Ever come across the theory about two main proto-human tribes way back there? One was cruder and less evolved, the other smarter and more advanced? And how the advanced tribe conquered the lesser beings, then went on to become who we are today?"

"I recall the theory," I said.

"You ever think maybe the other tribe won?"

# 41

We stopped by my place and I got the same answer on Mix-up.

"He's probably dead," I said. "Or taken by someone."

"He's a big dog, Carson," Cherry said, patting my back. "On size alone he probably scares the coyotes. And, uh, he's not the sort of adorably cute critter people want to snatch up. He's out there and he'll come back."

I nodded, thankful for Cherry's optimism, but not convinced. We returned to her place. "I'm going over the lives of Burton, Tanner and Powers with a fine-tooth comb," she said. "Find out what they could possibly have had in common with Crayline, where paths crossed . . . It's a nightmare."

"It's tough," I sympathized, yawning. "But basic detective shoe leather. I usually start with interviewing neighbors, move on to—"

Cherry interrupted me by taking my hand. She led me outside, pointing to the west. "What do you see?"

I smiled, unsure of what was happening. "Uh, mountains, more mountains. Trees, valleys."

"And all around us? East, North, South?"

"More of the same."

"Woslee County is almost three hundred square miles of area, Carson. With a population under six thousand people. The biggest town is Campton, four hundred people strong. The tallest building is three stories. There's two small apartment complexes, a few trailer courts. Most everyone else is scattered over the remaining three hundred square miles. People come and go as they please, no eyes around to see. Except for a few nosy-parkers, no one keeps tabs on anyone else."

"Ah," I said, getting her drift. "Not a lot of neighbors to interview."

"It's hard for urban folks to have secret lives; they're surrounded by casual onlookers, curious eyes, surveillance cameras. They might have a hundred neighbors in a single apartment wing. In country as sparse as this, secret lives are a lot easier. Bobby Lee Crayline could have dated Tandee Powers for all I know. Or played poker at Sonny Burton's house three nights a week. The thing is, no one would ever know. I can't get that through Krenkler's head."

"Sorry. I didn't realize."

She kissed my cheek. "You're forgiven. But only because you're cute. I've got to take the sparse input on the vics and squeeze it like a stone, see if I can get out that little extra juice that turns the case. All in between Krenkler's running me ragged."

I went to the porch swing and sat, doing my part to revisit the cases. In my head I listened to people we'd interviewed, re-walked the murder scenes. Ten minutes later I was replaying my tag-along to Berlea Coggins's house and the input from the Tongue.

"I want to visit Mr Tongue again," I said.

"Miz Coggins's daddy? I thought he bounced off Powers a few times and that was that."

"I remember him saying he gave her up because she got too nasty for him. I thought he meant her lesbian tendencies. In retrospect, I'm thinking it would take more than that to be nasty to Coggins."

"You think you can get the old letch to open up?"

"Reply hazy, ask again later. I'll need to be alone with him."

Cherry checked her watch, "Berlea's been trying to get me to lunch or supper for eons. I know she wants to give me a good proselytizing. Maybe there's still time tonight. That's all you need . . . me to get her gone for a while?"

"I need pornography," I said, building my plan on the fly. "Lots of porn."

She shook her head. "You mean like movies? Pardon me if I'm naïve, but it's not exactly my field of interest."

"Movies. Magazines. Anything and everything. Magazines for sure. I need to flash them."

"You mean *Penthouse, Hustler,* that kind of thing?"

"I need the ugly stuff. The kind of thing you can smell from across the room."

"Jeez, Ryder, you're making my stomach turn."

I clapped my hands. "That's exactly what I need. Got access to any?"

She tapped her chin with a delicate digit. "No local place would carry it, the church types would reach critical mass. I've found plenty porn in busts. Seems preferred reading at meth labs and among dope dealers. I carry the crap to the garbage bin with tongs, pitch it out. There's an X-rated bookstore on Interstate 75, about an hour away. Or you can get it in Lexington."

"No time. Not if we want to try today."

I saw a light dawn in Donna Cherry's eyes. She dialed her cellphone. "Hang tight, Ryder. If there's any sleazy, greasy porno around, I know where it's at."

Cherry had planned to re-stock her fridge tonight until waylaid by new plans, so she ran off to do that while I scratched through the notes for the hundredth time. A half-hour later I heard a vehicle outside, opened the door. It was Caudill, carrying a paper shopping bag.

"Special delivery," he said, looking embarrassed.

"What do you have for me, Judd?" I asked, rubbing my hands together.

Caudill pulled a six-inch stack of magazines from the bag, followed by a dozen DVD cases. "Sheriff Beale keeps a big batch of the porno we turn up. He goes through, selects out what he wants and hides it in an evidence box with a fake case number. Everyone knows it's there, but the sheriff thinks it's his big secret."

"You have to get it back?"

"It's a big evidence box. I don't think he'll miss a teensy bit like this."

I looked at the material. On top was a DVD with a pair of leering women dressed as nurses, tight, low-cut uniforms overflowing with silicone breasts. The ladies appeared to be taking the air's temperature with their tongues. The title was *Oral Medication*. The teaser proclaimed, *Take as needed and as often as necessary!* I shuffled through the rest, saw titles like *Boob Madness. Anal Holiday. Pink Dreams. Spurtfest IV* . . .

I shifted my attention to the magazines. *Wet Candy. Bush Fever. Triple-X Panty Party* . . .

"Pure hot raunch-a-roni," I said, clapping Caudill on the shoulder. "Well done."

# 42

We had a little luck for a change. Berlea Coggins was delighted to be asked to a restaurant by Cherry. We figured I had two clear hours with her daddy. I gave Cherry a bit of lead-time and showed up at the Cogginses' house carrying a briefcase borrowed from Cherry. It bulged.

The old man opened the door and looked up, the oxygen hose dangling from his nose.

"Whatcha need?"

"I need to ask a couple more questions about Tandee Powers, Mr Coggins."

He rolled backwards, invited me inside with a flap of his hand. "I told you 'bout Tandee. She loved this." He drooped out the tongue again, let it flap against his collar.

"What woman wouldn't," I said. "Tell me more."

"Ain't nothing to tell. We got hot and we hooked up when we got the chance. In a car down a lonesome road, or a room in one of them gambling places on the river. We didn't talk a whole lot, you get my drift."

"Did you know any of her other friends? Zeke Tanner, maybe? Sonny Burton?"

His eyes flicked away. "I seen Burton a time or two. He was a big ol' boy, mean in spite of all that toothy grinnin'. That's all I knew. Tanner was a bigmouth preacher full of big talk. I know what ever'one else does cuz Tanner and Burton live around here. Or did. Listen, mister, I got my programs about to come on the TV. I gotta go watch."

"Sure. Just one fast question before I go. Tandee was hot, right?"

Coggins did the open-close hand thing again. "That pussy loved to exercise."

I leaned against the wall, crossed my arms and affected perplexed. "Did Tandee finally become too much for you to handle, Mr Coggins? You couldn't satisfy the woman's needs so you beat a retreat? I can understand how that might happen, you being older and—"

"Weren't never no woman I couldn't handle," he snapped.

"I'm confused," I said. "The other day you said Tandee had become too much for you. Those were your words."

"You need to get your ears cleaned out, mister. You missed half of what I said. I said she got too *nasty* for me. It ain't the same as too *much* for me."

"Too nasty for a man of the world like you?"

He frowned. "Some stuff ain't right."

"Gay stuff?"

He waved it away. "Tandee went both ways. I didn't. But sometimes it put another woman in bed with us, y'know. Some mornings I'd get up and my tongue'd be too tired to talk. I'd have to point at things."

"Tell me what Tandee Powers did. The stuff that wasn't right."

"I'm gonna go watch my TV," he said, rolling away. "You gotta git."

I stayed at his side. The TV remote, universal style, was lying on an overstuffed chair. I swept it into my pocket, followed Coggins.

"Mr Coggins, I think there were a lot of things going on back then. A closed little world with a few people who got deep into sex. Drugs maybe. Gambling. Were children involved in any way?"

"I'm a sick ol' man. Go away an' let me see my shows."

"Yeah, sure," I said, surrender in my voice. "Thanks for your time. Before I go, let me turn on the television for you."

"Do that, wouldya? I can't find the fucking remote. It was right here . . ."

While he patted beneath chair cushions I walked over to the equipment – monitor, DVD player, an old cassette player – stacked together on a shelf. Simple-looking gear, somewhat outdated, few buttons to figure out. Good.

I turned on the television while standing between Coggins and the equipment. I slipped a DVD from my jacket pocket, slid it into the player. I advanced the disk to an opening scene I found particularly artful. Hoping everything was set correctly, I pressed Play.

*Wet sounds, moans, the hiss of flesh over sheets, low throbbing bass line marking time in heartbeat tempo . . .*

Coggins's head jolted toward the sounds pouring from his television.

"Holy shit," he whispered.

On the screen a man with a tongue nearly as prominent as Coggins's was using it in the service of a twentyish woman with a truly amazing body and an unruly mane of blonde hair that shivered with every overblown moan. As if harmonizing, Coggins loosed a groan.

I hit Pause.

"Hey, keep that thing playing!"

I moved between the old man and the frozen image. "Been a while since you've seen anything like this, I take it?"

"I tried to get some hot stuff from mail-order," he panted, eyes unwavering from the stilled action. "Goddamn Berlea was right there when the mailman come. My name on the package and she's openin' it like it's hers. Now she gits the mail sent to a post office box and checks through it. My own flesh-and-blood daughter an' she's got the sex drive of a tube of toothpaste. She cain't understand what I'm goin' through, stuck in this chair and this house."

I made the jack-off motion. "You must have memories to work from."

"I used 'em up," he hissed. "I been thinking about that sweet Cherry ass. Only thing I got that's new, an'

I'm gettin' wore out on it." He strained sideways, trying to see past me at the screen. "Git that teevee started up again."

"First I want to show you some other interesting items."

I retrieved a magazine from the briefcase and opened it just out of grab range. I flipped through pages. "Oh my lord," Coggins wheezed, eyes wide. "I'm about to loose a load just looking. Slow down."

I set the magazines aside and opened the briefcase, showed him the thickness of the stack within. He was panting so hard I wondered if I should turn up the oxygen.

"They're yours, Mr Coggins. Hide them. Look at one magazine a day, one video a week. By the time you get through, the old ones will be new again."

"Gimme," he wheezed, his old claw grabbing for the pages like junk to an addict. "Pleeeeease."

"When you give me what I need."

"Whaaaat?"

I leaned back and set the magazines on the table, a foot from his reach. I popped the DVD from the player and set it atop the books with the others.

"I need history, Mr Coggins. History."

# 43

After a fifteen-minute conversation with Lester Coggins, I went to Cherry's office and waited in the lot. Two phone calls about dogs came through in ten minutes. After a few questions I determined neither was Mix-up. Cherry arrived twenty minutes later.

"Are you converted yet?" I said, stepping from my truck and handing back the borrowed briefcase, empty now.

She pushed open the door and we went inside. "I'm a believer, Ryder, but on my own terms. Fact and reason shouldn't negate faith, but enhance it. Why does religion have to be four hundred years behind everything else?"

"I'm not the one to ask about theology. I just finished whipping an elderly man into a sexual frenzy."

"Was it worth it?" she asked.

"You be the judge. Coggins ran with Powers for about two years, coupling like ferrets on Viagra. On back roads, in local motels, now and then grabbing a hot weekend at one of the casino boats on the Ohio River."

"We knew that from before."

"Powers also liked money a lot and spent it fast when she got it. Plus she had a thing for cockfights and dogfights. She loved the noise and action and being one of the few females in the crowd, a hundred men eyeballing her. One time she and Coggins attended a dogfight. Coming back, Powers alluded to being friends with folks in the biz, and suggested Coggins might put some of his money in a special investment."

"Dogs?"

"Powers got coy, called it an 'educational opportunity'. She alluded to risks, but the money came in hard and fast. She also added that the risks had recently been reduced. Something about being put under a star."

"Educational dogfights? Under a star? Doesn't make a lot of sense."

"We're lucky Lester Coggins remembered that much. He hears through his tongue. Anyway, the pair went back a week later. No fight, but caged dogs were visible. Powers was, according to Coggins, 'stoned about two planets away'. She laughed and said the place was a school."

"A school for dogs?"

"Coggins saw small sheds tucked in the trees. Standing in the doorways were a raggedy band of kids, a half-dozen boys, 'sulky looking', in Coggins's description. A couple of them had bandages on their faces. He thought the boys looked about as stoned as Powers."

"Coggins recognize the kids?"

"He thought he'd seen one around Campton a few times, a kid with the first name of Donald."

"Donald what?"

I shook my head. "Coggins remembers every sexual encounter he ever had because sex is all that's important in his life. The kids were just faces. He only remembered the kid's name because it reminded him of Donald Duck."

"I'd love to see this so-called school. Where was it?"

"Coggins had no idea. Powers did all the driving. He thought it was east somewhere."

"Daddy Coggins refused the offer to invest, I take it?"

"Coggins was a glutton for sex, not money. He made a good living as a union miner. Coggins blew Powers off by saying he couldn't get money without his wife finding out. They started drifting apart about then. Seems Tandee found a new significant other named – I need a drum roll here – Sonny Burton."

"I should have seen that one coming. When nasty meets nasty, is that nasty squared?"

"There's more. The night Powers took Coggins to the dogfight? There was a main parking area filled with cars. There was also a second lot tucked away behind the barn, something like VIP parking. There were a few cars and trucks there . . . and one large white step-van."

"Maybe Burton was already hanging around, you think? One of the originals? He's always had white delivery vans." She stepped to the window and studied

302

the distant peaks while rubbing her temples. "You know what this resembles, don't you?"

I nodded. "What Crayline went through in Alabama around the same time, eighteen to twenty years ago. Except there was nothing that could be called educational in Crayline's history."

"Education, education . . ." Cherry mumbled, scooting to her desk and riffling through the paperwork overload. She snapped a page from the heap and began reading.

"Tandee Powers was a substitute teacher, Carson. Almost twenty years ago. It didn't seem to agree with her, she taught at the local junior high a few dozen times. I checked all that, no ties anywhere. But she also filed for a home school certificate eighteen years ago, kept the papers active for five years. Zeke Tanner had teacher aspirations, too."

"Tanner?"

"I remember him talking about setting up a school when he first started as a preacher. Talking about adding a TV link to services, building a network, turning the church into a major venture like what's-his-name down in your state, Ryder. The chunky guy in the big scandal?"

"Richard Scaler." I recalled Scaler's empire, his college and TV outlet. Compared it with memories of Tanner's trailer-church, folding chairs in front of the pulpit that numbered less than thirty.

"Did Tanner do anything about the school?" I asked. "Like getting it off the ground?"

"Big dreams with no follow-through, that was Zeke.

As far as starting a school, you file an application. It's a formality. You don't need a teaching certificate, experience, anything. There are illiterates teaching home schools."

"Eighteen years back. Would there be a paper trail?"

She picked up the phone. "No one in the Kentucky bureaucracy ever throws anything away. It's finding it that's the trick – could take months. I've got a friend in the system and a favor to call in. Keep your fingers crossed."

"I'm running back to the cabin to check on Mix-up," I said. "Keep yours crossed, too."

We waved our crossed fingers at one another.

# 44

No sign of my dog. I fought the visions of wounded animals crawling from car strikes to die miserably at the side of the road and forced down a power bar for supper. I grew steadily angrier at my brother for luring me here. He'd wanted company and someone to keep the law from checking his background, and I'd nearly been killed and worse, lost my dog.

Jeremy hated any kind of pet – dogs especially – and his mention of poisoning Mix-up wouldn't leave my mind.

It was almost dusk when I crept through the woods behind his house, thinking I might push him on Mix-up, make sure he was telling the truth. Or maybe I just wanted him to give me an excuse to punch out a few of his lying teeth.

Now and then I take a mood.

But Jeremy's Subaru was gone. I checked my watch:

eight-fifteen. My brother often took late meals at a café five miles distant, fuel for a night scanning the Asian stock markets. When I turned to head back to the cabin, something stuck my feet in place and I felt a strange tingle in the pit of my belly.

What if I was wrong, though, and Jeremy *had* taken Mix-up?

I had visions of my dog imprisoned in Jeremy's version of the pit where Crayline had kept the hapless Jessie Stone.

I crouched low and ran to his yard, stepping from dense forest into manicured grass and neat beds of bright flowers. The doors and windows were locked tight, the door locks too complex for my simple abilities at picking. I stepped back and scanned his second floor. A back window to his office appeared lifted a few inches. I went to his tool shed and retrieved a twelve-foot ladder most likely used to clean leaves from his gutters, angled it against the roof. I listened for sounds and heard only the breeze in the leaves and the far call of a whip-poor-will.

Within a minute I was inside his office. I ran downstairs, opening doors, looking for a basement or even a large root cellar. Nothing. It hit me that the land here was a foot of topsoil over sandstone or limestone, not conducive to excavation. A fool's errand, I realized; desperation and fear. I scrambled upstairs to escape.

The computers hummed as the screensaver etched its endless line across the screen. A question came to mind:

Jeremy had alluded to making his money playing the market, but had also said he'd only learned about making money after his arrival here. My brother lied so often even he forgot when his falsehoods crossed paths.

I pulled close the chair and played my fingers over the keys. I had a few stocks of my own, a portfolio worth about enough to buy an entry-level car, but it provided a sense of control over my money. And it had given me an insight into reviewing charts and graphs and other financial records.

I discovered Jeremy's online trading accounts were password-protected, and my brother would never have used the birthdays and names common to most mnemonic passwords. He would simply have assigned each account a meaningless term and remembered it, his mind thriving on minutiae.

I studied the desktops in turn until seeing a file named TXREC. I opened it and found tax records: gains and losses and estimated quarterly taxes he needed to file. I stared for several seconds at the amounts of the gains. My brother was indeed a canny reader of the market.

I continued my fast scan until hearing an engine sound. I scrambled to the front window.

Jeremy!

His vehicle was canting down the road and approaching quickly, downshifting to turn the bend at his drive. I exited his file, pushed the chair into place. Heard the crunch of gravel beneath his wheels stop as he pulled to the gate. By the time my feet were feeling their way to the ladder

307

rungs, I heard the clatter of the gate chain as he undid the lock.

When my feet hit the ground, I heard him pull through the gate. Then stop to relock it. I started to slide the ladder closed, forgot the spring-driven stop mechanism. It slapped over a rung like bell. I winced, dropped the ladder to the ground and began feeding it into itself with one hand while the other held the mechanism from the rungs.

Jeremy pulled to the porch, less than forty feet away, on the other side of the house. His door was opening as I grunted the ladder to the shed. Ducking inside, I replaced the ladder on its wall mount, the sweat of fear pouring into my eyes.

His back door opened. I edged to the wall and found a slender crack between boards. My brother stepped outside and studied a thermometer mounted on a porch post. He nodded as if pleased by what the day was doing for him and went back inside. I slipped from the door, backed carefully away with the shed as my shield. In seconds I was back in the covering safety of the woods.

My scan of my brother's records confirmed what I'd suspected – none of the stock records pre-dated his arrival. He may have fostered his particular insights into the market before arriving, but had only profited once here.

Which sparked a curious question: Where had my brother gotten the money to buy his property?

# 45

McCoy was at my door the next morning at seven thirty, the normally composed master of the woods looking pale and distraught.

"What is it?" I asked, hobbling out to the porch while pulling on the second shoe.

He produced a small black laptop and tapped the keys. "The geocache website. I checked it out of habit a half-hour back."

He spun the screen to me. I leaned close and saw map coordinates, above them the dreaded symbol.

$$=(8)=$$

My heart sank. Crayline was dead. This couldn't be happening.

"Where is it?" I asked.

"Over by Star Gap. Donna's heading there now. She wanted me to show you this, then meet her there."

"It has to be some kind of joke," I said, stumbling into the vehicle, wondering if I was having a full-blown nightmare.

We returned to the Forest Service SUV and McCoy pulled up and out of the hollow. We were closing on the site fifteen minutes later, Cherry waiting and pacing, her face tight with tension. We followed McCoy, walking left, then right, guided by the arrow on the GPS screen. He angled around a house-sized boulder, arriving at a muddy clearing in the forest floor, the mud lightened by dissolving shale, gray, rarer in the area than the dark soil or sand that generally prevailed.

I heard McCoy gasp. Cherry ran up. Her lips moved but no sound came out. Caudill arrived and stopped dead in his tracks. He turned away and began hyperventilating.

I stepped into the clearing. Beale's naked body was on the ground. It took my mind several reality-bending moments to fathom the scene. What had been done to Beale was almost indescribable, requiring a sharp knife and hideous surgery.

"Is it him?" Cherry asked, only able to look at the body in glances. "We can't see his face without, uh . . ."

"Those are his tattoos," Caudill whispered. "It's the sheriff."

Cherry called the state forensics and medical people and asked for their most experienced team to unravel the nightmare of Sheriff Roy Beale.

310

"Why Sheriff Beale?" Caudill asked, shaken to his bootstraps. "What did he do?"

"An authority figure, maybe," I ventured. "Or a threat."

"There was nothing to Beale, threat-wise," McCoy said. "If the killer had only Beale to deal with, he could kill half the folks in the county before Beale Junior even noticed."

"Beale *Junior*?" I said.

"I thought you knew his daddy was sheriff, Carson," McCoy said.

"I do, I just never had to make connections to it before, see it on the timeline." I turned to Cherry. "Could old Sheriff Beale have known anything about the camp?"

Cherry said, "I heard a few bad tales about Beale's daddy, but every county sheriff makes enemies who—"

"I knew old Beale," McCoy interrupted. "If there was anything illegal going on, I expect he got paid for not noticing."

"He was that bad?" Cherry asked. "You never told me that."

"Old Beale was dead and gone. No sense spitting on his memory."

Something stirred in my mind. "Mooney Coggins recalled Powers talking about 'being put under a star'," I ventured. "Could that have meant a protective alliance with old Beale . . . the sheriff paid to overlook the camp?"

McCoy did the money-whisk. "If there was enough of this in the picture, I expect Beale senior would have pretended that part of the county didn't exist."

I re-thought the situation with the new input. I walked from behind the boulder and studied the savaged corpse for a few seconds.

"What's another term for not seeing what's in front of you?" I asked.

Cherry shot a glance at the wreckage of Roy Beale. Her eyes closed and her shoulders slumped.

"Having one's head up one's. . . ." She couldn't finish.

"I rest my case," I said.

# 46

If Krenkler and her crew had been in mop-it-up-and-hop-it-up to DC mode, they pivoted on that dime. We were summoned to the cabin by the park, told to the minute when we should arrive, which had Cherry mumbling under her breath as she took her seat at the conference table, awaiting an appearance by the woman she'd taken to calling The Peroxide Queen. Krenkler stood outside the cabin talking into two cellphones at once, her lacquered hair the only item not in frenzied motion. Three agents swirled around her bringing notes, coffee, chewing gum.

Caudill arrived as the sole representative of the Woslee force. He didn't look comfortable with command, pushing the furthest chair back even further and avoiding eye contact.

"Christ Jesus," Krenkler barked as she strode into

the room, looking at Cherry and me like we did this on purpose, producing a body after she had most likely told HQ the case was wrapping up. "How many nutcases are loose in this goddamn wilderness?"

"One more than Bobby Lee Crayline," I said. "At least."

She fed the red mouth a strip of Juicy Fruit and shot me the hard eye. "You got no anonymous calls this time, Ryder?"

She was flogging that horse again, obsessed with that damn call. "I'll answer for the next fifteen times you ask, Agent Krenkler, and I'll say it slow so you can understand it. I – never – received – any—"

"Not funny. Answer the goddamn question."

A light dawned in my head. "Wait a minute," I said, staring her full in the eye. "There's something you're not telling us, isn't there?"

She looked at the floor. I hadn't figured Krenkler capable of guilt, but there it was.

"What?" I pushed. "Out with it."

"Someone called us here anonymously," she said, rolling her eyes. "Just like you."

"Wait a minute . . . you're just now telling us that—"

"Sheriff Beale didn't call us in. I'm not sure Beale – rest his dull soul – could have found the FBI's telephone number without a guide dog. The Bureau got a call three days before Charles Bridges was found. The caller predicted a string of murders here and invited us to take a look. The Bureau gets more weird calls than Jerry Springer. By the time we checked into it, the victim now known as Charles Bridges had shown up. We called Beale and convinced him it was in his best interest to request our presence."

Cherry stared at Krenkler. If looks could kill, hers were cyanide laced with strychnine.

"What kind of lunatic killer invites the FBI to a killing spree?" I said. "And why didn't you share the information from day one, so we could all know—"

"Here's the way it's going to work," Krenkler barked, over-voluming my question. "Everything will continue to be run directly from this office with my full—"

"No way," Cherry said.

Krenkler froze as if slapped. Surprised faces turned toward Cherry.

"You surely weren't talking to me?" Krenkler said.

"I'm talking to exactly you." Cherry stood and put her palms on the table. "Detective Ryder and I may have found a new investigative path. We are going to look into it. WE, as in Detective Ryder and me. I can't have you treating people like ignorant savages because they don't live in a city, Agent Krenkler. We need them to talk, not stare at their shoes and mumble."

Krenkler snapped her gum like gunshots. "How good are you at running a cash register, Detective Cherry? You're digging your grave here, career-wise."

Cherry said, "Only if I screw up, and I'm not planning on screwing up. If we discover something, we'll tell you immediately, a gesture of professional respect you seen incapable of giving to us."

The room was as silent as the far side of the moon. The cluster of agents were too stunned to do anything but stare at the backs of their hands. Krenkler's voice dropped to a whisper.

"I'm not used to being spoken to like this."

Cherry said "Guess what, I've got four years of college, eight years of on-the-job training, a host of commendations. And I'm not used to being a copy machine."

Krenkler stared but found no response. Cherry nodded for me to follow and the door closed at our backs. "Tell me you have something," I side-whispered as we high-tailed it out of the cabin before Krenkler sent the agents after us. "Either that or I'm going to have to send you to store-clerk school."

Cherry nodded to her vehicle. Amazingly, she was smiling. She patted my back. "It's just wonderful what some folks can leverage with a handful of dirty pictures. Get in my ride and I'll show you what Powers meant by education."

We jumped in. Cherry pulled a few pages from her briefcase.

"A friend who's a clerk in a state office came in early and started digging for me, bless her bureaucratic heart. Turns out the state keeps a record of kids being home schooled so districts don't send out truant officers to the homes. It's just a list of names, but names nonetheless. I did some cross-checking, some elimination because of dates and ages, and presto . . ."

She snapped a page in my face with a flourish and

assumed a look of detectively success. That or she'd recently devoured a canary.

"Seven names from way back when . . ." she said. "Jessie Collier, Elijah Elks, Bemis Smith, Jimmie Hawkes, Creed Baines, Teeter Gasper, and Donald Nunn. Seven names of boys aged eleven through thirteen listed as attending the Solid Word home schooling and camp program under the stewardship of Ezekiel Tanner, pastor, the Solid Word Church of Campton, Kentucky."

My heart skipped a beat. Maybe several.

"Jesus, Cherry, you struck gold."

"Silver, maybe. Let me read what it says under Purpose. 'The Solid Word School Program and Wilderness Camp is a rigorous and extensive program of care and discipline designed to strengthen students in mind, body and spiritual teachings.' I've heard both Tanner and Powers talk and I can tell you that phrase got stolen from a legitimate home-school program somewhere."

"We've got to find those kids," I said. "They're the key."

"I've already started: Jessie Collier and Donald Nunn are deceased. Collier of an OD when he was twenty, thirteen years back. Nunn got shot in a drive-by in Ashland eight years ago; I'm thinking that he might be the Donald remembered by Daddy Coggins. I'm just crosschecking names and approximate ages with crime stats. Hawkes is in the state pen. Nothing yet on Smith and Nunn."

"Our only source is in prison?" I said.

"Maximum security at LaGrange."

"Which is where?" I asked.

She jammed the vehicle in gear, whipped away from the FBI cabins. "Buckle up. We'll be there in a couple hours. I got things covered."

We booked for the prison, me looking out the back window for the FBI every few miles. If it looked like a parade of hearses, it was them. But it appeared we were on our own.

Cherry knew the warden at LaGrange and arranged a private room for meeting Jimmie Hawkes, twenty-nine years of age, and a one-time student of the Solid Word home school and camp for disadvantaged children. I hoped Mr Hawkes would have plenty to say.

We stopped at the guard station outside the visitation room. A heavyset guard with caterpillar eyebrows sat at a desk absentmindedly thumbing through a Bass Pro Shops catalog.

"We're here to see Jimmie Hawkes," Cherry said.

The caterpillars flicked up from a page of camo hunting gear. "You ain't eaten recently, have you?"

"Could you explain that, please?" Cherry asked.

The guard walked to the control plate on the wall and pressed a button. The steel door at his back rolled open. "Hawkes is here for trying to rob a Korean grocery in Paducah. Trouble was, the store owner kept a twelve-gauge under the counter. The guy whipped that shotgun up and fired. Took the docs eight years just to git Hawkes where he is now."

"I can't wait," Cherry muttered.

We took our seats at the table. The door opened and Hawkes entered the room in profile, all we saw was the right side of his face. He seemed a series of jitters, each part of his body driven by a different rhythm, spasms in motion.

When he turned to us I heard Cherry stifle the gasp: Hawkes looked like a character from a Batman movie, if there'd been a character called Half-face or maybe just Nightmare. The shotgun blast had torn off the left side of his face from mid-cheekbone outward, blowing away bone, flesh, ear, hair, a third of the mandible.

The result was a face normal on one side of his nose, with no face on the other – just a sloping plain of gray scar tissue rebuilt in the rough shape of a head. There was nothing where his eye used to be, not so much as an indentation. I imagined the left side of his skull was some form of inner prosthetic. His skin resembled lizard hide. The right side of his mouth was normal, the left truncating in the scar, unable to close, making a permanent downcast hole.

"Jesus," Cherry whispered. I took her hand, squeezed it.

"Guards say you want to talk," Hawkes said in a strange, lisping rasp. "Got a half you want to talk to?"

# 47

"Home? What the fuck is a home, lady?"

Hawkes answered Cherry's opening question, asking where home was in his childhood. "Didn't have no home. Got run from place to place. Uncles, aunts, mamaw. I learned to stay outside, keep outta the way. Run in, EAT! Go back out, winter, summer, didn't matter. One day a preacher an' a sexy lady come around, said they was starting up a bible camp and they was gonna school ME for FREE." He turned in his chair and waved to an invisible woman. "BYE-BYE, MAMAW, YOU OLD WHORE."

Hawkes shivered and jittered. I wondered if the shotgun blast had left a bunch of wires hanging loose in his brain, sparking at random to cause the jumping and twitching.

"Did you like the idea of going off with Reverend Tanner and Miss Powers, Jimmie?" Cherry asked.

"Didn't give a sh-shit. I figured they'd send me some-where elst soon enough, like always."

"So you went to the Solid Word school."

"Words and turds, turds and words," Hawkes said, disgust on his half-face. "Dog turds, dogs everywhere. Barkin' and growlin' all the time. Everything stunk of dog turd. Never cleaned it up, just waited for the rain to wash it away."

"Tell us about the school."

"Started off nice. GOOD EAT! Lived in little house things. NO RAIN NO PAIN."

"Did you have school lessons?" Cherry asked.

"We learned this . . ." Hawkes jumped up and started throwing air punches. He spun to kick something only he could see. The man's kicks and punches were tight, hard, and controlled. He knew what he was doing.

"Sit, Jimmie," the guard cautioned. Hawkes sneered, but sat.

"You ended up fighting?" I asked.

"PIN A NUMBER ON YOUR DICK!" he bellowed into our faces, his breath treacherous. "BUST THEIR ASSES AND GET SOME EAT IN THE BELLY!"

"You fought and you ate?"

He backhanded away spit dripping from the keyhole mouth. "Food without maggots. Real EAT! EAT AND EAT MORE. DOPE AND WHISKEY AND GETTIN' ALL FRISKY! WIN AND FILL THE MOUTH-HOLE!"

"What happened when you lost?"

Hawkes stopped moving as if a spring mechanism had

321

spent its energy. His mouth drooped and his one eye turned inward. He became absolutely still.

"Coach'd come in and have his party," he said, turning away.

"The coach?"

Hawkes leaned back his head and screamed, "HERE COMES THE SNACK TRUCK!"

I turned to Cherry. The blood had drained from her face. "Is that what Coach said, Jimmie?" I asked.

Hawkes jumped up, planted his feet wide, made the motion of grabbing a head while being fellated. He knifed his hips forward and back. Grunted, "Here . . . comes . . . the . . . snack . . . truck . . . uhn, uhnnn, uh-HUUUGRG!"

"Did anyone ever try and get away, Jimmie?" I asked, holding up my hand at the guard, *Don't interfere*.

"Yesssssss," he hissed.

"Did they make it?"

Hawkes's single eye burned into mine. He made a throttling motion with his hands. "HE did this to a dog. Then HE hung Mister DOG from a TREE."

My mind's eye presented a limp canine swinging from a limb, the symbol of the failed escape. "It was to tell you what happened to the boy, right?"

Hawkes gestured me close with his forefinger. "Read the dog, mister," he whispered. "The dog knows the future."

"Who killed the dog, Jimmie?" Cherry asked. "The coach? The preacher?"

"The Colonel," he said.

"Colonel, Jimmie?"

322

Hawkes cupped his hand over his crotch. "PUT ON YOUR CUPS AND COVER YOUR PUPS," he barked, as if giving an order. "STICK A NUMBER ON YOUR DICK, BOYS! MAKE THE COLONEL SMILE!"

I said, "The Colonel was part of the camp?"

"YES-FUCKING-SIR, MISTER COLONEL! Colonel was always there." Hawkes did the money-whisk with both hands. "BIG FUCKING SUGAR! NO MAGGOT FOR THE COLONEL!"

"Maggots?"

"PREACHER-MAN WAS FOOD MAN. MAGGOTS AND SLOP AND PUKE 'TIL YOU DROP. WIN AND GET THE GOOD EAT!"

I glanced at Cherry, shook my head, turned back to Hawkes.

"What did the Colonel look like, Jimmie?"

Hawkes craned his head toward the door, as if readying an escape. He didn't want to talk about the Colonel.

"Time for me to GO!"

"Just a couple more questions," I said, whipping out the photo in my jacket pocket, Bobby Lee Crayline.

"This guy," I said to Hawkes. "Ever see him? Was he ever with you in school? He would have been about your age."

Hawkes scowled at the photo. Turned away. "GUARD," he yelled into the air. "I WANT THE YARD!"

"Jimmie," I pleaded, "just a couple more minutes."

"I WANT OUT!"

The guard shrugged at us and opened the door.

"Jimmie," Cherry called to Jimmie Hawkes's retreating back. "One question, Jimmie. Please? Just for me?"

Hawkes jittered and twitched. He paused in the doorframe.

# 48

We stood in the sun of the parking lot, five sheets of paper spread across the dark hood of Cherry's cruiser. Heat rose from the metal as Cherry shifted the sheets like puzzle pieces. She'd asked Hawkes to draw us a map to the "camp".

"Think this is worth anything?" Cherry squinted at lines and images Hawkes had scribbled.

"You're expecting accuracy in a map drawn by a man with two-thirds of a brain? Aiming us at a place almost two decades gone?"

Cherry leaned over the hood, shuffled the pages yet again. "I might be able to dope out landmarks he was talking about. Here . . ." she pointed to a lollipop shape Hawkes had scrawled beside a line representing a road. "He called it the cow tree."

I did dubious. "And?"

"There's a pasture by the county line with a huge beech, the tree near the road. There's a spring-fed creek by the tree and the farmer keeps salt blocks there as well."

"Shade, water, salt. Cows?"

"Usually a couple dozen at least, all ringing the tree. And here's what Hawkes called Beer Stop. If this is the tree I'm thinking about, there's a little grocery a mile down the road that sells beer and wine. It's been there since I was a kid."

Cherry pulled a sheet from the bottom of the arrangement, set it on top. Joined the lines Hawkes called roads. She tapped on the center page. "This so-called map, Ryder? It might actually make sense if I can figure out Hawkes's other landmarks."

"This wavy line," I said, pointing to a wavering doodle. "He said that was a creek, didn't he?"

"Yep. And this triangle over here was – what did he call it? – the big boat rock? It could be a big pointy boulder that looks like a battleship pushing out of the mountain. There's one like that a mile or so from the grocery."

I tapped a dark smear of ink. "He called this big muddy field."

"It fits the landscape," she said. "I'm thinking we tape these pages together and go a-hunting."

It took two hours of driving, circling, doubling back. We ended up at a chained gate blocking a dirt lane overgrown with weeds. The chain was crusted with rust, the lock a red block of oxidation.

Cherry said, "This is where Hawkes's map leads, as far as I can figure."

"No one's been through this gate in a long time," I said. "We're on foot from here."

We crawled warily over the barbed-wire fencing running from the gate in both directions and followed the lane for several hundred feet before encountering a second and taller perimeter of barbed-wire strung with rusted cans, a cheap alarm system. We found a tumbled section and pushed through, following the lanes to a two-story house of logs tucked in a tight hollow surrounded by hundred-foot cliffs, too sheer to climb without bolts planted for climbers.

There were a half-dozen windowless outbuildings on the hillside sloping to the cliffs, little larger than outhouses. Rhododendron had grown up over the years, the shacks almost hidden in the green. Behind the row of houses was a half-acre motley of hurricane-fence enclosures and tumbledown doghouses. The topography put the canine area a few feet above the outbuildings. Hawkes had been right about dog excrement, it would have washed down the hill directly beneath the little boxes.

*"Dog turds, dogs everywhere . . . Everything stunk of dog turd."*

Neither Cherry nor I uttered a word as we angled toward the house. The place was empty, save for the bats. No furniture, no fixtures, not so much as a scrap of newspaper on the floor. Chinking had fallen from between the logs and birds had nested in the empty spaces.

We went to inspect the row of outbuildings: sheds, reeking of animal urine from years of possums, rats, birds and raccoons. Each shed had the remains of a mattress on the floor, now no more than rotted fabric filled with insects. Cherry swung a creaky door on heavy iron hinges, studied a latch.

"The doors lock from the outside, Ryder," she said. "And this was supposed to be a school?"

"The one-room schoolhouse from hell," I said.

At the furthest end of the hollow was an old barn, large, the wood weathered almost black. We circled it, spying a huge cage on its side in the bushes.

"That cage is big enough to hold a doggone horse," Cherry noted.

"Or a couple of humans," I added.

We came around to the front again, no other openings in the building. The sliding door was frozen with rust so we pulled it back enough to slip inside, turned on our flashlights. On both sides of the structure were four-tier bleachers, twenty feet long. I estimated the place might hold a hundred-fifty screaming onlookers.

In the corner was a tabletop set-up, behind were shelves screwed into the beams. The bar area, I figured. The only liquor allowed at events had to be purchased there at ten bucks a pop. Another profit center. Plus oiled-up gamblers wagered more money. The bar also explained the shards of busted glass glittering from the floor: bottles dropped, or banged on the bleachers in bloodlust frenzy. I kicked loose glass that had been stuck in the dirt for years.

The floor between the bleachers resembled a perverse three-ring circus. On one end was a square pit about twelve by twelve, a yard or so deep. On the other end was a slightly smaller and less-deep pit, circular. Dogs and chickens, respectively.

In the center of the floor was a rectangular hole about twelve feet by five, four feet deep. Cherry's beam touched the pit, pulled away as if repulsed, returned to light the damp and scuffed bottom.

"Remember what came out of Crayline's memory?" she said. "The kids fought in a long pit nicknamed the grave. You think that happened here, too?"

"The other kids Crayline fought had to come from somewhere."

"But Crayline was kept in the Alabama mountains. He was never in Kentucky that we know of."

"Because he got trucked in and out in the dead of night," I said, my beam climbing the rafters, finding a row of broken light bulbs cupped by gray, sheet-metal shades. They looked like lamps from Auschwitz.

We retreated down the lane, escapees from Sodom. Cherry turned for a final look. I saw her shudder. "It's like a Ray Bradbury nightmare, Ryder. A carnival of horror."

"A horror that was filled by Powers," I said, the blanks

in the puzzle beginning to take shape. "She found isolated, troubled kids from hideously dysfunctional homes. Told parents about her special school where kids would get fed, receive a righteous education, whatever. She just needed permission, a few papers filled out. She'd been a . . . what did you call her?"

"A classified teacher. It's an assistant's position that doesn't need a teaching certificate. But anyone needing to check Powers out would see teaching in her background. Plus she knew the jargon when submitting the home-school forms, not to set off any alarms."

"And, of course, she had the church-lady talk."

"Miz Powers had everything covered," Cherry said. "The parents simply gave the kids away."

"Happy to get them gone, I expect. Putting Billy or Bobby's leash in the hands of folks spouting chapter and verse made it easy."

"Tanner was the head spouter, I imagine," Cherry said. "The Pious Teacher and the Man of Faith. Maybe Tanner believed it at first. Then the money started and he got hooked. I'll bet he still deluded himself, telling himself he'd use the gambling proceeds to build the grand religious edifice in his mind."

We climbed the barbed-wire again. Cherry said, "Eighteen years back would have been about the time Zeke got sick with all the old-timey religion, the save-yourself-from-Satan spiels."

"A pure man of God couldn't be throwing himself into rampant sex and gambling and cruelty to children.

330

It must have been Satan acting through him. By attacking Satan, he could still claim the high ground of an alliance with God. It's aligning symbol and metaphor to absolve yourself of baser instinct. When you're not at fault, every low and self-serving wish can be freely granted."

Cherry shook her head, holding down a strand of wire to help me over. "I swear religion like that is a form of madness. How about Burton?"

"Burton didn't need to re-arrange private symbolism to suit his needs. He was simply amoral, taking what he needed with no bothersome conscience."

"He was also a boxer, Ryder," Cherry reminded me.

I nodded, recalling the air punches and kicks Hawkes had demonstrated. The moves had been drilled into him so deeply they were fluid and powerful years later.

"The boys needed a coach, right?" I said. "Can't make money unless you win, can't win unless you know what you're doing."

"There's one more person in this hell broth, Ryder. The Colonel. I got the impression from Hawkes that the Colonel was the top dog, so to speak."

We reached the gate and turned for a final look, seeing only the rustic tranquility of trees and meadow and birds flitting tree to tree. Butterflies tumbled round red spikes of sumac. Insects rasped in the warm air.

"This whole dirty scheme needed a leader," I said, chipping rust from a barbed-wire point with my thumbnail. "And someone to bankroll the start-up. Buying this place and building the houses. Double-stringing the area with barbed-wire. Building bleachers and fight pits."

Cherry wrinkled up her nose. "Let's get gone from here. The reek of dogshit is making me sick."

We were a half-mile from buildings where dogs hadn't been kept for years. There was no smell left; Cherry's mind was supplying the odor.

I began to smell it, too.

Followed by the feeling of eyes on the back of my neck. A tingling, like an ice target painted across my spine. I picked up my pace, shooting glances at the ridge-line above. Though I saw nothing, I continued to feel the cold eyes even as we drove away.

# 49

"I'm gonna get the state property evaluator's office on finding out the owner of that property," Cherry said, driving with one hand, dialing with the other. "It's part of tax records. The last thing the state's gonna misplace are tax records. It may be a day or two, but we'll get something."

While Cherry wound her way through the bureaucracy and backtracked toward civilization, I studied the map scrawled by Jimmie Hawkes, one more relic of this bizarre case. Jimmie Hawkes had lived amidst the stinking boxes, fought the bouts, ate the maggoty food. His mind was a stream-of-consciousness retelling of the horror.

I didn't know if he'd entered the camp a damaged child, or been damaged while there and during the crime-ridden post-camp years of his life. Given that his pre-camp life was spent shunted from relative to relative and living most of that time outside like a farm dog, I figured – from a fair amount of experience – that Jimmie Hawkes was pretty much broken from the git-go.

I stared at Hawkes's childlike symbols: a wavy line for a creek, cross hatches for the plowed dirt of a field, lollipop shapes designating trees. Simple signs.

I put his map in my lap and replayed our prison experience in my mind, the half-faced man bouncing from toe to toe and firing tight, hard punches and whipping kicks at head height.

Saw Hawkes cup his hand over his crotch. "*PIN A NUMBER ON YOUR DICKS, BOYS! PUT ON YOUR CUPS AND COVER YOUR PUPS!*"

Athletic cups. The only fight protection the boys wore, according to Mickey Prince. A cushioned plastic and fabric semi-oval covering penis and testicles, held in place by slender straps around the hips. I thought of skinny boys wearing the protector, recalled Crayline wearing a cup and nothing else when he'd been spotted by the surveyor. I picked up a pencil and made a few loose sketches. Felt my heart skip a beat.

I turned to Cherry. "You have to call LaGrange and check on their video capabilities. I need to show Jimmie Hawkes something."

"What?"

"It's too strange. I have to run it by Hawkes."

Fifteen minutes later we pulled into her office. Her computer set-up had a camera for video conferences and

334

I sat and played with the controls while Cherry confirmed a similar set-up at LaGrange.

"Do they have the technology?" I asked.

She clapped her hand over the phone. "There's a secure room with video capability, used for depositions and the like. Hawkes is headed there now."

I pulled a black marker from my pocket, slipped a sheet of paper from the copier tray and drew a simple picture. Cherry ran in, tapping her watch.

"One minute to show time."

We sat in front of the monitor and camera. Jimmie Hawkes appeared on our screen. The cheap lens flattened his face to create the impression of a bizarre mask, half a face of an intense-looking man with pronounced features, the other something clipped from a lunar landscape. The shadows on his face moved when he moved, creating the impression the landscape was pulsing.

There was an institutional-yellow wall behind Hawkes and I saw the arm of a guard behind and to the side of the man. Hawkes gave us his splayed grin and leaned close to his camera, face ballooning to fill the screen.

"Yo! Anyone in there?"

"We're here, Jimmie. Detective Cherry and me, Detective Ryder. Look at the computer screen."

Hawkes's face turned to the monitor at his end, giving us a full shot of the ruination of the eyeless left side of his face. "I wish they'd have put the camera on the other side," Cherry muttered.

"Ssssh," I cautioned, knowing the mics could be surprisingly sensitive.

"I thought this was the side you liked, Miz Cherry," Hawkes giggled. He flicked his tongue in and out and moved his damaged face to the lens until the screen went dark with shadow. He jolted back. I saw the guard's large black hand on Hawkes's shoulder, returning him to the chair.

*Thanks, buddy,* I thought to the guard. Maybe his presence would calm some of Hawkes's wilder antics.

"I take it you hear us fine, Jimmie," I said.

"This is fun, I never been on the tee-vee afore. Want me to sing you a song?" He leered into the camera and sang in a raspy falsetto.

"*There once was a sweetie name of Cherry, who had a sweet pretty butt . . . and ever' time I think of it, my peter starts standing straight up.*"

I saw the hand come down and put the squeeze on Hawkes's shoulder, heard a cautionary voice, deep: "Behave, Mr Hawkes."

Hawkes shot a dark look at the guard. "He'd never a done that if I was Hank-fucking-Williams!"

"You know Hank Williams, Mr Hawkes?" Cherry asked.

"That shit played all day and all night when I was a kid. I'd sneak in the house while the record was on and Mamaw'd yell YOU MADE HANK SKIP! NO EAT FOR YOU!" Hawkes canted his head and leaned it closer to the camera. He winked. "I'd sure a-liked to eat Hank Williams. BETTER THAN PREACHER MAN MAGGOT SLOP!"

"Maggot slop?" Cherry asked, shooting me a glance. "Are you saying Brother Tanner fed you bad food, Jimmie?"

Hawkes poked his finger in his mouth, gagged. "GARBAGE CAN MEAT WHAT GOT THROWED AWAY AT THE STORE!"

I figured Tanner must have cooked with rotting ingredients scavenged from dumpsters behind groceries. It made sense: the killer had returned the favor by killing Tanner with poisoned food. I pasted a bright smile on my face and winked into the camera.

"I want to show you something, Jimmie. I want your impression."

I reached to the side of the desk and retrieved a drawing done a few minutes before we'd fired up the theater of the weird.

"I want you to say exactly what comes into your mind, OK, Jimmie?"

I held up the paper, reproducing a symbol much in my mind of late:

$$=(8)=$$

Hawkes's eyes widened. He screamed, "PUT ON YOUR CUPS AND GRAB YOUR PUPS! IT'S WHUP-ASS TIME!"

He started bouncing in his chair, agitated. "What is it, Jimmie?" I asked. "Tell me what you see."

"COVER YOUR BALLS SPLATTER BRAINS ON THE WALLS!"

"Jimmie!"

"STRAP IT TIGHT AN' WEAR IT RIGHT WE GONNA HAVE THE EAT TONIGHT!"

"What is it, Jimmie? What did I draw?"

He stood from his chair so all we could see was from his belly to mid-thigh. He cupped a hand over his genitals, jerked his hips at the camera.

"SOMEBODY'S NUMBER EIGHT TONIGHT! FIVE-FOUR-THREE-TWO-ONE . . . PUNCH THAT MUFUKA!"

Hawkes went crazy, flinging kicks and punches. Guards rushed in and the scene turned to tumult. It was over and I snapped off the video feed. Cherry pulled down the edge of my drawing so she could take a long look.

"I see it now," she said. "It's an athletic cup, right?"

I nodded. "A simple and effective representation. The equals signs are the straps, the parentheses form the cup, the number is the fighter's number."

Her eyes widened. "Is it possible that—"

I shook my head. "There's no way to ID a fighter by the numbers. They were drawn fresh each fight night. But Crayline is number five."

"The number on the symbol when Bridges got killed. Crayline killed Bridges, right? He had it in for the guy."

"I figure Bridges served two purposes. One was revenge, Crayline carrying through on his threat. Two was a demonstration of how a kill was done. A teachable moment, as they say."

Cherry made a face. "Ugh. But it makes sense. What

338

doesn't make sense is posting the information on the geocache site. The athletic-cup symbol of a fighter. The coordinates. Again, why post info that draws people to the murder scenes? It made it more likely to get caught."

"Like calling in the FBI, it added the element of risk," I said. "Get it?"

Cherry paused. I saw her re-playing the day Taithering died. Hearing my brother's explanation for his public display of vengeance against a dead man.

"Danger, destruction, display," she said, turning to me. "Charpentier's criteria for symbolic victory over the past."

I nodded. Cherry walked to the window and stared outside, finger at her pink lips. After a long minute, she turned to me, a strange light in her eyes.

"Who says only one kid from the backwoods fight club made it to the XFL?"

# 50

Her words were a Zen punch that left me reeling with a drunken clarity, like the world was spinning, but in perfect focus. My fingers were shaking so much it took me two tries to dial the number fished from my notebook.

"Mickey Prince, please," I told the receptionist. "It's Detective Ryder." A pause as the call was announced. I could almost feel Prince's hand hovering over the phone. He picked it up and launched his false bonhomie.

"Hey, Detective Ryder. Great to hear from you. We still cool?"

"We're as cool as we'll ever be, Mick."

"Uh, sure. Good, I guess. S'up?"

"You put new names on most of your fighters, right?" I asked.

"Like I said, you can't seem tough if your name is Lester Doodle."

"I'm gonna read you a list of names, all right?"

"Go for it, Detective."

I turned my notepad to the boys in the Solid Word program and commenced my recitation, omitting Hawkes's name because we knew his history.

"Jessie Collier . . . Elijah Elks . . . Bemis Smith . . . Creed Baines . . . Teeter Gasper . . . Donald Nunn." I finished, said, "Well, Mickey, know any of them?" I held my breath and looked at Cherry.

"Sure," Prince said. "Teeter Gasper. Ain't that a silly fucking thing to name a kid? I guess if he was twins the other'd be Totter."

"Who did Teeter become, Mick? What did you name him?"

"Teeter was the guy that whipped Bobby Lee," Prince said. "Then got stuck in the ground for his efforts. Teeter turned into the Mad Dog . . . Jessie Stone."

I set the phone down, stunned.

"What?" Cherry said.

"Jessie Stone never went to Ireland," I said. "He came home to the mountains to destroy his past."

"Stone and Crayline had to know one another as kids, right?" Cherry said after taking several head-shaking moments to process the information. "They were fighters from different camps?"

I saw in my head the Appalachian mountain range stretching from the Talladega mountains in north Alabama up to, and past, Kentucky. Saw nondescript vehicles ferrying young fighters under cover of backwoods darkness. Vans pulling beside barns filling with raucous drunks, pockets thick with rolled bills, yelling odds as they sucked down bottles of beer, shots of whiskey. The kids stripping off their clothes and pulling on their cups as their trainer-coaches bellowed incentives.

I nodded. "Forced to beat the shit out of one another. Only two kinds of bonds come from that: Fierce hatred or total allegiance."

"I'll put out an All Points Bulletin on Stone," Cherry said. "Then I'm gonna go fill everyone in, even Krenkler."

"I think she'll be happy with this news. You're saved from a life sentence at Wal-Mart."

"You coming?" she asked, slinging her bag over her shoulder. "Bask in some of the glory?"

"You can have my share. I've still got thinking to do. Be careful out there. Stone's lost his buddy and it may cause an explosion. He killed Beale, who had no part in the fights except for his genetic connection. It's an insane jump, but . . ."

"But Stone's insane," Cherry completed. She zipped away to brief the county guys. I paced the room, writing down all the information on the murder scenes instead of the victims. I made coffee and studied timelines. Compared them to sunrise data. Scribbled, erased, scribbled again.

Nearly an hour passed. I was making ties and conclusions when my cellphone rang.

"Detective Ryder? This is Judd Caudill. Detective Cherry

left there yet? She was heading over here to give us some new infor—"

I looked at my watch. It was a ten-minute drive. Cherry should have been there forty minutes ago.

"She hasn't shown?" I asked, feeling sweat prickle beneath my arms.

"Huh-uh. Any idea where she could be?"

I told Caudill to get some cruisers on the road, check for an accident. I also advised to avoid usual communications modes, switching to alternate channels or phones when possible. I didn't want the info broadcast on the air.

I called McCoy. He was out on a trail but showed up twenty minutes later, fear darkening his eyes.

"Let's not start worrying yet, Lee," I said. "A lot of little things could have happened. A flat tire. A stop at the store. A visit to her home to pick something up."

"Those are rationalizations," he said quietly.

"I know."

When another hour passed with no sign of Cherry, McCoy and I went to check her home. The door was locked. "She keep a key anywhere?" I asked.

"I've never been here. She kept trying to have me over for supper, but schedules never worked. We always ended up at a restaurant."

The oak door built by Cherry's Uncle Horace was castle-quality. I broke a side window and unlatched it, crawling through and opening the door. It was cool and dark inside, scented with a woman's potions. A plate and

343

coffee cup sat in the sink. The bed was made. I looked at the wall and saw Cherry's favorite photo, her with Uncle Horace. She beamed her bright child's smile into the empty room.

"Everything looks like it would have when she left this morning," I said.

"There's a couple of messages on the phone machine," McCoy said. He pressed the Play button. The first was a bank trying to upgrade Cherry to the new Super Titanium credit card. A pause and the machine beeped to a woman's voice with a central Kentucky accent, warm vowels, consonants softened at the edges. The time signature placed the message as arriving fifteen minutes back.

*"Hello, Detective. This is Daisy Lutes at the state property evaluator's office. I've been trying your mobile phone and can't get you. Give me a call when you get a chance, please."*

Lutes finished by leaving her number. I sat on the couch and called, explaining that Cherry and I were working together.

Lutes said, "Detective Cherry wanted me to check on a parcel of land. I guess it's about forty-six acres."

The fight camp.

"See, what happened was a foreclosure," Miz Lutes continued. "The owner stopped paying."

"Who was the owner?"

"Allen Eckles."

"Who?"

"This was . . . lemme see, twenny years back. I'm

344

looking at the paperwork. Right here, Allen Eckles. Lived in West Liberty back then. Looks like Eckles died and the government foreclosed."

"The state owns the property?"

"That's what I couldn't find out because things back then aren't on the computer. We had to root through boxes. What I found was the land got bought at auction seven weeks later. Price was eighty-seven thousand dollars."

"Who bought it?" I asked.

"Now I just had that sheet here . . . daw-gone, bet I left it in the copier. Hang on a second."

I held the phone to my cheek and looked over at McCoy. He stood riveted before the wall of photos and objects. "I wish I'd gotten over here for supper," he said, shaking his head.

"Why?"

He nodded to an arrangement of wood and metal implements on the wall, the odd tools that had given me an uncomfortable feeling.

"Donna didn't have any idea what this stuff is, did she?" he said.

"She found it in Horace's shed. Some kind of farm gear, she supposed. You know what it is, Lee?"

He blew out a breath. "That piece of wood on the right is called a break stick, used to separate dogs when they're fighting. That lead and leather gizmo is a weight collar to build a fighting dog's neck strength. Beside it is a—"

Miz Lutes popped back on the phone. "Mr Ryder? I got the name of the guy that bought the place from the government."

"Horace Cherry, right?" I said, feeling lightheaded.

"Horace *Thurgood* Cherry," Miz Lutes said, adding, "Ain't that some fine kind of name?"

# 51

"Horace Cherry was the Colonel?" McCoy asked. "You're sure?"

I nodded. "The impresario of the circus from hell."

"What does this have to do with Donna?"

"She's Horace Cherry's only surviving relative. She once called herself the last Cherry left on the tree."

It took McCoy eight seconds to get it. His voice fell to a hush.

"Stone killed Beale as a stand-in for Daddy."

"Now Cherry's a stand-in for Uncle Horace," I said. "She's the only available symbol of the Colonel."

"Why Colonel?" McCoy asked. "Horace was never in the military. Or anything else I can recall."

I went to an arrangement at the far end of the wall, the framed-certificate subdivision. Cherry's papers, mainly, a couple of diplomas, training certifications and so forth.

I pointed to a framed document that looked straight from a physician's wall.

"Right here, Lee. A certificate naming Horace T. Cherry a member of the Honorable Order of Kentucky Colonels."

McCoy scoffed. "I'm a Kentucky Colonel. Every third Kentuckian is a Colonel. It's what Kurt Vonnegut called a granfalloon, a proud and meaningless association of human beings."

"Burton was Coach. Tanner was the Preacher. Powers was the Lady. It makes sense for Horace Cherry to be the Colonel."

"Come to think of it, that sounds right. Horace was a human granfalloon. A blusterer, full of himself. Loud. Drank too much. Gambled too much. Thought himself above everyone, the law included. He used to boast about screwing the government out of taxes."

"Why does Cherry think so highly of him?"

"After high school she was rarely around Horace, just her memories of him. Memories have softer edges. And it seems like most people have someone – friend, relative – where they have a blind spot, right?"

"I, uhm, guess. How did Horace make his money?"

"Whatever turned a buck. He'd own a coin laundry for a couple years, sell it, buy a sandwich shop, trade it for a trophy store. To hear him talk, he was Donald Trump."

"All the more reason to affect the Colonel moniker," I said, not going into the insecurities involved. "How did he die?"

McCoy pointed to the overlook. "Conventional

wisdom has Horace taking some kind of fainting spell at the edge of the cliff. He didn't make bottom, but got hung up in a tree. I led the recovery team and had to rappel to the body."

"Conventional wisdom?" I asked.

McCoy stared into my eyes as if weighing something. "When I was wrestling Horace into the basket I saw a scrap of paper pinned to his shirt. The words were so small they seemed whispered. He never whispered."

"What did it say?"

"*I'm sorry for everything.*"

"What happened to—"

"I pulled it off and hid it. It would have produced nothing but hurt. And nothing would have changed."

McCoy went to marshal his forces, rangers and park personnel driving every back road in the area, looking for anything that might lead to Cherry. He was going to alert the FBI and tell them that Cherry was missing. I advised that his people use alternate communications like phones unless an emergency, avoiding tipping their location over the police and emergency bands.

Finding anything was a tall order. Given the ability for concealment learned from Crayline, I figured Stone could stay invisible until his mission was accomplished.

But I had accumulated enough information to make a few conjectures.

They all led to my brother's door.

# 52

I cut the engine and drifted up Jeremy's drive. His car was in the side yard with a coiled hose beside it, the vehicle freshly washed. The residue was blue-gray, the color of the clay where Beale had died. I looked inside the Subaru as I passed and saw a stick shift.

My brother wasn't on his porch or in the garden and I figured he was playing with his scared children and blustering drunkards. I turned the doorknob. Locked. I started to knock, but ended up kicking in the door. It swung around and banged the wall.

Coffee break: Jeremy sat in the living room, cup in hand, wearing a three-piece suit with a pink shirt and red striped tie. The Bloomberg channel was on television, stock quotes crawling across the screen.

Jeremy's eyes went wide. "WHAT DID YOU DO TO MY—"

I strode to his chair. When he tried to jump up, I shoved him down. I said, "What's the difference between a Hindu ascetic's cave – a hole in a hill – and a hole dug in a barn floor when it comes to getting in touch with one's inner self?"

"What are you babbling about?"

"Teeter Gasper, aka Jessie Stone. Crayline didn't kidnap Stone, right, Brother? Crayline was hardening Stone for a warrior's journey. Teaching him to turn off outer influences – like living in an open sewer."

"You've lost me."

"Burying himself alive, that was Crayline's magic. When his mama OD'd he sought refuge in a root cellar. Five years old and that's where it started."

"Where what started, Carson? You worry me when you get like this."

"It's where Crayline learned to shut off the outside. When he was eight years old he turned off time to get a larger share of candy. When he was being trained to fight, he stayed imprisoned in a lightless basement, tucking inside himself and getting stronger. When he escaped from the Institute, he lived in a pit under a house for weeks, waiting for the search to die down. So when Stone was readying to meet the past, Bobby Lee put him in a pit. Stone was to retreat inside himself and invent the symbolism necessary to destroy his tormentors, a rite of passage prescribed by Bobby Lee Crayline. Where did Crayline get that idea, do you suppose?"

My brother's faced changed. The aggrieved professor-businessman-gardener mask fell away, as did the wisp of accent. His eyes were totally his: clear and blue and as cold as the laughter in his voice.

"Bobby had things clanging inside him, Carson. I told you that." He looked at my hand on his chest. "May I stand? Or are you determined to be a boor?"

I stepped away. Jeremy stood and paced the room. There was no trace of a Canadian psychologist.

"The clanging inside Crayline was the horrors of his past?" I asked.

"Far worse, Carson. The horror that he'd never escape his past. He killed his tormentors in a rage, Carson. No symbolic journey and, consequently, no salvation."

"Thus his crying to you at the Institute?"

"I had just confirmed Bobby Lee's worst fears: his direct and simple vengeance lacked the power to destroy his past. He would never be free."

I walked to Jeremy's bookshelves, saw Jung's *Man and His Symbols* and *Modern Man in Search of a Soul*. They nestled against Joseph Campbell's *The Power of Myth*, *The Hero with a Thousand Faces*, *The Inner Reaches of Outer Space: Metaphor as Myth and as Religion*. A dozen similar books ran the shelf, held in place by Frazer's *The Golden Bough*.

I ran my finger slowly down the covers, making a ticking sound. I turned to my brother.

"You got paid a helluva lot, Jeremy. Am I right?"

"Paid for what, Carson?" he crooned, almost a taunt, enjoying himself and proud of whatever he had done.

"To judge whether the murders met the proper criteria

352

for danger, destruction and display. You said Taithering's journey lacked only one element, the validation of a higher authority. Someone had to study the signs, produce the white smoke of success. You were Jessie Stone's higher authority, right? A man who spouted all the right terms about magic and symbols and was regarded as no less than a past-killing wizard by Bobby Lee Crayline."

My brother flicked a piece of lint from his cuff. "I did nothing wrong, Carson. I took innocent morning walks."

"Innocent? You were a killing inspector," I said, using Judd Caudill's perceptive term. "Did you stand before the carnage and give a thumbs-up, Jeremy? You posted your acceptance on the geocache website, right? It was you who invented the visual pun of the athletic cup."

His eyes twinkled. "Took me all of two minutes of playing on the keyboard. Did you like it?"

"What did you promise Crayline he'd get from assisting with Stone's journey . . . the mentor's cut of redemption?"

"Bobby Lee helped Stone because of his love for a fellow warrior. A brother in arms. Bobby Lee might benefit, but never enough to be free."

"You told me you hadn't spoken to Bobby Lee since the Institute. Years."

"Not aloud. You never mentioned correspondence. There are quiet corners of the Web, Carson. Places to meet. Bobby Lee notified me that he had a friend wanting to free himself by erasing the past. He needed a shaman to read the entrails."

# 53

I looked at my watch, fear boiling in my belly. It was time to change the angle of my questions.

I stepped close to my brother, hands in my pockets, voice gentle.

"Stone has Cherry, Jeremy. He needs to kill her."

He grinned. "That'll certainly make things quieter around here."

My punch caught him between the eyes, snapping his head back. He stumbled into the wall. My brother studied my face as his eyes refocused.

"Oh my," he sneered, rubbing his forehead. "You finally slipped your tongue into the pie, Carson. Was it tasty?"

"Where's Stone?"

"I have no idea."

"I'll say it one more time. Where's—"

"You don't understand, Carson. I didn't know who Bobby was working with. Coordinates of, uh, various events arrived on my computer. I'd slip out and inspect. If the event had sufficient poetry, I signaled acceptance. All I know is the victims were people who tormented children and deserved what they got. People like our male parent."

"Beale never tormented children. Neither did Cherry. They're stand-ins for the dead."

My brother did wide-eyed innocence. "You can't expect me to have predicted that."

I wanted to slam my brother into the wall. Instead I looked out the window and breathed slowly, controlling my emotions. I looked over his beloved garden, seeing a bright cardinal flash in the open sun. Beyond, the bees sizzled in their white hives. I saw the white chair where he sat in the shade and read his books. I'd never known my brother to feel a kinship with a locale before, one place as good or bad as the next. But something was different here: He'd set down roots, literally and metaphorically. It was a first step, but something in him was changing, perhaps even moving toward the elusive peace he seemed to seek in more rational moments, but never find.

"Do you like it here in the forest?" I asked.

"It's my home. I've never been able to say the word before. I love it here."

I checked my watch. "I'll give you a three-hour head start beginning right now. Then I'm blowing the whistle."

His mouth dropped open. "What?"

"You like anonymous calls? Here's mine: one to the FBI that suggests a fast and close inspection of one August Charpentier."

"YOU CAN'T DO THAT!"

I nodded toward the garden. "Kiss it goodbye and remember it fondly."

"YOU CAN'T DO THIS TO YOUR OWN BLOOD!"

"*Tempus fugit*, Brother. Best get packing."

He glared at me, fists clenching and releasing. "I KNOW WHAT'S GOING ON, CARSON. YOU WANT ME TO FIND YOUR LITTLE SCREECH OWL. CHECK THE GODDAMN RV PARKS."

"Stone knows we know about them." I glanced at my watch again. "You're down to two hours and—"

"ENOUGH!" Jeremy howled, dropping his face into his hands. "LET ME THINK!"

I went to the porch and waited. It took ten minutes until Jeremy called me back. He was lying on the floor and looking up. It was his preferred manner of thinking: projecting thoughts and ideas on to the ceiling like watching a movie.

"Where is she?" I asked.

"If I tell you, I stay here. If I'm going to lose my home, I'll lose it today. But you'll lose . . ."

"Deal," I said. "Tell me."

He stared at the ceiling like he was watching a scene come into focus. "If Stone has entered a world where someone related to a tormentor is a perfectly acceptable metaphor for the actual tormentor, he's in a world of pure symbol. He'll need to be at a magic node for the finale."

"A what?"

"A place where the present intersects the past, and all is possible."

"That's useless to me," I snapped. "Be more specific."

"I can't tell you *where* Stone is, Carson. I can only tell you *how* he is. What he needs right now is past and future together, Alpha and Omega."

"The camp," I whispered, seeing the completion of a circle.

I pulled out my phone to call Krenkler and the crew, but I couldn't get my finger to press her number. Thinking she was racing to the solve, Krenkler had gone stormtrooper on the poor tormented Taithering, causing needless destruction. Stone was a man without limits; he needed to kill Cherry to regain his soul. There would be no bargaining, nor would he tolerate any form of stand-off. While Krenkler raised her bullhorn, Stone would butcher Donna Cherry, destroying the hated Colonel.

If I called Krenkler, the situation could turn bad in an eyeblink. On my own, I had control.

It took under twenty minutes to get to the rusted gate outside the camp. There was no other vehicle nearby and my heart sank until I realized Stone would use a back entrance; surely there was a hidden entrance. I parked at the gate, the dirt still puddled from the earlier storms. The air was blue with twilight, night falling fast. I checked my weapon, patted pockets filled with bullets, knife, and flashlight, climbed over the barbed wire, and began running to the camp.

Recognizing the final bend, I slowed. High ridges blocked the waning sun, making it seem an hour later here in the valley than in the highlands, almost full dark now. When I saw lights in the barn, I ducked low and sprinted to the tumbledown house for cover, crouching in the soupy dirt.

I heard dogs growling nearby, deep-throated rumbles. The sound chilled my spine. A whiff of dog excrement hit my nose, fresh. I peered around the corner and saw a bright RV, boats and bikes strapped aboard.

I sprinted to the corner of the barn and heard a dog start baying. I hoped it wasn't announcing an intruder. The huge cage Cherry and I saw outside the back door was missing. I put my ear to the warped barn slats and listened. The growling of dogs. I crept another six paces, listened again. Heard a sound at my back and turned.

I saw a huge fist as if in slow motion.

Stars. Black.

# 54

Dogs barking. Followed by the reek of excrement. Followed by the smell of mud. I opened my eyes and saw I was caged in a six-foot cube of quarter-inch bars set four inches apart: the cage from the bushes behind the barn, now positioned beside what had been the bar area during fight days.

My gun was gone.

Stone stood two dozen feet away beside a similar cage containing a trio of black, snarling dogs, two Dobermans and a pit bull. He wore nothing but a white athletic cup, his overbuilt body gleaming with sweat. The metal-shaded lamps in the rafters produced a hard white light that lent the feel of a theatrical performance.

I studied the scene through a half-opened eye, twitching each limb slightly, testing for pain and response. Everything seemed to work. Stone had missed a chance to incapacitate me, totally focused on Cherry, perhaps.

Stone turned, pushed open the door and went outside, the dogs snarling and high-hackled. Dog excrement had been mounded around the floor, part of the symbolic tableau, I figured.

Seconds later, Stone re-entered the barn, tugging on a yellow rope with one hand, holding a wad of clothes in the other, throwing to the floor a blouse, jeans, panties, bra. Cherry followed, the rope tight around her neck. She was dressed in a man's suit jacket, cream-colored and outsized, sleeves past her fingertips, the bottom inches above her knees. A tan hat was on her head, a dollar-store purchase resembling the hat Horace Cherry affected. I saw trails of brown crust in her hair and realized the hat had been glued to her head.

Outside of the costume, Cherry was naked. She looked worn and frightened, but angry as well, watching Stone like he was a deadly snake, one she might kill if she found the chance.

I looked through slitted eyes as Cherry saw my crumpled form. Her eyes dropped in despair. I had no way to signal her without alerting Stone to my consciousness.

Stone rope-dragged Cherry to the far end of the structure, tying her to an iron hoop in the wall. My eyes searched the ground and saw a brown glint in the dirt a yard away, glass. I wormed through the mud, scraped at it with my fingernail, unearthing a semi-triangular shard from a beer bottle, shorter than my thumb. It was thick on one end where the wall of the bottle joined the butt end, pointed on the other. As a weapon, it was lacking – short and brittle – but it was something. I cupped it in my palm, shot a veiled glance at Stone.

He was staring at me.

"I saw you move," he whispered.

He was reaching for a dark wooden bar when I closed my eyes, heard feet pounding my way. I made myself go limp, knowing what was coming.

The feet stopped beside the cage. The stick probed my back, jabbed my side.

Slashed down on my legs, the pain like a dozen simultaneous hornet stings.

*Don't move . . . don't move . . .*

The rod slashed down twice again. Finally satisfied I was unconscious, Stone padded back toward the dogs and prodded them with the stick. The emptiness in his eyes was spooky. Stone was foreign in time, inhabiting a world his body had left twenty years ago, but where his mind remained in a prison beyond anything of rock and iron. It was not the world of his miserable childhood, of the XFL, of the hole in the barn floor. Stone was in the twilight of all his worlds, and they intersected on these unholy grounds where, long ago, children had fought in the pit they called the grave.

When the dogs were foaming and furious, Stone went to Cherry and began untying the rope from the iron ring.

"Come on, Colonel," he said, jerking her across the floor toward the pit.

"I'm not the Colonel," Cherry gasped. "I'm—"

Stone calmly backhanded Cherry. She caromed off the

wall, slipped in dogshit spread across the floor, fell to her knees. Stone grabbed the back of her hair, lifting. She groaned and fought to her feet, the hat sideways, glue tearing away. Stone replaced the hat atop her head, slapped it down. The blow must have been like a pile-driver, but Cherry stayed standing.

"Time to meet the boys, Colonel," Stone said.

I wondered if I was seeing a fantasy created while he had retreated inside himself during his false abduction. He'd fantasized killing Powers by dressing her in whore garb, inverting logic by "baptizing" her in the pond. He'd crushed Burton beneath the kind of vehicle in which the man likely raped the young Teeter Gasper as he had William Taithering. Stone had fed poison to Tanner, a dark echo of the preacher feeding spoiled food to the boys in the camp.

I wondered what Stone imagined for the Colonel.

I heard a moan and saw Cherry stagger and seem to falter. It was a ruse. She snapped a kick into Stone's belly that doubled him over. Cherry kicked again, catching Stone in his head. But Cherry's kicks were nothing compared to punishment Stone had absorbed from professionals; his open hand swatted her like a troublesome fly. She spun away into the dirt.

"Get up, Colonel," Stone whispered. "Up and up."

Cherry tried to rise, hands squishing in the mud. Stone again lifted her to her feet with her hair, the hat tumbling away. He pushed Cherry into the pit and she sprawled across its mud-slick bottom. Stone retrieved Cherry's clothes from the floor and used the dark stick to push them between the bars of the dog cage. The enraged animals shredded the cloth in seconds. Stone put his back to the cage and began skidding it over the floor to the pit, his heels digging into the floor.

"We're going to be free," he called over his shoulder to Cherry. "We're free tonight, Colonel."

Stone's eyes glittered with an electric glow, haunted by his need to tear free of the bonds of his childhood. Stone grunted the cage toward the edge of the pit, the grave. The dogs tore at the metal, aching to sink their teeth into flesh.

Stone had only to release the latch and the dogs would cover Cherry. He stood back and took a final look at the scenario, an eerie smile on his face, beatific calm. My mind raced to fathom the shapes in Stone's head. What had eleven-year-old Teeter Gasper seen in this place eighteen years ago? Who had he known?

Jimmie Hawkes.

With Stone's eyes turned to his tableau, I stripped to white briefs and rolled the sides into straps, a white pouch over my genitals. Stone moved toward the cage and put his hand on the latch. The dogs fought at the door, establishing which came first to Cherry's throat.

I dipped my finger in the mud at my feet and scrawled a dark shape on the white cloth, like a number, feverishly trying to recall what Jimmie Hawkes screamed in LaGrange.

"YEEEEEE-HAH!" I screamed maniacally, leaping

from one side of the cage to the other. "PUT ON YOUR CUPS AND COVER YOUR PUPS!" The sound echoed through the barn. The dogs stopped fighting and looked my way, sensing more quarry.

"PIN A NUMBER ON YOUR DICK!" I howled. "BUST THEIR ASSES AND GET SOME EAT IN THE BELLY! EAT AND MORE EAT."

Stone halted, his face turning to me. "Jimmie?" he said, confusion clouding his eyes.

"DOPE AND WHISKEY AND GETTIN' ALL FRISKY! WIN AND FILL THE MOUTH-HOLE!"

"Jimmie? Is that you?"

I drummed down my body, jerking my hips, Stone was frozen in the black hole of his mind, mouth open and aghast at whatever images I was creating in his brain. His hand fell from the latch. I pointed my hand at him like I was delivering an ultimatum.

"READ THE DOG, BUDDY! THE DOG KNOWS THE FUTURE." I bounced from side to side of the cage like a trapped animal. I stopped, stumbled as if seized by a terrible thought. I craned back my head and screamed.

"HERE COMES THE SNACK TRUCK!"

*No,* Stone mouthed, his face seized by fearful awe.

"HELP ME TEETER," I cried. "I WANT OUT FROM THE GRAVE!"

Stone seemed as numb as a zombie as he plodded to my cage, yanked open the door. He came to me with arms wide.

"Jimm—"

My hand flicked out and slashed his left eye with the shard. When reflex pulled his hand to the eye, I jammed the shard so deep into the right eye I felt it hit bottom, whatever that was.

He screamed like a scalded banshee but instead of grabbing at his eye he closed his massive hands around my neck, as if everything in him had burned away but the instinct to fight. I jabbed at his face with the glass but he tucked it between his arms and all I could do was scrape at his crown. His hands seemed ready to meet in the center of my windpipe and I heard the roar of unconsciousness closing in, felt the final rush down the vortex. The roar turned to a series of noises I figured would be the last sounds I ever heard. It sounded like twigs breaking in a moonlit forest.

Was Crayline after me in the next life, too?

# 55

"You're a hot dog, Ryder," said the voice in the sky. "And you just about got what hot dogs deserve. Cooked."

Krenkler's voice. It zoomed down to stop just past my splayed feet. I opened my eyes. The agent named Rourke was crouched beside me, palpating my neck.

"Nothing broke," he said to Krenkler.

"You can't win 'em all."

"Cherry!" I said, my head snapping upward.

"Outside getting medical attention," Krenkler said. "She's all right, outside of cuts and bruises."

My eyes came to focus on a human form, horizontal and still, the body of Jessie Stone face-down in the mud of the barn floor. I smelled cordite in the air and realized the cracking twigs were gunshots.

"The cavalry arrived just in time," I said, feeling my head clearing. "Thank you."

"It was close," Krenkler said. "Luckily we had a window into your ridiculous attempt to fly solo."

She nodded toward the door of the barn. Entering, surrounded by a half-dozen FBI agents, was my brother, hands behind his back. Krenkler had probably started digging into Jeremy's background from the moment he'd stepped into Burton's visitation. He'd told me how he'd put one over on Krenkler, asking to be part of the investigation. It appeared he'd misread the lady. His life in the forest – his life in the real world – was over.

Jeremy said something to one of the agents. The guy looked at me and laughed. My brother shot me a wink and a wave.

No handcuffs.

The agent patted Jeremy on the back, nodded at me. They both laughed like I was the butt of a joke.

"Doctor Charpentier came to us an hour ago," Krenkler explained. "He said you were at his home earlier. You were looking for some place tucked way in the north of the county. You couldn't raise McCoy on your cell and you thought a hiker like the doctor might know how to get here."

I shot a glance at my brother. "I, uh . . . yes, that's right."

"The doctor also said you were acting pretty squirrely. He began to fear for your safety and called us. You owe him big time."

Rourke extended his hand and I let him pull me to standing. I closed my eyes with my hands on my knees

367

for a few seconds, getting my bearings. My brother had walked into the lion's den to save my life.

Krenkler shook her head at me for a final time, then trotted over to inspect the body, snapping orders to the agents like they were errant bellhops. I went to Jeremy, now alone.

I said, "Thanks, Doc."

"This has been very instructive," he said quietly, sliding his hands into his pockets and leaning against the wall, totally at ease. "I've been quite the curious fellow on the way here, asking the boys how they dig into people's backgrounds and so forth."

"The boys?"

"And, of course, dear Miss Krenkler. They've been most informative without realizing it. With a little more work I can harden my identity."

I shook my head in amazement: My brother had once again fallen upwards. I went outside and found Cherry about to be taken to the hospital for a checkup. The paramedics were kind enough to allow us a few quiet moments together, and I followed the ambulance to the hospital.

Cherry's exam and several X-rays took a half-hour. McCoy stopped by for a few minutes. After she was pronounced in remarkable shape, given her ordeal, we retreated to her home and stood in a steaming shower until the water ran cool. She poured us bourbon over ice, enlivened with a few ounces of seltzer. We sat on the porch as the stars wheeled overhead.

"How well did you know Horace?" I asked.

A long pause. "He laughed a lot. Bought me birthday gifts, graduation gifts. Things Mama couldn't afford. I loved to be close to him because he smelled so good, his aftershave or cologne. I'd sit in his lap with my arms around his neck when I was little. One time I . . . he . . ."

She fell silent, her eyes far away and looking inside.

"Talk to me," I said. "Don't hide it."

"I-I must have been ten, eleven. My birthday party. I was sitting on his lap and spooning ice cream into his mouth. I felt his hand on my legs, then . . . something tickled and I wriggled away. The ice cream fell on to him. I remember seeing this startled look on his face. I thought I'd done something wrong."

"Do you think—"

"I think he was testing something, that he might have even scared himself. From that point on he started telling me I'd gotten too big to hold. For a long time I thought it was because I'd spilled ice cream on his lap. Then time sped up and it was junior high school and I was in the band and on the newspaper and then high school and I was in clubs and there were boys, whoopee. College and studies came next. I really didn't see him much after I was thirteen or fourteen, too much happening in my life."

"But he left you his home."

"Horace had changed over the years, become a recluse. His big laugh went away. He had an enlarged heart that

369

was expanding. I'd come to visit and he really seemed to appreciate the company and, uh, and . . ."

Reality crashed in and her words choked into tears. She stood and wiped them away with the back of her hand. She paced the porch until her voice was steady.

"I can't believe what a monster he was, Carson. What a disgusting monster. I can't live here any more, knowing what he was. I can't."

"Maybe Horace changed at the end," I said.

"People like that never change, Carson. Their souls are too broken."

She fell into the chair and put her head in her hands. I moved close and put my arm over her shoulder.

"Did you know Lee McCoy was on the recovery team when your uncle fell?" I asked.

Her face turned to me, puzzled. "He never mentioned it."

"There's something else Lee didn't mention."

I told her a brief story about a ranger rappelling to a body in a tree and finding a scrap of paper pinned to the corpse's ice-cream suit. I handed her something McCoy had kept for three years, figuring it might someday be needed. I'd asked him to bring it to the hospital.

Donna Cherry stared at four words written in a whisper:

*I'm sorry for everything*

She folded the note, closed it in her hand, and we walked to the edge of the precipice, lit in the soft light from her porch.

"Two men involved in the fight camps died down there, Carson. One created horror, the other was trapped in it. Both were looking for freedom from their pasts. Why did they both die here? What does it mean?"

"Whatever you need it to mean," I said. "Whatever it takes to work the magic."

"Magic? What do you mean by . . ."

But I was already climbing the steps to her porch. I went inside and stripped her walls of the half-dozen implements used in training dogs. I took them outside and told her what they were.

"They're all that remains of the bad," I said. "If you kill them properly, you can set your home free."

Cherry stared into my eyes for a long moment, nodded understanding. She went inside, returning minutes later in a simple gown of white. Her feet were bare in the warm grass. She was wearing Horace Cherry's hat.

Cherry stood at the precipice with her eyes closed for five minutes, praying or chanting or simply wishing . . . it was only hers to know. She bent and picked up the bite stick and flung it high and away, watching it dissolve into the night sky. One by one I watched the other angry tools disappear into the dark. They reminded me of old knives sucked beneath green waves.

When the last device was gone, she pulled the hat from her head and launched it out over the valley. It floated on the breeze for a two-count, then tumbled into the depths. She turned to me.

Asked, "How'd I do?"
"Not mine to judge," I said. "How do you feel?"
She pulled me close. Whispered in my ear.
Said, "Free."

# 56

It was nine a.m. before Cherry and I rolled from bed, Cherry answering the strident phone. "Good morning," she said. "Uh –huh. Not long, I expect. Take care." She hung up.

"World's briefest survey?" I asked.

"That was Lee. He wants to, uh, meet up for supper tonight or tomorrow, maybe turn it into drinks."

"I'm up for it. I'm hoping for another hike with him."

I had time remaining in my vacation and planned to spend the bulk of it with Cherry. She drove me to Road's End for fresh clothes, passing Jeremy's cabin. He was in his garden, pruning something or other. He looked up and grinned, making the OK sign. Cherry waved back and yelled a greeting.

"You still think he's weird?" I asked as she pulled her head back into the vehicle.

"He saved our lives. If he's weird it's the best weird ever."

We rolled down the lane to Road's End. Turning the bend for the last hundred feet, I noted motion on my porch. Saw a wagging tail. Heard a triumphant bark.

Mix-up had returned.

He bolted for the car as we drove to the cabin. I bailed out the door while the car was in motion, thumping, patting, petting, all at once. I couldn't stop laughing. I threw a stick, he ran and fetched. I ran in a circle and he darted between my legs, knocking me to the ground. I tumbled him over in the weeds and thumped his huge chest as he pedaled his feet at the sky.

Something struck me as strange. Mix-up's coat was mat-free and as shiny as fresh silk, not expected of a furry beast lost amidst a forest's brambles and burrs. I found no mud on his feet. No ticks in his fur.

Had he been bathed and brushed? Perplexed, I went to the kitchen and filled his food bowl. He finished half of the meal, then wandered outside.

The way he acted when recently fed.

I followed Mix-up outside to the porch, where Cherry was smoothing the fur on his broad back. A strange thought touched my head. I'd handed Cherry two dozen LOST DOG posters to disperse. But the only posters I'd ever seen were ones I'd distributed. The only calls I had received were from people who saw posters I'd put in place.

And why was Cherry always so optimistic about Mix-up's return?

"*Good doggie . . .*" Cherry said, now scruffing Mix-up behind the ears, his favorite site for attention. But I had been with Cherry when Mix-up disappeared, my mind reasoned. We'd been on the run all day.

"*He's a good doggi-woggie . . .*"

But . . . that six-second call from McCoy a half-hour ago. Was it really about going out to eat? Just saying *How about we all head to a restaurant for supper some night this week?* took about six seconds. And that was as stripped down as a telegraph message, without the standard pleasantries associated with Lee McCoy. And how did Cherry's response – "*Uh-huh. Not long, I expect*" – fit with McCoy's message?

My head tried a sample dialogue.

McCoy: "*I'm sneaking the dog back to Road's End. You'll be at your place a while, right?*"

Cherry: "*Uh-huh. Not long, I expect.*"

Was I over-analyzing? Had my Detective Meter gone to overload mode?

I watched Cherry smiling and patting Mix-up's flank. His tail whisked at her face; his clean, fluffy tail. She scratched him between his cow-sized eyes. Patted his belly, which he loved. She rubbed Mix-up's ears. My mutt looked ready to ascend toward canine Nirvana. When had Cherry found time to learn his special spots?

"Uh, Donna," I said, swallowing hard and walking closer. "I've got a question . . ."

But if Cherry and McCoy had dognapped Mix-up, it was because they needed me on the case, doing what

I did best, right? It just made sense: I was, after all, the hotshot hard-on from Mobile. In hindsight, I expect I'd have done the exact same thing if faced with the prospect of losing me.

"What, Carson?" Cherry said, turning the beautifully idiosyncratic eyes my way. Was that a shadow of guilt in the left one?

"I, uh – say, how about we head over to the skylift for another ride?" I took her hand and lit up my most sincere smile. "I just purely love that thing."

# ACKNOWLEDGEMENTS

To the librarians in the Powell County and Wolfe County Public Libraries in eastern Kentucky, keepers of the lighthouses. To the exceptional folks at the Aaron Priest Literary Agency. To Julia Wisdom at HarperCollins UK for her overview and suggestions. To Anne O'Brien for sharp-eyed editing. And to the professional staff at Kentucky's Natural Bridge State Resort Park, whose multi-faceted programs are instrumental to my knowledge and appreciation of the Red River Gorge.

Coming soon from HarperCollins*Publishers*

The next thriller in the series featuring
Carson Ryder, the detective with a unique
perspective on serial killers

Enjoy an excerpt now

# 1

*Three Weeks From Now*
*There's something I got to give you, Harry, something important . . .*

It was hotter than a potter's kiln in Harry Nautilus's attic. Sweat rolled down his face and into his eyes. He ducked under a joist, pushed past a broken kitchen chair he'd forgotten to repair, came face to face with a wall of cardboard cartons.

*I got everything I need, Zing. Lay back and relax*

The cartons were packed with outsized clothes. A year ago Nautilus had been ambushed by a blow to the head and nearly killed. During his convalescence he dropped thirty pounds he'd been trying to lose for ten years. A heavy-shouldered man of six-four, he was determined to stay at two hundred ten pounds. Still, he'd been unable to donate the duds to Goodwill, which he took as subconscious admission his former body was biding its time within. He shouldered aside the cartons and kept moving ahead.

*I need you to get in my closet there, Harry. Grab out that brown box in the corner, would ya?*

Nautilus palmed sweat from his brow. The roof angled low at back and he duckwalked the final few feet to a dark corner, reaching a small green box, metal, no larger than a shoebox. When he reached for the box, his hands faltered.

*What the hell's in here, Zing . . . a brick?*

He closed his eyes and forced his fingers to close around the box. He backed out of the corner and retreated down the staircase, closing the attic door. He took the box to his office and set it on his desk while he patted his face dry with a bandana.

Above Nautilus's desk, the wall was a montage of commendations, certificates and awards. Three medals of valor. Two awards for Officer of the Year, one as a patrolman, one as a detective. There were certificates of advanced training from the FBI. Recognitions from neighborhood associations. Letters from schoolkids thanking him for visiting class. There was a picture of a young and uniformed Nautilus laughing as his eight-year-old niece tried on his street-cop hat. Centering the wall was an eight-by-ten photo of Nautilus standing beside Carson Ryder, his partner and friend of many years. They were jointly holding a framed certificate.

*What do you want me to do now, Zing?*

The picture was from a few years back when the pair shared Officer of the Year status. Harry Nautilus was in a dark suit ironed hard as masonite, his wide black face somber behind the bulldozer-blade mustache, eyes stern and official. Ryder's white linen sport jacket was rumpled and his tie hung askew, his belt buckle an inch off center in the jeans. His dark hair looked like someone had wounded his comb. Still, he was standing straight with his usual semi-smirk replaced by a serious and suitably dutiful face. However, as Carson's left hand held the framed commendation, the right one had snuck up to put rabbit ears behind Nautilus's head.

*Open the box, Harry. Careful now . . .*

Nautilus felt guilt pool in his gut and he turned his eyes from the photo. His heart had started racing. He took a deep breath and opened the box, removing a zip bag brittle with age. The bag tore, pouring forth the smell of steel and gun oil. He pulled out a greasy towel and folded it open, revealing a black 40-caliber revolver. It had a five-round magazine and a one-inch barrel. The stock grips had been replaced with fingerprint-resistant burlap, now rotted into threads.

Nautilus ran his thumbnail over a depression in the frame of the revolver where a serial number had once resided.

*Jesus, Zing, what is this? What happened to the . . .*

The number seared away with acid.

*You know what it is, Harry. What it's for.*

The gun came from Zing Johnson, Nautilus's long-time

mentor in the Mobile, Alabama, Police Department. Harry Nautilus was thirty-two years old the day he'd received the weapon. Zing Johnson was fifty-one, seventeen days from his death by cancer.

*I don't want the damned thing, Zing. I don't even want to look at—*

Johnson pushed up from the bed, the stink of disease rising from his loose skin like hot fog. *Shut up and lissen, Harry. I ain't got no time left to fuck around. You're one of the few men able to understand a gun like this means there's no options left. I can trust you with it.*

Nautilus had nodded at Johnson and put the weapon back in the box, thinking first chance he got he'd throw the damned thing off a bridge into the bay. Johnson fell back into the covers, his strength depleted. Standing, bidding his friend farewell, Harry Nautilus went to the door with the box beneath his arm.

*Harry?* Johnson rasped, struggling upright again. Nautilus turned, eyebrow up in question.

*You know that if that gun is ever used, the user will never be the same again. You know that, Harry, right?*

Nautilus sighed and set the gun on the desk, staring at a blunt machine modified for one mission: Deliver death and disappear. The weapon had bided its time in his attic for over fifteen years, Harry Nautilus never truly understanding what Zing Johnson had been talking about.

Until yesterday.

# 2

Spring in coastal Alabama is a violent time, weather-wise. Two inches of tumultuous, lightning-driven rain in an hour is not unusual, nor is it rare for blue to rule the sky shortly thereafter, as if all has been forgiven. Gulls return to the air and the foaming whitecaps on Mobile Bay settle into a mild green chop beneath warm breezes built for sailing.

But this morning, as I drove to work from my beach-front home on Dauphin Island, thirty miles south of Mobile, we were stuck in the first movement of the meteorological symphony, purple-black clouds laced with bolts of jagged lightning, rain sweeping down in roiling sheets. Smarter drivers had pulled to a halt beside the road, or taken shelter in coffee shops and donut joints. I was plodding along at fifteen miles an hour, peering through my windshield and trying to recall when I'd last had the wiper blades replaced.

*Three years ago? Four?*

My cellphone rang and I pulled it from my jacket pocket, the words HARRY NAUTILUS flashing on the screen. Harry was my best friend and detective partner in the homicide division of the Mobile, Alabama, police department. Harry kept me grounded in reality and I kept him ... I'm not sure, but it'll come to me.

I punched redial, Harry answering before the first ring faded. "Hey bro," his voice rumbled, "don't go to the department."

A semi passed in the opposite direction, adding another five gallons of water to my windshield. I peered into rippling gray and slowed to ten miles an hour.

"I can turn around and go home? Cool."

He ignored my attempt at humor – typical. "I'm at the morgue, Carson. There's a strange situation here."

"What is it?"

"You'll find out. Just get your ass to the morgue, pronto."

"My wipers are shot, Harry. I can't see through my windshield. I'm stopping."

"You and that damned ancient truck. Where you at?"

My truck was old but not ancient, perhaps suggesting antiquity by being the color of the pyramids, roller-coated with gray ship's paint. Say what you will about aesthetics, I've never been bothered by rust or barnacles.

I said, "I'm just off the DI Parkway near the city

limits sign. I'm pulling into the parking lot of the fish shack by the creek."

"Hang tight and I'll send the cavalry."

"The what?"

Harry hung up. There was a coffee shop just past the fish restaurant, but to get there meant crossing twenty feet of open pavement, getting as soaked as if swimming the English Channel. Lightning exploded above and I sank lower in the seat.

A minute passed and I heard a howling. I first thought it the wind until it turned into a siren, flashing blue-and-white light filling the cab of my truck as a Mobile police cruiser pulled beside me. I wiped condensation from the window with my sleeve and saw a face on the driver's side, a hand gesturing me to lower my window.

Rain whipped in and the face – a pretty young black woman in a patrol cap and uniform – yelled, "You can see out the windshield a little, can't you?"

Perplexed, I nodded the affirmative.

"Stay on my bumper," she said, "but not too close, right?"

I saw the plan, pure magic. The cruiser whipped away and I stood on the accelerator, pasting myself fifty feet behind the MPD wagon. When we hit the highway another set of flashers slid in fifty feet behind me. I was bookmarked by light and sound and we blasted toward the morgue at perilous speed, though I can't say how fast exactly, never once taking my eyes from the lights of the leading cruiser, my sole point of navigation.

Fifteen white-knuckle minutes later our impromptu caravan rolled to the entrance of the morgue, more correctly the pathology department of the Alabama Bureau of Forensics, Mobile office. It was a squat and solid brick building by the University of South Alabama. I spent a fair amount of time here for two reasons, one being its function as a waypoint in the passage of murdered humans, the other being the director, the brilliant and deliciously lovely Dr Clair Peltier, was my good friend. Take that as you wish, you can't go wrong.

I pulled under the protective portico and parked beside the nearest NO PARKING sign. The cruiser protecting my flank sped away, dissolving into sheets of gray downpour and leaving only the vehicle driven by the young officer. I waved thanks as she pulled to a stop twenty feet away, on the far side of the portico, rain drumming across her cruiser.

The driver's-side window rolled halfway down and the pretty face reappeared, frowning at my trusty gray steed. "You really ought to get rid of that truck, Carson," the woman called through the downpour. "You've had it for what – eight years now?"

Her familiarity took me aback. "Almost nine," I said. "How did you know how many—"

"Carson Ryder . . . " she said, studying me and tapping her lips with a slender finger, like recalling a story. "Swimmer, kayaker, angler, cook, jazz buff. A man whose intuition battles his logic, perhaps to the betterment of both. A secret fan of poetry. Poorly informed folks might add womanizer to the list, but that's far too harsh. How about lover of beauty in both mind and body . . . " A puckish twinkle came to her eyes. "How'd I do? Was I close?"

I felt my mouth fall open. Her other descriptions aside, virtually no one knew of my taste for the poems of Cummings, Dickey, Roethke, and a few select others. My mind raced to identify the face. Even through rain and the twenty-foot distance, I was sure I'd never seen it before. And she was too pretty to forget.

"We've met?" I said, flummoxed by the surreal exchange.

"Don't you remember holding me in your arms, Carson? Or the time we kissed?"

"Uh . . . "

Her radio crackled with a dispatcher's voice. She canted her head to listen, then looked at me with a sigh. "Lightning blasted out a string of traffic lights along Airport Road," she said. "I've got to go. But I expect I'll see you soon enough."

She winked and did a little finger-wavy thing, chirped, "Bye-bye, Carson." Her window rolled up and she disappeared into the gray as if never existing. I stared into the rain before recalling the building at my back and the reason for the wild ride that had started my day.

*Get to the morgue pronto,* Harry had said. *There's a strange situation . . .*

Giving a final glance to the space where the woman's cruiser had resided, as if the drenched asphalt held a clue to her identity, I turned and pushed through the door to the morgue, finding – as always – a dry and cold atmosphere spun through with molecules of violent death and human despair.

# The Hundredth Man
## by J.A. Kerley

'Superb debut novel. A headless torso, the
heat-soaked Alabama nights, a detective with
a secret. Fantastic' *Sunday Express*

A body is found in the sweating heat of an Alabama night;
headless, words inked on the skin. To Detective Carson Ryder's
eyes it is no crime of passion, and when another mutilated
victim turns up his suspicions that this is the work of a serial
killer is confirmed.

Famous for solving a series of crimes the
year before, Carson Ryder has experience with psychopaths.
But he had help with that case – strange help, from a past
Ryder is trying to forget. Now he needs it again.

ISBN: 978-0-00-718059-2

Also available as an audio book

# The Death Collectors
## by J.A. Kerley

Thirty years after his death, Marsden Hexcamp's 'Art of the
Final Moment' remains as sought after as ever. But this is no
ordinary collection. Hexcamp's portfolio was completed with
the aid of a devoted band of acolytes – and half a dozen
victims, each of whom was slowly tortured to death so that
their final agonies could be distilled into art.

When tiny scraps of Hexcamp's 'art'
begin appearing at murder scenes alongside gruesomely
displayed corpses, Detective Carson Ryder and his partner
Harry Nautilus must go back three decades in search of
answers.

ISBN: 978-0-00-718061-5

Also available as an audio book

# The Broken Souls
## by J.A. Kerley

**Blood was everywhere, like the interior had been hosed down with an artery . . .**

The gore-sodden horror that greets homicide detective Carson Ryder on a late-night call out is enough to make him want to quit the case. Too late.

Now he and his partner Harry are up to their necks in a Southern swamp of the bizarre and disturbing. An investigation full of twists and strange clues looks like it's leading to the city's least likely suspects – a powerful family whose philanthropy has made them famous.

Their strange and horrific past is about to engulf everyone around them in a storm of violence and depravity. And Ryder's right in the middle of it . . .

ISBN: 978-0-00-721434-1

Also available as an audio book

# Blood Brother
## by J.A. Kerley

Homicide detective Carson Ryder catches killers. Jeremy Ridgecliffe is one of America's most notorious murderers. But these two men with death in their veins share a dark secret – they are brothers. And now Jeremy's escaped and is at large in New York.

A mysterious video at the scene of a shocking mutilation-murder demands Ryder be brought in on the case. With Jeremy as the chief suspect, a man-hunt begins – and the body count rises. Ryder is trapped in a game of life, death and deceit – with an unknown number of players and no clear way of winning . . .

ISBN: 978-0-00-726907-5

Also available as an audio book

# What's next?

Tell us the name of an author you love

J.A. Kerley

Go

and we'll find your next great book.